blood
sisters

Blood Sisters

Lesbian Vampire Tales

BIANCA DE MOSS

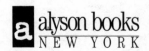

alyson books
NEW YORK

Manufactured in the United States States of America.
This trade paperback original is published by Alyson Books.
P.O. Box 1253, Old Chelsea Station, New York, New York 10113-1251.
Distribution in the United Kingdom by Turnaround Publisher Services Ltd., Unit 3,
Olympia Trading Estate, Coburg Road, Wood Green, London N22 6TZ England.

First Edition: June 2006

06 07 08 09 **a** 10 9 8 7 6 5 4 3 2 1

ISBN 1-55583-883-9
ISBN-13 978-1-55583-883-6

Library of Congress Cataloging-in-Publication Data has been applied for.
Designed by Victor Mingovits

Contents

Introduction

I will never forget when I made my first blood pact. Alyssa and I were pressed tightly against one another, our fifth-grade bodies fit neatly into the crawl space beneath the stairs in my childhood home. Her pale face shone innocently in the half-dark as I pricked her index finger. After pricking my own, we pressed our fingers together, our eyes locked. I could feel the electricity of our connection lighting up our bodies. We were suddenly blood sisters, united forever. I had made her mine.

That ritual was the beginning of my life-long obsession with blood and darkness and eventually the erotic life of vampires, and that's why this collection thrills me: The writers whose work is showcased here take us to the darkest blood-tainted places.

Start your nocturnal journey with Kristina Wright's "Bound by Blood," when an intoxicatingly beautiful girl with silken pale hair incites Monique to risk her lover's rage. Vampire or not, anyone who suffers from unrequited desire will wilt with satisfaction after Amanda Tremblay's "Taken," when our hero finally takes possession of her girl. Betty Blue, Jewelle Gomez, Leslie Anne Leasure, Rakelle Valencia, and many others lead us, innocents that we are, down tortuous paths, ultimately feeding our every craving. It's as if the vampires they write about are reaching up from the page to ensnare us.

There's no turning back now, lovelies. It's time to satisfy your hunger before the sun rises . . .

Bound by Blood

KRISTINA WRIGHT

"She is very sweet, sister, but hardly your type."

The words were a hiss against the back of my neck, nothing soothing or familial about them. I didn't turn to witness Giselle's knowing smirk. "I have known you for over a thousand years, Giselle. You are no more my sister now than you were then. *Back off.*"

Giselle's laughter danced across my cool skin. "Ah, Monique, you are terse with me tonight. Your hunger is getting the best of you."

I ignored her. Giselle was my—pardon the poor cliché—cross to bear. I heard the rustle of her dress and the soft closing of the door as she left me to my thoughts, which were on the beauty outside. She was not as young as Giselle or I when we were cursed, but she had the soft, gentle curves of a woman in the waning blush of her youth. She was waiting for a bus, as she did each night at precisely two-fifteen in the morning. She was, I knew, a waitress at the restaurant across the street. She was also an avid reader, with a book in her hand as she waited for the bus to take her home each night.

Butter-yellow hair glinted beneath the phosphorescent glow of the streetlight. My fingers clenched at my sides, longing to touch that long hair, to feel the smoothness of her skin beneath my fingertips.

As if sensing my gaze, she looked up from her book. This had become a ritual for me. For weeks I had watched her until she glanced up. Then I withdrew to the shadows of the room, to avoid frightening her away. I always wanted to stay in the window, though, to have a clear view of her pretty face as she looked up. Tonight, perhaps egged on by Giselle's taunts, I did just that.

Her mouth was a blood-red O, tantalizing and desirable. She looked startled, afraid, timid. My breath quickened as I watched her, watching me. Desire drove me closer to the window, until my nose nearly brushed the glass. I knew the expression on my face was anything but friendly—predatory and feral would be a better description—and I waited for her to quickly look away or perhaps even to flee. But she did neither; she did the unthinkable: She gave me a small smile and waved.

I uttered a startled gasp as I did what I should have done in the first place and withdrew from the window, shaking the heavy draperies into place. I sat down on the edge of the bed, unable to gather my wits about me. With my next breath, I cursed Giselle.

Once we had lived away from people. It was better that way, safer. It allowed us to pick and choose the moments of our hunger, to not be ruled by the passion trapped within us. But impetuous Giselle had bought this house, this big, ornate mansion on a heavily populated street of Charleston, and I'd had no choice but to follow her as I had so many times, and so many years, before. She teased me about being a recluse, which was all too true. But here, now, sitting on the edge of my bed with my body betraying my lust, I knew my way was better. Time may have eased our aversion to light and to all things holy, but time could not ease the ache and the need of a curse so strong it kept us from the grave.

I sat there, trembling, for fifteen minutes before going

downstairs. I found Giselle sitting with her needlepoint by the dormant fireplace in the sitting room, her dark, wavy hair tumbling over her shoulder so that her face was shielded from me. Her floor-length dress was spread about her like a cape, the burgundy fabric reminiscent of a previous century, though I could not recall when it had been purchased. Personally, I preferred more modern attire.

She did not look up at my approach. "She is not for you, sister," she said, her words tainted with anger. "Leave her be and choose another."

My head throbbed. I sat on the divan at the far side of the room. "It's your fault. I didn't want this."

Giselle *tsked* softly. "Do not play the petulant child, Moni. You need to be among people, even if they're not our kind. But do not choose from those so close; it is not safe, as well you know."

She was right; I did know. To choose a victim, we went miles and miles from our homes and then took only as much as we needed. It was the only way to ensure our survival, though I often wondered—bitterly, to be sure—if survival was worth this half-life. The times we had chosen unwisely, few though they were, had ended with frightening consequences that threatened our existence. I would not be so brash this time, I vowed.

Giselle tilted her head toward me. "I know what you're thinking," she sing-songed. "If only you were so strong."

I cursed her silently. She had made me what I was and never allowed me to forget it. I hated her, I loved her, I needed her. She knew all that, which only made her more powerful. I turned my head to the wall, refusing to give her satisfaction.

"She is waiting for you." Giselle's fingers stilled on her needlepoint. "She waits just outside the door, feeling the pull of you as strongly as the tides feel the pull of the moon."

"As strongly as I felt your pull?"

Giselle chuckled, and it was an indulgent sound. "Not as strong as that, sweet girl. Our desire shall last eternity."

She was wrong. My desire for her had long since waned. I think she needed to say the words to feel safe, to pretend she could not lose me. I hadn't left her in a millennium and there was no reason for her to think I ever would, and yet I could feel her insecurity.

Perhaps it was her need to appease me that made her say "Go to her, Monique. But be careful, please. I do not wish to deal with a mess of your making."

I hesitated for the briefest moment, surprised at her quick acquiescence, having resigned myself to yearning for that which I could not have. Then I was gone, without a backward glance.

"Quickly, my love," Giselle called. "Take her home, but be back before the sun."

I did not need the warning, but I knew Giselle felt compelled to refresh my memory about the rule. She would let me stray to sate my hunger without her, but never, never was I allowed to bring the object of my desire to her home. Not our home, *her* home. It was a stinging reminder of our stations in life, but it did not trouble me so much this night.

The night air stirred around me as I opened the door and stepped out into darkness. She was there, as Giselle had said, waiting by the marble stairs, looking up at the house with equal parts awe and apprehension. She took a step back when she saw me, then quickly stepped forward, as if afraid of offending.

"I'm sorry," she said softly, her voice lyrically southern. "I saw you there, in the window, and thought you looked familiar."

I forced a smile, every fiber of my being telling me to go slowly, gently. "I have lived here for six months. Perhaps you've seen me on the street."

"I work at Flannigan's. Maybe you've been in there?"

I never had, but I shrugged. "That's probably it. I'm Monique Dupres."

She did not give me her hand. "I'm Sarah Cooper."

"Sarah. That's a pretty name," I said, wondering if she could hear the impatience in my voice. "It looks like your bus is late."

She shrugged. "It usually is. That's why I bring a book."

I wanted to sweep her into my arms and take her to my room, but Giselle would never allow it. "I'd be happy to drive you," I said, though I loathed driving. Still, Giselle made sure we always kept a car in case we needed it. And now, my need was great enough to overtake my dislike of that particular modern convenience.

"Really? That would be so nice. Normally I don't mind waiting, but I have to get up early."

I led her around to the narrow driveway tucked in beside the house. The car Giselle had purchased for us was sleek and black, some sort of sports car, though I'd never paid much attention. Sarah, however, seemed impressed.

"Pretty car. I wish I could afford something like this."

I didn't bother to respond, my impatience getting the better of me. I let her get settled in the car while I stood beside the closed door, getting a grip on my emotions. It wouldn't do to lose my control now.

We drove through the quiet streets of downtown Charleston, desolate but for an occasional car. All my attention was focused on the mechanics of driving, having never been all that interested in Giselle's lessons. My fingers gripped the steering wheel until my knuckles went even whiter than they were naturally.

Sarah didn't seem to notice. She prattled on about her job, the classes she was taking at the community college, her family in Georgia. I simply drove, taking in the melodic sound of her voice and the directions she gave until we were parked in front of a nondescript two-story apartment building in North Charleston, amid the strip malls and laundromats.

"Here we are. Thanks for the ride," Sarah said brightly.

Panic gripped me. I could not stand to let her go. "Would it be too much trouble to use your bathroom?"

She hesitated only the briefest of moments. "Sure, come on up."

I followed her up the narrow stairs and waited while she opened the door. My fingers burned to touch the curtain of hair that cascaded down her back, but I resisted.

The door swung open to darkness, and I followed her inside. My body hummed with an intensity I hadn't felt in a century or more. I needed this girl, this beautiful young woman. Needed her as I'd only ever needed Giselle.

"The bathroom is over there," she said, gesturing off toward a short hall. "Pardon the mess. I haven't had time to clean."

The apartment was small and cramped with furniture, with no style or fashion to speak of. It wasn't her home I was interested in, though. I made the pretense of using her bathroom, taking my time to calm myself. I studied my face in the mirror, taken by how bleak and gaunt I appeared. Is that how I looked? Is that how she saw me? It couldn't be; otherwise I would have scared her off. I looked away from my offending image and gripped the bathroom sink.

"Control," I hissed to myself and almost imagined I could hear Giselle's laughter.

Sarah was waiting for me in the small living room. Her expression seemed knowing, amused.

"I was wondering when you'd come out. It's not nice to keep me waiting."

I shook my head, my short hair brushing my neck and making me shiver. "Excuse me?"

Sarah reached out her hand to me. "I know, Monique."

I took her hand, not comprehending her words but longing for her touch. She was as warm and soft as I had imagined, her fingers gripping mine tightly, pulling me closer. I went into her arms, burying my face in the silk of her pale hair, brushing my mouth against her cheek.

She murmured softly against my ear, "I know who you are."

I stiffened in her embrace and pulled away to look at her. "What did you say?"

Her smile was small, secretive, teasing. "I've seen you watching me, night after night."

I could not deny it.

"So, one night when I saw you leave the house, I went to the door. Your sister answered. She told me about you."

I was speechless. This lovely creature had spoken to Giselle? It wasn't possible. Anger coursed through me, displacing the heat and the passion of only a moment before.

"What did she tell you?" I asked, my voice sounding fierce even to my own ears as I gave her a small shake. "What?"

She only laughed. "She was right, you are impatient." My grip on her tightened and her eyes widened ever so slightly. "She told me you've lived for hundreds of years. Is that true?"

"Longer," I said through gritted teeth. I wanted to cast her aside and leave this bourgeois place, but her scent was intoxicating, and I could not resist her.

As if sensing my need, she tossed her head back, her hair cascading over my arms as she bared her neck to me. Instead of pristine flesh, two neat, red circles spoiled her purity. Giselle had already marked her as her own. I growled and thrust her away from me.

"Why?" I rasped, feeling lightheaded from more than hunger.

"She knew you wanted me. She said you have betrayed her before."

A wail of agony tore from my body. Giselle, my lover, my mistress, my enemy. I turned to leave, but Sarah's voice stilled me in my tracks.

"You can still have me," she whispered. "It's you I want. Only you."

Never had I taken something that was Giselle's. Never. "I can't. She would be angry."

"Take me." Her voice was seductive and taunting. "Take me."

I knew the effect was part of Giselle's bond with her, but I didn't care. I embraced her then, devouring her lips and tongue in a ravenous kiss, crushing her to me until she whimpered. I moved to release her, fearing I would hurt her, but she clung to me.

"Don't," she gasped. "I want to feel your passion."

It was she who guided me to the bedroom, who drew me down to the bed, who stripped off first her own clothing and then mine. Our bodies rubbed together sinuously, like two halves of the same serpent. I stroked her breasts, belly, and thighs, and she mimicked my motions, sliding her hand lower, between my thighs, cupping and pressing my swollen cunt.

I drove my fingers into her at the exact moment she did the same to me, and it was like fucking myself. She matched my rhythm stroke for stroke, grinding against my hip while my fingers pressed into her, feeling her arousal. She threw her head back to reveal her ravaged neck, her breasts heaving, the nipples tautly drawn. I bit one, then the other, drawing blood from both until twin rivulets ran down her rib cage.

Her cunt felt good against my hand, warm and slick. I slipped my fingers from her gripping walls and tasted her honey. So sweet.

I moaned as she slid down my body, her mouth on me like fire, her tongue dipping into my cleft, stroking my clit. I bucked and whimpered against her mouth, feeling the rise of my desire. She drove me higher, her moans humming against the lips of my cunt as her tongue plunged into me. I cried out and came, passion overtaking my control, raking my nails down her shoulders until blood flowed from there as well.

She did not stop. She devoured my cunt like a starving thing, until I ached to be still, to be left alone. I pushed her away at last and drew her up my body, sexual desire giving way to a deeper need, a more powerful hunger.

I kissed her mouth, tasting myself. I licked and sucked her lips as my fingers slipped inside her once more. She gripped me tightly, with her hands, with her cunt, driven now by her own passion.

"It will hurt," I murmured against her mouth. "But the pleasure, I'm told, is sublime."

"I know. Giselle showed me."

At the mention of Giselle, I froze. Giselle had marked her already, Giselle had tasted her and left her for me. I was Giselle's pawn, now and always.

Sarah moved against my stilled fingers. "Do it," she urged. "Don't let her win. Don't let her keep me for herself."

I twisted my fingers inside her, two, then three. I fucked her hard, knowing Giselle would have spared her nothing. Giselle enjoyed inflicting pain whether it was welcome or not. I only enjoyed it when it was wanted. Sarah wanted. She wanted the pain and she wanted me, and I would not leave her wanting.

I slid my mouth from her lips to her cheek, down past the curve of her jaw to her neck. I felt Giselle's marks beneath my tongue and made to mark her in the same place, to spare her a new wound. But she turned her head and offered me the untainted side.

"Here," she said. "Make your own mark. Now." Each word was enunciated slowly, carefully, as if the power of speech was beyond her abilities.

My lips caressed the skin she exposed for me, my fangs pressed lightly. I ached to gore her, to penetrate her neck the way I penetrated her cunt. But now that I'd been given sexual release, I had enough control to bide my time, to make her come.

I fucked her slowly with four fingers and she opened to me, wet and swollen. I tucked my thumb into my fingers, wondering if she could take so much, if she would want it. Her thighs gripped my forearm as I pushed into her, my fist being absorbed into her body like it belonged there.

"Oh God, yes!" She held me tighter, body quivering with need. "Fuck me," she groaned. "Fuck me hard."

I fucked her as if her life depended upon it, which in some ways it did. Having been tasted by an immortal, her desires would run higher, hotter, deeper. If too much was taken, she would become like Giselle and me. But before that threshold was reached, she would know a craving so intense it would drive her mad if it was not fulfilled. She wasn't there yet, but she wasn't far. Giselle had taken much, and I could take but a little, I thought bitterly.

When I felt her orgasm approaching, the walls of her cunt contracting so hard around my fist that she would have crushed my hand had I been mortal, I pressed my fangs into her flesh. The first taste was sweet, pure, incredible. I had waited so long for it to be like this, this precious gift. I drank as she came, drank her life's blood as she twisted and groaned in my arms.

I lifted my mouth from her neck and looked into her eyes. She was still in that passion-induced stupor from having been with one of my kind. She smiled sleepily.

"That was . . . amazing," she said, words coming with great difficulty. "It hurt much more with Giselle."

I had no doubt that it did.

Silently, I left the bed and went to the bathroom. My mouth was a crimson stain. I filled the sink with water and scrubbed at my face until the water was colored strawberry red. The metallic tinge of blood made me feel sick as it so often did when I had not fed in some time. But this . . . this had not been a simple feeding. I felt different, stronger. Powerful.

I heard Sarah calling me from the bedroom. Reluctantly, I returned to her. I was anxious to go home, even if it meant facing Giselle.

"Stay with me," she said, reaching out. "Stay with me for a while longer."

I shook my head even as I was reaching for my clothing. "I cannot. Dawn will be here too soon." What I didn't say was that I would not have stayed even if I did not fear the sun. Sarah's hand dropped to the bed as if weighted. "Giselle said you'd leave me. Giselle said you never stay."

"Stop talking about her," I said, though my words had no fire. I was strong, full of energy, and I could not waste it on this girl. "You should not have taken such a risk, first with her and then with me. It was foolish."

Sarah sat up on the bed, clutching the bloodstained sheet to her waist, her pale, blood-streaked breasts gleaming in the faint lamplight. "I want to be like you," she said. "Giselle promised I could stay with the two of you."

I laughed, the taste of blood nearly as bitter as my heart. "Giselle was playing with you, child. She wants no one but me."

"And you? What do you want?"

I turned my head away and finished dressing. At the door, I looked at her one last time. "Do not come to our house again. Do not speak of this night or your time with Giselle."

"Is that a threat?" Her false bravado was useless; I could smell her fear.

"Giselle will kill you, Sarah. She has killed before, and she will again if she feels threatened. Do not cross her."

She lay down on the bed, a contented smile on her face. "You won't let her hurt me."

There was nothing more to say. She believed she was safe because I cared for her, without knowing anything of my reality. I left her apartment and drove back home through the silent streets. I knew Giselle would be waiting for me, and I was not wrong. I found her naked on my bed, her hands stroking her hardened nipples.

"Was she as delicious as you expected, my darling?"

I stripped off my clothes, making her wait for my answer. "She tasted of you," I whispered. "Why, Giselle? Why did you do it?"

Giselle stretched on the bed like an exotic cat. "Because it pleased me," she said simply. "Now come, while we have time."

Her outstretched hand reminded me of Sarah. I went to her, unable—or unwilling—to resist and sank down beside her on the bed. She touched me in ways Sarah never could, with a thousand years' experience and an immortal thirst for sex. Her fingers found my cunt, still wet from my time with Sarah, and she fucked me hard, harder than a mere human could handle. Her lips were at my nipple, sucking fiercely until she drew blood—Sarah's blood.

I writhed beneath her ministrations until I was moaning for release. Then, before I could come, she withdrew. Her fingers, her lips and teeth, the press of her body, they were all gone from me.

"Giselle, please," I whimpered with need, reaching for her. "Please."

Someone who did not know her might have said her expression was cold, unfeeling. But I could see the glaze of desire in her eyes, her need as hot and hungry as my own. "You know what we must do," she said.

I shook my head, my brain feeling foggy with my lust. "What Giselle? Tell me."

"We must visit Sarah together."

I mouthed the word *no* even while she was slipping her fingers back inside my swollen sex. "Not that, Giselle. Please."

"We must," she insisted, driving her fingers up into me. "You know we must, Moni. We will share her; she will be ours."

"No, no," I gasped. Sharing Sarah meant making her one of us, and I couldn't do that to her. I could never do that to one so innocent.

"Why not, sweet? Did you not like her? Did she not please you? If she upset you in any way, I will—"

"No, Giselle," I interrupted. "She pleased me, but we can't do that. I don't want to do that." I could barely form the words as she bared her fangs to me. "Please, Giselle, give me what I need."

Her tongue glided across white teeth, the barest tinge of blood on her lips. "Then give me what I need, my love."

I held her hand between my thighs, afraid she would withdraw from me once more. I held her head to my breasts with my other hand, wanting to feel her mouth on me when I came. "Take her blood from me," I gasped. "Take her blood and let me come."

"Such a naughty girl you are, such a needy girl," she said, stroking me. "Tell me what I need to hear, Moni, or we shall go tomorrow night to see Sarah."

I groaned, aching with a need that Giselle had fine-tuned to wicked perfection. "Please Giselle, do not say that. Not that, not her."

"Why not, Monique?" Her nails scraped the walls of my cunt, the feeling an exquisite blend of pleasure and pain. *Tell me!*

"I don't want her," I screamed. "I want only you, Giselle. Only you. Always you. Please!!"

She mounted my body then, her hand pressed between my cunt and her powerful thigh. Her eyes were filled with an animal lust. "Only me, Moni? Are you sure you don't want the pretty blonde to play with and fuck?"

"No! No! You, Giselle! I want you, I've always wanted you," I moaned, and I believed my own words. "She meant nothing. She was a plaything."

With that, Giselle bit down on my breast, just above the nipple, her fangs sinking into my flesh to draw forth the life source so precious to us both. She drank from me as I came, my back arching off the bed as if I were having a seizure. The pleasure drove all thoughts from my mind as she rode my body like a succubus, her cunt rubbing against my thigh, leaving me slick with moisture.

When she came, I thought she would rip a hole in my flesh. I held her to me, my orgasm still cresting, lasting an eternity. She collapsed on top of me, her body feeling delicate and fragile, though I knew better. I cradled her gently, loving her in this moment.

Later, when the moisture had dried on our bodies and Sarah's blood had flaked from my skin, she looked at me. "We must bathe and prepare for bed," she said, her tone brisk. "Dawn is upon us."

I nodded and made to rise, feeling empty, hollow, desolate.

"Moni? Tell me something?" she asked, vulnerability creeping into her voice. "Please?"

"Anything, Giselle," I said wearily.

"Promise me you will never leave me."

I looked toward the window, the heavy drapes blocking out

the real world, the human world. Then I looked at the creature on the bed, so heartbreakingly beautiful and so frighteningly cruel. Whatever Giselle was, she was mine. For always.

"I'm yours forever, Giselle."

The words were as cold and dead as my heart.

Taken

AMANDA TREMBLAY

It was selfish of me, I know. But at the time I thought I deserved it. I deserved her. And because I hated loving her, it was the only thing I could do.

Corinne and I had been friends for over a year. I wanted more, but I didn't know how she felt. From the very beginning she knew I was a lesbian, and she told me she was straight. But as our friendship grew, I began to wonder about her preference. She liked to flirt with me and tell me how cute I looked. Then she would touch me on the leg, resting her hand on my thigh, knowing the effect it had on me. But she always played it safe. She only flirted with me in front of other people. It was a game to her.

If I invited her to go out with me, she would come up with an excuse to bring someone else along. Soon, I realized she was afraid to be alone with me. I think she knew that if we were alone together, all her past advances would finally be reciprocated. Since I would never get that chance, I began teasing her back. Of course, we always had an audience. But the truth was, I wanted her, and I didn't bother hiding it.

It was obvious she liked the attention. It was an ego boost for her to have a lesbian friend who was attracted to her. The sexual tension, at least on my end, was intense, and I thrived on it. She was the ultimate challenge, and my ego was just as big as hers. I thought I could break her down.

In the back of my mind, I knew I was in danger of actually falling for her, but I ignored it. No matter how hard I tried, I couldn't stop wanting her. It became the classic case of the gay girl crushing on the straight one. Ten months into our friendship, I gave up trying to figure her out because I was completely taken with her.

My friends were convinced she was a closet-case, and they tried to convince me of it. They kept telling me to just fuck her and get it over with. But that wasn't an ideal solution because, despite my physical attraction to her, I took our friendship seriously. I figured if she was a closet-case, then I didn't want to take advantage of her vulnerability. Maybe flirting with me was a safe alternative until she was ready to come out. As her friend I wanted her to go at her own pace.

On the other hand, if she *wasn't* a closet-case, then I thought she was cruel for leading me on. I wasn't about to give her the satisfaction of turning me down if I made the first move. I went back and forth like this for months, and not knowing what to do was driving me crazy. Closet-case or not, coming on to her was out of the question. It started to hurt just being around her. In the end, I decided to distance myself.

When she noticed I'd stopped hanging around, she called me.

"Where have you been?" She didn't even say hi, first.

"I've been busy."

"Too busy to see me?"

I sighed. I didn't know what to say.

"Hello?"

"Yeah. I'm still here." My voice sounded weird.

"I'd like to see you."

I laughed, shaking my head. She had a way of making it

sound like I was more important to her than I actually was.

She continued, "You wanna come over tonight?"

I knew it wasn't an exclusive invitation. "I can't," I lied. "I have to work." I think it was the first time I'd ever said no to her.

That night, it was all I could do to stay away. By nine o'clock, sitting at home was too depressing, so I decided to go for a walk. I don't normally go for walks alone at night (or at least I didn't used to), but at the time, I lived in a nice neighborhood and knew that the police patrolled until midnight. Deep down, I didn't care if I was being careless; I was too busy thinking about Corinne.

When I reached Connelly Park I didn't hesitate to find a bench and sit. There was a street lamp about fifty feet away, so I didn't feel like it was too dark to stop there. A small car was parked to my right. I noticed a young couple sitting in the backseat, kissing. I felt safe enough.

I must have sat there thinking about Corinne for an hour. I wondered who was at her house. I wondered what she was talking about. I started to fantasize about her. I wondered what she smelled like. How she kissed. I wondered if she was thinking about me. And I remember wishing that I could read her mind because not knowing how she felt about me was maddening.

I wasn't paying attention when the teenagers in the car drove away. And I certainly didn't realize I was completely alone until the street lamp burned out. It didn't flicker first as if to warn me. It just turned itself off. I blinked my eyes, trying to adjust to the darkness, but it didn't help. It was pitch black. I decided I'd better head back home. I stood up from the bench and stretched. It was getting chilly, so I started rubbing my hands together, and that's when it happened.

I felt a hand touch my face. The fingers were ice cold as they brushed against my cheek. I thought I would pass out from the sheer terror of this. The worst part was that I still couldn't see anything. It was as if someone had just blindfolded me.

I didn't want to be a statistic. Rape was one of my biggest fears in life, not to mention being murdered in a park. I cursed myself for not carrying a can of mace with me. I was frozen to the spot, having these thoughts all at once yet only for a split second. I took off running. I couldn't see where I was going and I didn't care. I just ran away. I don't know why I didn't scream at this point. Maybe a part of me couldn't believe this was happening.

Something hit me from behind. I flew forward as if I'd been pushed, and I fell hard from the momentum. I landed on dirt and realized I was on the playground. That meant that I had run farther into the park. I became furious with myself. This time I screamed when I was abruptly picked up by my shoulders. I punched and kicked at what I'd hoped would be the man's face and groin, but I missed. I must have blindly swung into the air.

And just as suddenly as it was taken from me, my eyesight was restored. I'd thought the street lamp must have turned back on. I saw for the first time what was attacking me, and I gasped. I had been so certain that my attacker was a man. I felt his strength when he pushed me down and in the way he picked me back up so effortlessly. But my attacker wasn't a man. It was a woman. And this shocked me more than anything. She still had me by the shoulders and kept staring into my eyes with no sign of guilt or remorse. It was paralyzing.

All I could do was stare back at her. I was frightened by her, even as I realized how beautiful she was. Her eyes were mysterious and black. Her skin was smooth and pale even though her lips were dark crimson. The contrast between her skin and her lips was startling. Severe. Sexy. She kept staring at me with those eyes. And suddenly I forgot I was supposed to be scared of her. I wanted to kiss her full lips. I wanted to taste her. She almost smiled as if she knew what I was thinking.

She dropped her gaze from my eyes to my neck. Her beautiful face turned sinister once more. I felt her icy-cold fingers through my shirt as her grip tightened around my shoulders. A shiver ran down my spine. It was as if I could feel death pouring out of her hands and into my skin. I felt my knees give out from under me but she easily held me up. I tried to grab her by the front of the shirt, as if to push her away from me, but I was powerless. I felt like I'd been drugged. At the time, I thought it was because I was in shock.

"You're very strong," she whispered.

I didn't feel strong. My body wasn't listening to my silent pleas to push her away. Instead, my hands slowly released her shirt, slid off her chest, and dangled at my sides. All at once, I understood what was happening. I couldn't believe it but I understood.

She was somehow controlling me. I was paralyzed because of her. Because of her, I had been literally blinded minutes before. The street lamp had never gone out. She literally took my sight and later gave it back. And I knew that I was now staring death in the face.

I don't know what came over me then, but I laughed. I think it was because of the fact that I wasn't going to be a rape statistic after all. At least not the kind of rape I'd grown up fearing. I understood what she wanted, and I knew that she would kill me when she was finished, yet I had laughed.

I think the sound coming from my lips was so unexpected that she snapped out of her trance to look at me. She was surprised by me, I think. I noticed her beautiful lips again.

"You find me amusing?" She purred, "Usually my victims

scream when they are about to be taken."

"Taken?" I whispered. It was barely audible.

But the vacant look in her eyes returned. I knew this was the end. I can't explain why I was calm as I faced my own demise. I was completely aware that it was about to happen, but I wasn't afraid. I think she had something to do with it. At least that's what I like to believe.

She sank her teeth into my neck so quickly that I didn't feel it at first. I opened my eyes and saw that her hair covered most of her face. And then I closed my eyes again. I didn't need to see anymore. I could *feel* everything. Her lips on my neck felt cool but quickly warmed as she took my blood from me.

I started dreaming. It was a warm, comforting dream. I saw my family and friends. I saw Corinne, and she was grinning at me. I always loved her smile. Then I dreamed she was kissing me. I leaned into the vampire's embrace. I knew she was watching my dreams with me, but I didn't care. I no longer cared what happened to me. I felt high, and I didn't want the dream to end.

Then the vampire started kissing me. I thought about Corinne and pretended it was her. I felt the familiar butterflies in my stomach spread between my legs. The vampire pressed her lips against mine, prying my lips apart with her tongue. I started kissing her back. I could taste my own blood on her lips, but I didn't care. All I could think about were her soft breasts pressing against mine. I stopped thinking about Corinne. She couldn't have kissed me like this.

I realized the vampire had controlled me physically, but she had let my thoughts remain my own. And now she knew I wanted her. She held me close, and I realized she didn't feel cold anymore. She was warm because of me. I wondered who she was.

"Kyrelle," she answered before sinking her teeth into me again.

And then the dreams returned, but I wanted Kyrelle to kiss me instead. I wanted her to fuck me. She abruptly grabbed me and lifted me off the ground. I couldn't tell if we were flying, or if she was carrying me. She had taken most of my blood, and I knew I was dying. As we left the park, I saw an empty patrol car parked underneath the street lamp. A policeman had seen us, no doubt. But he would never find us.

I don't know if I actually died that night, but I do know that Kyrelle had every intention of killing me. I can only assume that when the police interrupted her, she took the evidence and ran. Later, perhaps she cast me aside, leaving me for dead. Instead, I woke up the next evening, and I was famished. I could still taste the blood on my lips from the night before and my stomach growled. I knew I had become one of them. Kyrelle had *taken* me just as she'd promised, and life as I knew it would never be the same.

I'm not sure how I survived those first few nights. I just did what came naturally, I guess. I had to drink blood at least once a night because the cravings were too intense to ignore. I didn't care who my victims were. I just cared about killing my own hunger.

As an inexperienced vampire, I felt like an infant discovering its new motor skills. It was both exciting and frustrating. I mostly learned about my abilities by remembering what Kyrelle had done to me. I controlled what people saw and I could paralyze them as easily as Kyrelle had me. But I wasn't interested in anyone's thoughts or dreams. My victims never knew the sensuality of being taken. I was swift and relentless when I was hungry.

Luckily, I had a large cellar beneath my house, so I slept

down there during the day. Of course, I locked myself in to keep intruders out. Like most women, I'd always felt safest during the daytime because nighttime made me feel more vulnerable. Now it was just the opposite. I felt more susceptible to danger while I slept because nothing could wake me before dusk. I was literally defenseless. But as soon as the sun went down, I became empowered.

I have to admit that at first being a vampire was disappointing. It's not as glamorous as people think. I went through a period of deep depression because I was extremely lonely. Corinne would leave messages for me to call her, but I never called her back. In fact, I didn't speak to anyone for almost three months. I didn't even bother to call my boss to tell him I quit. What was the point?

I missed my friends the most. I often wondered what would happen if I came out to them as a vampire. I knew exactly how each one of them would react, and it made me miss them even more. We could never remain friends now that I had changed. What if I killed one of them in a moment of weakness? So I remained hidden until little by little, my friends gave up and forgot about me. All accept one.

When I refused to call Corinne back, she wrote me a letter. I never read it because I didn't want to be tempted to contact her. But I kept it, unopened, in the cellar with me. I imagined it was hate mail because she didn't like to be ignored. This helped me to decide not to open it.

I went on like this for another month. Then, just as quickly as I had become a vampire, I snapped out of my depression. It literally happened overnight. I woke up and wasn't hungry for once. Instead of rushing out to feed, I went out to observe. I craved to see people who were happy and not terrified, as I always made them feel. I wanted to hear them laugh instead of scream. I needed to feel alive again.

I went to a nightclub, of all places. It was the only place I could think of. I was a little nervous at first. I didn't want anyone to notice I was different just by looking at me. But as I entered the nightclub and walked through the crowds of people, they didn't pay any attention to me at all. They just kept dancing and laughing and drinking and living. I actually smiled for the first time in six months.

"Would you like to dance?"

I spun around and came face to face with Corinne. My smile faltered for a second. She was more beautiful than I remembered, and she was grinning back at me. I felt a wave of relief wash over me. I needed a friend now more than anything, and I was glad to see her. My smile broadened.

"I saw you walk in," she said, "Where the hell have you been, anyway?"

She smiled again, and my heart skipped a beat. I looked her straight in the eyes.

"You wouldn't believe me if I told you."

She stared back at me for a moment as if she wanted to press me further but thought better of it.

"You look different," she finally said.

I looked down, afraid I might scare her.

"Your hair is darker," she continued. "It brings out your beautiful blue eyes."

She was flirting, as usual.

"Don't even start with me," I joked.

She laughed and hugged me. She smelled sweet. I was careful not to look at her neck.

"Come on." She grabbed my hand to lead me to a table. "Let's go catch up."

I took my hand away and followed her, hoping she hadn't noticed how cold I felt. We found a table with a dim lamp hanging over it. A couple passed us, laughing. I watched them sit at a table together, and I envied their carefree attitude. Corinne watched me, closely.

"Everyone's been worried about you."

I shrugged, "Worried that I might be dead?"

She frowned. My voice had sounded incongruous.

"Yes, as a matter of fact," she stated.

We looked at each other for a moment.

"I'm far from dead," I replied, smiling, "as you can see."

We talked for awhile, and I drank with her, though the alcohol had no effect on me. It tasted bitter, and I didn't care for it. I was used to drinking warm blood, not iced drinks. I marveled at this for a moment, until I realized she was watching me again. She looked very sad.

"What's wrong?"

"I was just wondering why you never wrote me back."

"Oh." I paused, trying to think of an excuse to make amends. I finally decided to tell her the truth. "I never read it."

"Why not?"

I thought for a moment and then sighed. "Because I didn't want to."

Corinne took another sip of her drink, absorbing my words. She avoided eye contact. I'd hurt her feelings.

"But I'd like to, now," I added.

"Forget it," she said, frowning.

I looked at her neck. My stomach was starting to hurt. I needed to get away from her.

"I have to go," I said, standing up. "I'm sorry, Corinne."

She stood and followed me as I made my way to the exit.

"Sorry for insulting me?" she asked, "Or for walking out on all of us."

I stopped in my tracks. This wasn't the way I wanted to end the evening with her.

Little did I know how much worse it was going to get.

"Go back inside," I warned her. "You don't want to be with me right now." My hunger was growing. I tried to walk away from her.

She grabbed hold of my arm, "You left because of me, didn't you?"

The pain in my stomach intensified. I needed to feed.

"No," I growled. I was telling myself no, because I wanted to grab hold of her. I wanted to kiss her. Or much worse.

She thought I'd just answered her question. She tightened her grip on my arm as if to keep me there.

"Stop lying," she demanded. "They told me how you felt about me."

"Who?" I hissed. I already knew the answer.

"Everyone," she replied. "They all told me you were in love with me."

All the old feelings came flooding back, and I was suddenly angry with myself. I did love her. And I was angry with her for knowing it. A group of people came out of the club, interrupting us. I could easily have left her then, but something kept me there: my ego.

"You were a goddamn cunt tease," I retorted. "You kept fucking with me, even though you knew I wanted you!"

She was shocked by my candor. I saw her pulse quickening in her neck. I gazed at it longingly. I swallowed hard and looked her in the eyes. I wanted to make her as angry as I was.

"But, don't flatter yourself," I sneered. "I was never in love with you. I only wanted to fuck you."

She looked at me as if she wanted to strike me, and I felt deeply satisfied knowing that I'd hurt her. I couldn't help myself. My stomach growled, and I didn't know how much longer I could control myself. It was then that I knew I would take her.

There were trees behind me. I backed away from her, as if to lure her into the shadows. I didn't have to control her. She followed me all too willingly into the cover of darkness. I backed myself against one of the trees, daring her to come at me, and she did. But instead of trying to hurt me, she grabbed me and kissed me on the mouth. It surprised me. Lust enveloped me as I started kissing her back. I was hungry for her in every way.

I slid my hand under her blouse and over one of her breasts. I played with her nipple and felt it swell between my fingers. And then I lifted her skirt, reaching between her legs. She was wet, and I could feel her opening up for me. She moaned and kissed me harder. I had only ever killed my victims instantaneously. But Corinne's death would be special; I still loved her.

I played with her and waited until she was about to come before I bit into her neck and started to drink. I could feel the fear and confusion rising up in her. I entered her mind, just as Kyrelle had entered mine. I willed her to not be afraid. She immediately relaxed in my arms as I continued to drink. My intense hunger finally subsided, and I could feel my body growing warm. This was better than sex, I thought.

Her dream had begun. I watched it as she melted into me. I knew her most private thoughts and saw the people who were important to her. I saw our mutual friends, and I was there, too. She was dreaming about me. I was reading her mind and I knew what she wanted. I stopped feeding to kiss her again. She felt the same pleasure I had once felt when Kyrelle had kissed me. When I drank from her I could hear what she was thinking. She wanted to be with me. She wanted me to make her come. I drank until her heart slowed. The letter entered her mind. She had written to tell me how she felt. She was in love with me.

All at once it was as if I woke from my own dream. I realized what I was seeing and what it meant. She still loved me. I stopped taking her blood, but it was too late. She was barely alive.

I gathered her up in my arms and ran. We reached my house and I carried her down to the cellar. I gently placed her on my bed. I was helpless as she lay there dying. All I could do was lay next to her and hold her close. She wasn't dreaming anymore. I kissed her, wishing we could finally be together. But she was unconscious and felt cold to the touch. I hated that I felt so warm.

"Corinne," I whispered in her ear, "stay with me."

I felt her take one last breath before she died in my arms.

I'd killed her, but I didn't want to believe she was gone. I held her for a minute longer before I remembered her letter. I jumped up and grabbed it off the shelf. I greedily tore it open and read it. It was all there. She missed me and wanted me to come back. My friendship was important to her. Our friends had told her how I felt. She was attracted to me and wanted to be with me. If I still loved her, would I come to her? She promised to love me back.

I read it over and over again. I was torturing myself, but I couldn't stop. I thought if I read it enough times, her own words would bring her back to life. It went on like this until I couldn't stay awake any longer. The sun was coming up and I needed to rest. I crawled back into bed with her and held her close. The last thing I remembered was the letter slipping out of my hand, but I was too tired to retrieve it.

That night I woke with a start. It was pitch black in the cellar, but my eyes adjusted immediately. I was still spooning Corinne's body, and she was warm from me holding her all night. I stayed with her, not wanting to get up. I just wanted to die. And the irony of it was that I couldn't die. I sighed and pulled her closer to me for comfort. And then it happened.

"You're squeezing the life out of me," she teased.

Surprised, I looked down at her. She turned her head and looked up at me, flashing that gorgeous smile.

Waif

TULSA BROWN

Heroin, I thought. The young woman across the desk from me showed the classic signs of long-term use. She was as thin as a fleeting hope and wore a long-sleeved sweater on a day when perspiration had welded my chubby thighs together beneath my cotton skirt.

But it was her pallor that caught my eye and made my stomach clench. Her skin seemed translucent, as delicate as a china teacup, the kind your fingertips glow through. Junk's calling card. I'd even noticed it in the waiting room, where she'd sat as still and composed as a blonde icon in the noisy, scruffy throng. I'd hoped one of the other assessment clerks would get her. Even after six years in social services, addiction rattled me.

Yet now she was here.

"Please take off your sunglasses." I smiled to soften it. "I like to see the person I am talking to."

"May I close the blinds?" Her voice was smooth and throaty, more resonant than I'd expected from her petite frame.

"Of course."

She rose and turned to adjust the Venetians. I felt a pang that was completely unprofessional. Her ass was perfect beneath her short skirt, saucy, enticing, ripe with health. How could that possibly be? And how could I live on wretched salads, rice cakes, and Diet Coke, only to have the same twenty pounds glare back from the mirror, year after year.

She had to be young. I scanned the application for assistance, looking for her age. But that line was black, as were all the lines, except for her name: Lucy Fenton.

The room was hushed in unnatural twilight now. Lucy sat down again, pushed her sunglasses to the top of her head, and pulled back the thick sweep of shoulder-length hair. My God. Her delicate, gamin features seemed to leap out at me, the haunting face of a silent-screen waif. Her gray eyes were large and luminous, perfectly balanced with her cherubic lips and willowy swan's neck. She looked poised in the breathless, teetering moment between girl and woman.

And she was needy. A vast hunger radiated out from her, burning even more brightly than her beauty. My womb moved.

Carol, stop it, I ordered myself. This is an adult with serious life issues. The only way to help her is to process her.

I cleared my throat. "Lucy, we have to fill in the rest of this form before we can proceed. Date of birth?"

"October fourteenth."

Tingles whispered over my scalp. That was my birthday. "Year?"

She told me and I looked up. "Really?"

"Why, yes. Is something wrong?"

I laughed, a silly, embarrassed flutter. "Oh, no. Nothing. It's just hard to believe that you're twenty-nine." The same age as me. Exactly. Another shiver shimmered over my skin.

I bent over the page and dutifully nailed down the facts of Lucy Fenton's life: sketchy employment, dozens of addresses, no family support available. I breathed a silent sigh of relief to discover she had no children; in this office, a woman her age could have six. When I learned she wasn't married, even common law, the revelation was a mild surprise, like that of a cat brushing my bare leg.

"You're blushing," Lucy said.

"Oh." I looked up, and the warmth in my cheeks flared to a blaze. How had she ever noticed in the low light?

"It's . . . so hot in this room. The air conditioning is from the stone age." Quick smile, clear the throat again. "Are you presently employed, Lucy?"

"I'm an artist."

I folded my hands on the desk. "Well. This isn't the National Endowment for the Arts. You have no dependents, and you seem fit and able to work. Lucy, why on earth are you applying for government assistance?"

"Because I'm desperate. And I wanted to meet you."

"Pardon?"

"I see you all the time on your way to work. You're so beautiful, vibrant, and strong. In control."

I felt stunned by the wash of praise, drunk on it. This exquisite creature thought I was beautiful?

"The sun shines on your hair; you just glow as you walk through the square. Then you stop at the doughnut shop and get a sour-cream double-fudge doughnut with sprinkles. I know you must be so late because you eat it so fast."

For an instant I was paralyzed by the shock of guilty pleasure, as if she'd found me with my hand between my legs. That's exactly what I'd done, more times than I'd let myself admit. Then the waves of shame ignited into outrage. Who was this woman? What the hell was her game? Lucy was gazing at me with a coy smile, a precocious child who'd caught an adult in a lie.

"Miss Fenton," I bristled, "my life is not under discussion; yours is. I'm trying to determine why you feel incapable of self-sufficiency. Do you have a history of substance abuse? Are you currently engaged in the misuse of illicit drugs, alcohol, or prescription medication?"

Her smile didn't dip, but it crystallized. "Define *abuse*."

"I think we both know what the means."

"And I think we're all addicted to something, Carol." My name in her mouth was a bold caress, a startling intimacy. "Some of those substances are socially acceptable, and some aren't. But we're all creatures of pleasure. And our greatest pleasure seems to be in judging each other for it."

The fiery glow of need I'd felt radiating from her earlier seemed focused on me then, like a spotlight. Her eyes said, I know you, the beast beneath your skin. Sweat filmed on my upper lip, trickled beneath the heavy curve of my breasts. My sex was slick, and I was . . . frightened.

I stood, my best Bureaucratic Bitch rising within me. "Thank you, Miss Fenton. Now, there are people waiting out there who genuinely need help."

She lifted an eyebrow, and in that instant became a steely debutante. "And you're going to save them?"

"Get out."

She glided to the door. With her hand on the knob, she turned and looked back at me, her eyes liquid in the strange twilight of my office. I felt a clutch. What was the color of longing?

"I mean it, you know. You are beautiful." Her gaze touched on the crowded waiting room. "And that may be the only bit of truth you hear today."

She lowered her sunglasses and was gone.

I went back to work with my usual smooth surface, mechanically processing the applicants who came through my office. But Lucy Fenton haunted me. I simmered between anger and wonder. Had she somehow researched me? It made me uneasy, but the other alternative was even scarier: that we did have the same birthday, that she had watched me and knew secrets beneath my skin. Even thinking about her gave me a dizzying rush. My clit pulsed, a tiny heartbeat between my legs.

Stop it. She came to you because she needs help, and you failed her. Even if she's not qualified for assistance, you should have told her what programs were available to help her battle her addiction. It was your moral duty, never mind your job,

I picked up the phone half a dozen times but never made the call. Late in the afternoon, a woman broke into tears in my office.

"If I don't come back with a check, he'll hit me. But what can I do? I just need that man. I need him." She was sobbing into her hands.

I moved around my desk and sat beside her, squeezing her shoulders. She was small like Lucy, a trembling little bird beaming ferocious heat. She leaned against me, and I felt strong, powerful.

"I want to quit that man, but I can't. I'll die without him. Oh, God. Somebody help me!"

I stroked her curly hair, floating in the roar of her need. Drinking it. Swimming between my legs.

I phoned my connection at Women's Services, who sent out two seasoned mobile workers. They knew every shelter and hustled her away with the swift skill of rum runners before she changed her mind.

Leaving, she seized my hand. "I'm so afraid."

The memory of her enormous, fluid eyes, the blaze of her compulsion, followed me down the polished government hall, while my thighs chafed against each other like rusted gears, and my heart beat in my throat.

Into the bathroom, into a stall. My quaking hands fumbled

to lift my skirt. I plunged past my thick, rainforest thatch into the scalding river beneath. I found my clit, an engorged, rearing little beast, and imagined sucking on Lucy's hard nipple, her voice crooning to me, smoke and steel.

We're all addicted to something, Carol.

Convulsing against the cool steel door. Terrible, sinful, exquisite electrocution. And as I twitched, lashed my bliss, hating myself, I wanted more. More and deeper. Terrified of it. More.

I leaned my forehead against the stillness, breathing rapidly even in my relief. I felt as though Lucy Fenton had peeled back a thin veneer from my body and what was underneath rose and churned like a dark sea. It had to stop. I would phone her tonight, discharge my duty. Exorcize her from my thoughts. I had to stop this.

She wasn't surprised to hear from me, and my apology seemed to amuse her.

"Yes, you were a bitch, weren't you?"

Her teasing, bluesy voice was a caress against my ear, a stroke down my shoulder. My nipple hardened, even though the words made my face prickle.

"I just . . . didn't behave as professionally as I could have," I agreed stiffly. "Listen, there are programs that can help you, Lucy, and they're free. I have all the infor—"

"You could bring it over. You know my address."

My irritation flared. "I'm not a caseworker, and I'm not a courier either."

"Carol." Her voice dropped like a veil. "I'm having a hard time right now. Please. I'd just like to see you."

That note under the words, a kitten's plaintive cry. I swayed, every molecule of my body awake.

"It'll take me half an hour to get there," I said.

I changed my clothes four times, but nothing was going to

hide those twenty pounds of secret indulgence or the fact that I was so nervous my face glimmered with an eager, anxious sheen. I finally settled on black jeans and a tube top covered with a gauzy blouse. My eyeliner smudged to blurry shadows beneath my eyes. With my short, dark hair I looked like a silent movie actor, not the tearful femme but the man who rescued her.

Lucy lived in a refurbished part of downtown where old, ornate apartments crowded each other like overdressed maiden aunts. I stood for a moment in the security foyer of her building, staring at the extravagant details. If she really lived here, Lucy Fenton did not have a problem with money.

For God's sake, the woman's playing you. Like the birthday. Get out now.

But the tingles of alarm felt just like excitement, the vertigo thrall of a cliff. Who could come this far and not look over the edge? As if it belonged to someone else, I watched my fingers press the button for L. Fenton. The door buzzed open without a word.

The hallway on the fifth floor was silent, sour, airless, and worn. But when I rapped on the heavy wooden door and Lucy answered, all other thoughts fluttered away.

Her beauty caught me fresh, like a slap. She was still pale, but there was a brightness to her skin, the cool, satiny surface of polished marble. Her hair hung thick and straight in astonishing shafts of color: sunlight to cedar, a blonde rainbow. She was wearing an icy-blue slip with spaghetti straps, and her breasts swayed underneath, small but firm, nipples pressing against the silk like shimmering buttons. I could have chewed through the blue straps with a single bite.

She fingered my chiffon blouse. "You might want to take that off. I have no air conditioning."

I followed her into the apartment, mesmerized by the

fluid rise and fall of her hips. She moved like milk, but the foundering, professional part of my brain managed to notice one thing: There were no tracks on her delicate little limbs. Lucy's dependency took another form.

I don't know what I'd expected inside. Not poverty—I'd already unraveled that lie, but disarray, a life distilled into a single pulse. I was stunned by the vast, airy swoop of ten-foot ceilings, the rich, dark elegance of antique furniture. My gaze darted everywhere, even as I chattered nervously about the pamphlets I'd brought.

" . . . includes a support circle that meets three times a week . . . *oh*."

My voice tumbled down a well. Lucy turned, twinkling.

"You like my paintings?"

The walls were covered in canvases, four-foot landscapes of flesh to tiny, astringent snapshots. They were all paintings of women—from buxom Renaissance beauties to long-legged gazelles, in cinnamon, coffee, caramel, cream—and they were all bound in some way: cuffed in steel, knotted in silk or leather. One woman was wrapped in bungee cords, black rubber cutting deep tracks into her soft flesh. Another was gagged with a pink belt, the quaint gold heart buckle just below her ear.

Their faces blazed out on me, dozens of vibrant flames, burning, needy.

I was abruptly molten. My sex was flowing, cleaved by the tight seam of my jeans, overripe fruit that had burst its skin. My gauzy blouse clung like a wet second skin.

I grappled for my Bureaucratic Bitch pose. "Very nice, although the symbolism is a bit heavy-handed. Are you trying to shock me? Is that why you wanted me to come over?"

"You don't look shocked; you look hot." She smiled. "I warned you to take off that blouse."

Enough fencing. I had to know. "You have a friend in Vital Stats, is that it? My birthday wasn't so hard to get."

Lucy settled onto the narrow, padded arm of the old sofa and crossed one leg over the other, miles of marble thigh, blue silk riding up.

"Did you know you trailed thoughts, Carol? They stream after you like perfume."

"Oh please." I let contempt curl the words. "I know you're not a mind reader."

"No, I can't read your mind, but I can read the thoughts you discard. The ones you toss away, can't bear to look at. Too embarrassing, too nasty. Thrilling. Like what happened in the bathroom today."

Horror flashed hot and cold, lightning against the clouds. "I don't know what your game is, Lucy, but it's sick, and I'm not going to play it." Sputtering, steaming. "I came here in good faith because I thought you needed help—"

"You came here to devour me."

I turned, a blind, furious bolt for the door. I don't know how in God's name she got there first, but she did. I almost ran into her. She was devastating against the old oak, a winsome siren with storm-gray eyes, a lost child slipped into a woman's body. My anger was undone, and I stood, heart thudding in my ears, wanting her.

"Have you ever thought about how easy it would be if someone already knew your secrets?" Lucy said. "Your dark, sticky fantasies, the ones you wouldn't dare whisper in a lover's ear? You'd never have to ask, never have to admit them. They'd just happen."

I felt lightheaded, stoned on the rush of desire. Her breasts under the slip were like plump, satin fruit.

"And what about your fantasies?" I whispered boldly.

"Come see my work-in-progress." The words were heavy

with promise. I was hooked, so slick I felt oiled. I followed her though a short labyrinth of narrow hallways, her pale legs whispering in the shadows ahead of me, two slender ghosts.

Turpentine. Linseed oil. The acrid scents made my nostrils twitch when we entered the room. Then Lucy clicked the light switch, and I saw that it was like any other studio, except for the accessories. A large iron ring hung from the ceiling. The handcuffs, belts, scarves, and even the rubber cords were scattered around the room. I stared for long minutes, my body humming, alarmed and intrigued. I recognized the paraphernalia from her paintings, but she'd said she could peek into my fantasies. Was I gazing at Lucy's need or at mine?

"Are you going to look at my work?" Lucy called.

I turned. The blonde crown of her head was just visible behind the canvas that rested on an easel. I felt a nameless leap of warning; I didn't want to see that painting. But Lucy's blue slip was draped over the edge now, as if it were an old-fashioned boudoir screen. She was wearing nothing behind the canvas.

Trembling steps. I unbuttoned and shrugged off the chiffon blouse, let it slide to the floor in my wake. When I rounded the corner, the sight of her was a sweet collision with my senses.

She was a cool confection, whipping cream and cinnamon hearts. Unveiled, her ass was a marvel, insolent curved slopes that jutted out farther than seemed possible on her graceful frame. The dainty, gingery muff of pubic hair barely hid the cleft beneath. My mouth watered. I felt like a dark beast next to her. There was a deep pile of cushions on the studio floor, and I wanted to lay her back on it, spread her wide with my tongue, a mewing dessert.

I reached out to cup her bare breast and her cheek. She caught both my wrists in a grip that opened my eyes. Lucy was strong.

"Look," she demanded.

I looked. On the canvas, loose strokes of color sketched out form, light, and depth with breathtaking simplicity. But the image was unmistakable: It was me clinging to that iron ring, my head thrown back in agony or rapture. I was bound by only one thing: a long snake wound around my nakedness, its slick, jewel-colored body strangling or embracing, its fangs sunk deep into my breast, over my heart.

Repulsion, then arousal, an aftershock. I knew I was looking over the cliff edge.

"Your fantasy and mind just happen to be a happy coincidence," she said softly.

As if in a dream I let her lead me to the ring. I reached up and closed my hands around it, the thin metal a piece of cool reality I could cling to. With my face tucked between my arms, I felt stretched and vulnerable; my labia throbbed with anticipation.

She peeled my clothes off, jeans, tube top, and panties. Her small hands danced over my bare flesh, coaxing and massaging, or tweaking me in sudden, bright nips of pain. She began to oil me, kneading my heavy breasts, squeezing my buttocks, edging close to my wet, aching pussy, then sliding away in a silky tease.

I writhed on the ring. "Please, Lucy."

"You beauty," she murmured. "So omnipotent behind that desk. Round, ripe, full of power. And their lives are stretched so thin in front of you." The words were wet, as if she was salivating. "Some of them splinter, and some melt. Do they ever beg?"

I felt a streak of scalding embarrassment. "Yes."

"Do you like it?"

"I thought I didn't have to tell you . . ."

"But you want to tell me, Carol." Lucy's voice was an oboe

against my ear, and she twisted my nipples expertly. Starbursts of pain. "So . . . do you like it when they beg?"

Slippery, squeezing shame. "Yes."

"Of course you do. You wanted me to plead with you. I could feel it across the room. You were hovering, waiting for it. Weren't you, you needy bitch?"

The welt of lust struck deep within me, a scalding V that made me moan. Lucy slid her hand over my ass, stroked it as if admiring the haunch of a fine animal. The other spread my eager legs wider and teased my clit by flicking a finger, snapping. I strained, thrusting my hips, trying to make deeper contact.

"I want to touch you," I gasped. She ignored my plea.

"It's your 'hit' isn't it? It's such a rush when they cry."

I saw the little bird from the afternoon, her frail shoulders under my arm, trembling as she sobbed. My cunt contracted.

"No."

"Liar."

Snap! I twitched at the pain that quickly bloomed into heat. Lucy slithered around me, hard nipples tantalizing my back. My whole being had become one craving, a grasping, twisting, desire. I clung to the ring like hope itself, afraid she'd stop touching me if I let go.

"It gets you high, gets you off. Say it." Feathery strokes between my legs, smearing my juice up the crack of my ass and down again. "Say it! Whisper 'I'm a needy bitch.'"

She plunged her fingers up into my cunt, and I gasped with the hard force and billowing pleasure.

"Again!"

I said it once more, reveling in the surrender of those terrible words and riding the exquisite thrust of her hand. Lucy tugged on me, finally urging me to let go. With relief I lowered my rubbery arms and embraced her, small, feminine curves snaking against mine. I caught her nipples between my fingers and squeezed. The little cry made me sway.

We melted onto the lavish mound of cushions. I reached between her legs, but she pushed me back, smiling wickedly.

"Close your eyes. Just relax."

I gave myself over to her, to my own pleasure. Her fingers slid in and out of my pussy, thumb swirling softly over the hard kernel of my clit. Lustrous pleasure. I moaned deep in my throat and pushed harder against her. Faster, harder, lights beginning to flash behind my closed eyelids. Oh, so close . . .

There. Spasms of joy clutched my body and released it, over and over. Sliding, pearlescent colors swept through my flesh, bloomed in my toes and fingers.

I flinched when her teeth sank into my neck, a brilliant needle of alarm that smoothed out into a strange, undulating calm. Revelation. Possible and impossible bayed like distant dogs. I only understood one word, a deep rumble at the base of consciousness: vampire.

She didn't need to hold me; I was transfixed, conscious that I was flowing into her and submitting to it. My body still reverberated with orgasm, and yet I was a languid liquid, honey. The heat of her skin was rising against me, the power of my blood in her body. I gravitated toward that hearth, even though I couldn't move. I was huddling around the fire of my own life, a beggar, and it didn't even seem wrong.

She finally released me and eased onto her back, gasping. I smelled my own blood, metallic, earthy, the scent of secrets.

"Oh, God." Lucy released the words in a sigh. For long minutes we simply lay together, riding the ebb tide. Awareness crept back into me like a thief.

"Will I die?" My voice seemed to float far above me, a vapor.

"Oh, no. You're too precious to me, too sweet."

I laughed dreamily. "Sweet? You said I was a bitch."

"You are." Lucy rose on her elbow and gazed down at me. Her eyes were a mesmerizing luminous gray, as if steel was translucent. "I mean you literally taste sweet to me. All the emotions that stream through your office: heartache, despair, bare, burning need. Someone else would just process those poor souls, but you . . . you drink it up. Feed on it. And I feed on you."

I prickled with cold, abruptly awake. Oh, God. She was going to use me like a siphon. Not only that, she made me sound like . . . No.

"A vampire?" Lucy caught the rejected thought before it landed. "Of course you are, you always have been. You drink desperation, and I drink blood. Why do you think I chose you?" She smiled, a crimson scythe. "It takes one to know one, darling."

Horror throbbed where once was pleasure. I pushed myself up and felt a dizzying wallop—blood loss. I struggled on, fumbling for my clothes. "I'm leaving."

"By all means. You can even try to stay away." Lucy tilted her head back, skin glowing delicate pink now. "But one taste is usually enough."

I looked back at her, a great, devouring demon refolded into a waif, like a slip of paper that becomes an origami bird. I knew what she was now, and still all I wanted in the world was to lay down next to her.

Everyone is addicted to something.

Night Crew

BETTY BLUE

There was the day crew, and the gay crew. Fairuza had made the joke first, with lesbian privilege, when the nightshift had been limited to herself and Honesto. Had it been one of the day shift word processors—Timothy, for instance—everyone would have frowned quietly and a perfectly clever nom de guerre would have been wasted.

"I don't know; we may have to change the name," said Honesto when Aisling signed onto the night crew so that she could go back to school.

"Oh, no," she said with a smile. "My ex-girlfriend Artemis 'gave me over to depravity' a year ago. I was her toaster oven. I think she's been working on the entire set of coordinated kitchen appliances since, although I understand if you hold onto your points, you can trade them all in for an Olivia cruise once you reach a thousand."

From then on, it had been the three of them, and it had almost become *fun* to go to work. Work orders trickled in until 10:00 or 11:00, and when those jobs were finished, there was often nothing to do until quitting time at 4:30 in the morning. Sometimes they did homework (Honesto was an art student, and Ruza was working on her PhD in psychology), but often they just sat around and drank Ruza's fabulous Parisian coffee ("American coffee is an insult to the name," she said) and read the personal ads in the *Bay Times*. Ruza and Honesto were determined to find a new girlfriend for Aisling—although somehow Honesto nearly always managed to find an ad for himself among the ones he skimmed.

Of course, they might not have been as thrilled to have Aisling on their team if they had known she'd killed her last lover. It was the real reason she'd joined the night crew—that, and the increasing allergy she had to the daylight.

And, really, Aisling had only technically killed Eloise. Eloise was still out there somewhere, painting some town red—Chicago, Aisling thought, but she wasn't sure. Eloise had never been comfortable with Aisling's continued friendship with Artemis, and when Aisling had finally brought her over and she'd discovered Artemis had given Aisling her first blood kiss, Eloise had challenged Artemis. No one ever won in a fight against Artemis.

Aisling had met Artemis at Club Q. She had danced Aisling dizzy and then taken her out for a bite at an all-night café after the bars had closed. Aisling had thought the burger and fries had been the bite, but when she'd driven Artemis back to her car, the pale, lithe blonde had scooted over on the seat to give her a kiss goodbye . . . Aisling could never quite remember it afterward; but in the morning she'd woken up in her own bed, dizzy and sick, as soon as the sunlight crept into her room. Artemis had slipped out before dawn, but the smell of her still lingered. When Aisling had staggered out of bed to yank the curtains closed, she'd found the crisp, white shirt she'd worn the night before laid neatly over the chair by her bed, two small spots of blood on the lapel, and a note from Artemis in the pocket: "Thanks . . . you tasted sweet."

She'd also left the number for Drinkers Anonymous. It turned out to be a twelve-step program for the newly bitten, to help complete their transformation; step number twelve was passing the blood kiss on to a new friend of your own. Eloise had been Aisling's step twelve.

Aisling was over it now, in spite of DA. You didn't *have* to drink to survive. It wasn't as Hollywood as that. It was a choice, and Aisling had chosen not to imbibe. She didn't need the hassle. Artemis teased her mercilessly about being "on the wagon," but Aisling thought she was secretly pleased not to have the extra competition. Naturally, there were a few changes she'd had to make after the full transition, like working nights, and giving up sunbathing, but she'd never tanned well anyway, and she was really enjoying the nightshift.

"Oh—my—god," gasped Honesto, "this is so you!"

Aisling shook herself out of her little skip down memory lane and swiveled her chair around to see what Honesto was talking about.

He was circling something in the paper and he slid it over to Fairuza across the workstation. "Does that not just have Aisling written all over it?"

"*What?*" Aisling demanded, but Ruza was holding the paper out of reach to read the ad Honesto had circled.

"Oh, absolutely," Ruza agreed. She folded the paper over and moved it to the other side of her computer, picking up her phone and punching in a number as she ran her finger down the page.

"What are you doing?" asked Aisling.

Ruza waved a curt hand at her. "Alo," she said to the phone, with her heavy French accent. "I saw your ad in the *Times* and I think we should chat. My name is Aisling and you can reach me at—"

"Fairuza!" Aisling hissed. She jumped up and tried to grab the phone away from her, but Ruza had already finished giving the number to the voicemail box and she dropped the receiver back in the cradle with a grin.

"You can thank me later," said Ruza, handing Aisling the paper.

Aisling scanned the page and found the red circle. "Goth girl with glasses seeks artistic geek with a dark sense of humor," she read aloud. "Oh, thank you!" She threw the paper at Honesto who dodged it, laughing.

"You're always eyeing those girls with the pale skin and the black bangs," said Ruza. "And this one has glasses; she's brainy."

"How does that follow?" Aisling laughed.

"She must read, or she wouldn't need the glasses," said Ruza. "And she wants an artistic geek. Of course she's brainy."

"People do wear glasses for other things," said Aisling, folding her arms. "Working, for instance. But let's get back to the real point, which is 'artistic geek,' thank you very much."

"It's a compliment," said Honesto with a grin. "Just embrace the artistic geekiness which is you."

Aisling rolled her eyes and sat back down in her swivel chair. "I can't believe you left that message, Ruza."

"Ah, I do what I can," grinned Fairuza. "Can't let you keep going out with that Artemis and blow any chance you have to pick up chics."

"I think you mean 'chicks'."

"You pick up chicks, I'll pick up *chics*, eh?" Ruza grinned. "Don't change the subject. You look like a couple. You have to let go of her apron strings."

It hadn't exactly stopped them from hitting on Artemis, thought Aisling. But Ruza was right; she did tend to use Artemis as a buffer; if women passed her over when they went out, she could always blame it on Artemis's long legs and striking Nordic looks, or just assume they must have thought Aisling was already taken.

So of course it was with Artemis the following weekend that

Aisling agreed to meet Vesta. Vesta, the "Goth girl with glasses," had left a return message on Aisling's voicemail saying she'd be at the Musee Mechanique near Pier 39 Saturday evening, and Aisling could find her by the antique peep-shows-in-a-box. "I'll be there around dusk," Vesta's message said. "They close a little after that, so if I don't see you by then, no sweat. I'll just take that as a sign you changed your mind."

"'Vesta'," said Artemis, listening to the message as they sipped their drinks at the café across the park from the mechanical toy museum, waiting for dusk. "You do seem to attract the classical types," she said, dropping the cell phone back into her suit pocket. The wink wasn't visible behind the dark blue rectangular shades, but she allowed just a touch of her sharp canines to show. She took a sip of her Bloody Mary (Artemis couldn't resist a pun). "You're lucky I adore you, Pooky. There are precious few people in the world who could get me out of bed before true dark to play watchdog on their blind date. But you, my darling, need to get some throat."

"You know, it really doesn't help me feel toppish when you call me Pooky," Aisling said dryly. She swizzled at her Bombay Sapphire and tonic.

The waning glow of indirect light from the last of civil twilight had finally cooled. Artemis slipped her glasses—a match to the color of the gin bottle and the night—down her aquiline nose. "There's your Goth girl," she said, nodding across the street, gray eyes flashing almost violet with approval.

A young woman with jet-black dyed hair tied in a high ponytail, Bettie Page bangs, and a pair of rhinestone-studded, cat's-eye glasses had paused in front of the Musee to look around before entering.

"How do you know that's her?" asked Aisling.

"How do you know that's *she*," Artemis corrected. "Please. Look at that cassock-style coat; it's straight out of the *Matrix*

Reloaded. Go get your Trinity, sweetie." Artemis gave her a little nudge, and with her predator's strength, it knocked Aisling's ass right off of her stool.

"All right, all right. I'm going." Aisling took one last, long draught of the Sapphire and tonic and set down the glass.

"And if you're not going to suck her," Artemis called after her as Aisling reached the door, "give me her number." The other café patrons gave Aisling a disapproving look as she passed. Somehow Artemis always managed to coolly deflect any negative vibes.

Aisling wandered into the museum, trying to act casual, looking for the long coat over the top of her own dark glasses— hers were red and round to complement Artemis's; Aisling really had been hanging on her coattails too long—and caught sight of "Goth girl" leaning over the ornate iron plate on one of the old-fashioned moving picture viewers. Aisling tucked her white muscle-T into the dark jeans behind her ratty leather biker jacket, wishing she'd worn something a little more hip, and approached.

"Are you Vesta?" she asked, and the girl straightened and turned around with a quizzical look.

"You don't sound French in person," she said after looking Aisling over.

"No; that wasn't me on your voicemail," Aisling explained, tucking her hands into her back pockets. "My friend. She thought she was doing me a favor."

Vesta raised a dark, high-arched eyebrow even higher above the pointed rhinestone frames. "And you don't think she did."

Aisling would have blushed if she'd had enough blood in her system. "No, that's not what I mean." She laughed. "I'm sorry. I haven't done this in a while." She took her right hand out of her pocket and held it out. "Let me start over. I'm Aisling."

"*Enchanté*," said Vesta, and brought the hand to her lips.

Aisling laughed, suppressing an unexpected shiver at the moist touch of Vesta's mouth against her skin. "Is that why you chose the Musee Mechanique? You thought I was French?"

"No, I just really like these old kinetoscopes," said Vesta. She dropped a quarter into the machine's slot and gestured for Aisling to take a look. "There's something really wonderful about the frank way they look at the camera."

Aisling bent down and watched the silent images flash by. Barely exposed flesh of calves and shoulders beneath 1920s boy-waisted slips was as risqué as they got, but the smiles on the turn-of-the-century faces were startlingly real, their eyes meeting the eyes of the beholder just beneath the veil of thick lashes. "You're right," she said as the picture ended. "Those are amazing." She smiled. "That one looked kind of like you."

The lights came up in the museum then and she grimaced distastefully.

"Yeah, I know," said Vesta. "They're closing already. But I really just wanted to find a nice public place to meet, just in case either of us wanted to back out."

"And do we?" asked Aisling.

"Not so far," said Vesta with a smile. "I don't see you running." She took Aisling's hand with ease and headed for the exit. "Plus, I like walking along Aquatic Park in the moonlight," she said as she drew Aisling along. "I know, cliché. But it's always been one of my favorite places in the city."

Out in the light evening breeze on the pier as they headed for the nearby park, Aisling sniffed appreciatively. "No, I know what you mean. It's one of my favorites, too." It always seemed like a local secret, even though it was so close to the densely packed tourist haunts at Fisherman's Wharf. There was certainly less of a crowd in this direction, and less light. Both good.

She hadn't planned to try to drink Vesta; she'd really

thought she was over that, had mastered that desire. But who was she kidding? The scent of Vesta's skin as the tail of her coat streamed behind them was a maddeningly tempting note beneath the piscine bay breeze.

Aisling leaned back against one of the worn wooden posts at the water's edge when they reached the end of the long fish-hook shaped curve and sighed. She was going to savor this one. Start it slow, kiss Vesta for a while, taking a playful nip at the soft skin of her throat. Maybe they'd even fuck before Aisling went in for the kill. It had certainly been a long dry spell since she'd had any of that as well. But she wasn't going to bring this one over. That was always a mistake. It was too bad, because Vesta would make a lovely apprentice, but Aisling couldn't afford the emotional upheaval right now.

Vesta moved around her—almost a predatory circling motion, Aisling thought—her slight smile amused.

"What's that look for?" asked Aisling, prodding the tip of one long incisor with her tongue behind her lips in anticipation.

"You. You think you're going to get lucky." Vesta traced her finger along Aisling's collarbone, and the slight touch where skin hovered over skin made Aisling's cunt warm. "You're thinking about how I'll taste, aren't you?" she whispered in Aisling's ear. "I know you are," said Vesta, "because that's what I'm thinking about you." Aisling saw the flash of silver in the moonlight just before Vesta struck.

"You bitch!" she gasped, feeling the bloodless cut the knife had made at her collar. If it hadn't been for the moonlight, she would never have known what hit her, wouldn't have had time to dodge the full attack.

Vesta circled her again, tossing the knife casually from hand to hand. "You're a bit faster than Ana guessed, but she was right; you're stupid."

Aisling felt a surge of fury and adrenaline as the blood at

last started to trickle down her front. "Ana," she said. "Eloise."

"Two points for you," sneered Vesta, slashing out again, but missing Aisling as she slipped to the side. Vesta didn't seem perturbed. She seemed prepared to settle in for a long skirmish. "Ana said you were a teetotaler, but I thought you'd at least recognize a sister, even if you were rusty in the game."

Aisling began to match her circling steps so that they danced slowly around one another. She never carried a weapon, but she had a few moves. She'd taken kung fu briefly before she'd been turned, not enough to be any good at it, but enough to keep a bitch like Vesta on her toes. And there was nothing like humiliation-driven rage to give a girl a little clarity. Aisling didn't like to be tricked. "That was you in the kinetoscope," she said.

"Oh, brava! Give the girl a cookie!" Vesta laughed.

Aisling stepped forward as Vesta lunged again, catching her off guard with the unexpected direction, and used Vesta's own momentum against her, swinging her elbow against the top of Vesta's spine and throwing her to the pavement. Blood poured from Vesta's nose as she scrambled to her feet; she had fed just before they'd met. That was the warm scent that had thrown Aisling off, making Vesta seem so lifelike. It also made her stoned.

When the younger woman (*correction, older,* Aisling amended) leaped at her again, Aisling went for the knife. This time she wasn't fast enough, and Vesta's dark eyes flashed red behind the cracked rhinestone rims as she spun and struck again, managing a deeper strike at Aisling's side. If it hadn't been for the old coat, she might have been able to bury the knife in Aisling's ribs. Aisling ducked low as Vesta stabbed again and swept out swiftly with one boot to knock Vesta off her feet. The silver blade struck the ground with a clatter as Vesta lost her grip. She leaped on Vesta as the girl scrambled for the knife, grabbing her by the hip-Goth ponytail. The knife slipped over the edge of the walkway into the bay.

"Well, look who's a little rusty after all, granny," Aisling hissed as she pulled Vesta's head back to snap it against the pavement. A sharp blow to her own head surprised her from behind.

Vesta was on her feet before Aisling could fully turn to see what had hit her. Aisling stumbled back and looked up as two pairs of boots planted themselves beside Vesta's. "God, I really hate you!" said Vesta, flinging blood from her broken nose with the back of her wrist. Beside her, Fairuza offered her a handkerchief. Honesto flanked Vesta's left.

"You've got to be kidding me," said Aisling, rubbing the back of her head.

Honesto dropped the rock he'd beaned her with, with an apologetic shrug and a guilty smile.

"It's nothing personal," said Ruza. "If that helps."

"No, it really doesn't," Aisling glared. "What did she promise you, anyway? Eternal life? The chance to kiss her ass and eat bugs for the rest of your short one?"

"There's no need to make insulting Renfield jokes," Honesto pouted. "It was either play the game or have our necks snapped. I really like my neck."

Vesta shoved the soaked handkerchief back at Fairuza. "You're good, but not good enough," she said, pulling off her broken glasses. "And you're going to pay for these."

"Yeah, well," said Aisling, getting to her feet, "girls who wear glasses shouldn't throw stones."

"Actually, I threw the stone," said Honesto and then shut his mouth at a look from Vesta.

"It's pretty sad that you need the help of not one but two Renfields to take me on," said Aisling.

"I don't need any help," said Vesta, waving her companions back. "They're just—"

"A little fortifying midnight snack after you burn all those blood calories you had earlier?"

Fairuza and Honesto exchanged glances.

"Save your breath for my teeth, bitch," Vesta snarled, lunging at her once more.

They went down, tumbling across the walkway at the end of the pier, tearing at one another, teeth and nails ripping flesh. Vesta darted in, fangs flashing, toward Aisling's jugular, but Aisling managed to sink her own teeth into the front of Vesta's throat first. The hot blood from Vesta's last victim sprang into Aisling's mouth and Aisling forgot for a moment that she was fighting as the rich notes of the blood, slick like melted 99 percent cacao Scharffenberger chocolate, swam against her tongue. Damn, she had forgotten how good this could be. The blood was already rushing through her as she swallowed, heading toward her cunt and hardening her tits.

Vesta tore away from her and slashed at Aisling's throat with her nails. She managed a deep enough cut to draw real blood this time, from what little Aisling had, but she was losing so much of her own from the jagged wound at her throat that she was losing the advantage of the strength of age.

She struck again, burying her razor-sharp nails in the side of Aisling's neck, and then fell forward over Aisling, gasping for air. Aisling had been fumbling at the edge of the walkway and had seen the silver knife perched on a support beam just below the pier. The knife was now buried to the hilt in Vesta's left breast. All of her stolen blood was now pouring over Aisling. "I really hate you," she gasped.

"You know, I really don't like you either," said a voice above them, and one of Artemis's boot heels struck the Goth girl's neck, snapping her spine. "That little snot Eloise left me a cocky e-mail," said Artemis, extending a hand to Aisling. "Said a friend of hers was in town." Aisling scrambled up and

Artemis looked appreciatively at the blood-soaked T-shirt. "I should have known my little Pooky could hold her own." She took a quick swipe at Aisling's throat with her tongue.

Fairuza and Honesto were still standing off to the side, not sure what they were supposed to do now that their mistress was dead. Artemis raised an eyebrow. "And who are your little friends?"

"The night crew," said Aisling. She and Artemis exchanged a glance, and Artemis gave a little shrug before moving with a motion so quick it was almost invisible, knocking both the human's heads together.

She held the dazed Renfields out by their throats, like naughty puppies. "I ate a little something earlier," said Artemis. "Which one do you want?"

Hope on the Mississippi

JEWELLE GOMEZ

Deep clouds covered the sky, turning the moon into a luminous back light. Their sensual glow hung low over the soft hills to the east, embracing the peaks. Gilda moved slowly along a road that showed signs of being taken back to nature's bosom. The lack of steady travel encouraged native grasses to take their rightful place and left the blacktop to crumble in peace.

Gilda had carefully unfolded and refolded worn motorist maps, long out of date; picking through what she recognized as remnants of highway. Studying computer-maintained maps online would have been too easily monitored and the feel of aging paper, frayed by use, felt good to her fingers. By identifying the local roads rarely used for long distance travel, she evaded notice. In over one hundred miles she'd passed a few trucks and cars but saw no one on foot. Even if she had they would have been unable to see her as she moved through the wind.

Her calculations indicated she was in Mississippi, quite near the winding river whose name was legend. "It just keeps rolling along . . . " Gilda hummed the lyrics of a song she hadn't heard in at least 75 years. *Yes, it rolls along,* she thought. After the last turn of the century and several years of unchecked storms, its banks had permanently overflowed. The river swallowed cookie cutter port shops, luxury homes, fishing shacks, hotels and stationery gambling barges, like they were colorful gumdrops. The result was a new and unpredictable shoreline for hundreds of miles, from the Gulf upriver to Chicago.

Water became the feared element, overshadowing the visceral response to fire. Hurricanes, torrential rains, tidal changes and pollution made living precarious. California, long the object of gruesome speculation because of the San Andreas and other fault lines, in the end, was victimized not by shifting ground, but by water. Without much preparation, valuable real estate succumbed to pelting rainstorms, crumbling cliffs and deadly tides. Cities, once landlocked, became the coastal ports of call.

And the east coast had no better fortune. By the year 2010 all of the barrier landmarks in the Atlantic—Long Island, Shelter Island, the Florida Keys—had disappeared. Water—long exploited, polluted, underestimated and overextended—was finally recognized as both precious and fearsome.

Over a twenty-year period small towns on the banks of the Mississippi had been washed away with the ease of soap swirling down a drain. They were quickly replaced by townships, once inland, now eager to establish new centers of business in their own backyards. It was in the wake of several natural disasters that corporate interests had begun to dominate. First came the rescue efforts, private industry stepping in where the government had ignored or failed stranded townships. Then came the rebuilding projects desperately needed even as they lined the pockets of profiteers. The change was subtle and insidious. Corporations controlled food, tents, building materials as well as the trucks and planes to deliver them. They began to rebuild towns that now belonged to them. Ultimately corporate control of the government structure continued as usual.

As Gilda made her way west and south the echo of desolation was disturbing despite the full leafy shadows cast in the moonlight. She avoided the periodic islands of activity that dotted the main roads except when the hunger came upon her. The unnatural white light which linked together food courts, gas stations, coffee shops and other points of consumption made her despondent. From a distance Gilda recognized the standard brand names that had taken over the landscape—coffee, books, schools, groceries, it mattered little where in the country you were. People needn't bother touring the United States—-each metropolitan area, every island of shopping had become a duplicate of the next.

Rather than cover the final few hundred miles rapidly, Gilda decided to continue her languorous pace so that she could sniff the air more deeply and try to sense the changes around her. For the first time in more than a century, Gilda was in the region of her birth. The Mississippi plantation, where she'd lived until her mother's death and her escape, was a sharp image among so many others—distinctly defined and fragrant.

She stood still as if the memories of slavery might hang in the air, projections from the dim past. Alone on the road with her eyes closed and the night air on her face she could almost remember the feel of her mother's hands as she braided her hair. Beside that image came one of blood trickling from the wounds on her hands as she'd pulled cotton from stiff branches.

She opened her eyes and looked around quickly. In the air she could also smell dawn. It was time to find shelter. Uncounted times over the previous century Gilda had lived that same thought. At the time of her escape in the 1800s she'd plowed her way through alien territory certain she could obtain freedom if she refused to stop moving. Walking and running for days, she always sought shelter at dawn, hiding from citizens who would raise the alarm at the sight of an unaccompanied slave girl.

As the world around her worked through its day she would let restless sleep overtake her. In the thick nightmares that had burdened her daily rest she was always caught, then dragged mercilessly into the light and returned to the fields where she'd last seen her sisters. She'd awaken, choked by her own stifled cry and would then calm herself by listening to the movement of trees, wind and small animals around her. When darkness fell she would venture out again, moving with the same relentless stride that she had now. It was as if that flight into freedom had prepared her for the gift of long life she'd been given, a gift that required that she shade herself from direct daylight and only fully live during the night.

Gilda found her share of the blood at the beginning of this evening when she'd visited a truck stop on one of the main highways. A young woman who had entered the public bathroom stared idly in the hard light of the mirror after washing her face.

Vietnamese, Gilda thought as she looked into the woman's dark eyes. They were ringed by exhaustion and some confusion. Gilda had held the woman's gaze until her eyes no longer saw what was before them.

"We take blood, not life." Gilda let the phrase drift into the woman's mind, assuaging her fear. Gilda held her gently as she took the blood she needed to survive. The fingernail of her small finger slid effortlessly across the oak-colored skin, initiating a slight seepage. Gilda pressed her lips to the line of red as she listened to the woman's body. Sifting through the thoughts, Gilda searched for something that might help untangle her confusion. When she touched it, Gilda marveled at how often she found the answer to someone's need inside them. Gilda planted a seed that would grow into clarity, then left the woman smiling at herself in the rest room mirror.

Once back out on the road Gilda decided to push on for just a bit more. If she didn't find the proper shelter, she would turn back to a spot she'd encountered earlier. This landscape offered fewer dangers than it had a century earlier. It also provided fewer safe places. Over the decades trees and grassland had been devalued; cement, tarmac and prefabricated buildings dominated almost every vista. In a frenzy of retribution, the forest had reclaimed much of the land, enveloping abandoned malls and gas stations with the abandon of a mother recovering a lost child. The foolishness of it all was so apparent now when all the man-made things began to sink back under nature's hand.

Gilda let the sensation of escape fall behind her and with each hour she became more entranced by the road and where it led, not with the reasons for her being there.

As she walked she laughed inside herself at how happy her brother, Julius, had been that she'd decided to finally leave the security of home. She began to understand his need for travel. New words, images, people, ideas might be frightening. But the new can be a portal to another world or a door to an unknown place inside yourself.

He was less enthusiastic about Gilda's plan to visit Nadine, with whom she'd exchanged correspondence for several years. In her eastern enclave Gilda felt safe communicating with Nadine. The world was hers with only the click of the keyboard; Nadine remained safely miles away. Gilda visited her far-flung family on a regular basis without ever risking a move out of her cliffside enclave.

Julius, the youngest of those she called family, had made the cities of the Midwest his home ground where he'd settled into local activist circles. Grassroots organizations fought against the absorption of their businesses and towns into the corporate entity that was now their national government.

"The business of America is business," Gilda remembered the words of a long dead president. He too had believed that profit was the only religion. And when assembly lines had led to unemployment no one could quite believe the connection between corporate greed and the death of their neighborhoods.

Julius lived among those whose ancestors had been disenfranchised by people like Henry Ford and those who sat in his corporate chair. Descendents of 20th-century workers were only now trying to recover their land and their lives. As she traveled, Gilda missed Julius. He was as close to her as one of her sisters, whom she knew must have been dead for over a hundred years. On the road, Gilda avoided use of electronic devices and relied on a feeling that he was near.

As if the thought of family had conjured up comfort, her shelter appeared before her. A small building stood back from the road overrun with brush and vines. The cracked paint and split wood marked its abandonment. It looked as if it had once been a weighing station for commercial trucks when this road was well traveled. Gilda peeled back the planks covering the doorway, dropped her pack and sleeping roll inside.

She tapped the concrete floor with a piece of the window molding which was half eaten through by termites—not her image of ideal accommodations but it was inconspicuous and in a way suited her. She slammed her booted heel down onto the concrete floor in two places. The dull thuds underrepresented the muscle behind the blow. She created fissures that ran jaggedly from the center of the small room off to two walls. After chipping at an edge of the flooring she lifted a section of concrete with little effort. She upended the five-foot-square section and tipped it back against the wall, careful not to overstress the rotting wood. She squatted and watched the scurrying life in the soil. Worms, ants, beetles, already alarmed by the force of her blow, now rushed away from the abrupt exposure. Gilda focused her attention on them, letting her intentions be sensed by the small things moving below.

Gilda dug quickly, tossing the dirt outside through a broken window that faced away from the road and toward the deeper woods. She spread out her bed roll—a futon pack which contained the soil of Mississippi—and then laughed at the redundancy. For the first time since 1850 Gilda stood on home soil; she would actually sleep in the dirt of Mississippi— a hole in the ground, not a bed roll or earthen bed, but the dirt itself. She recoiled the bed roll and set it aside. As she lifted the concrete slab into place over her, she thought of how few times she'd had to endure this coffin-like experience.

For centuries mortals had imagined her tribe reclining romantically in locked boxes lined with satin. Gilda shivered at the thought and settled deeply into the cool, damp soil, which was unnaturally still around the spot where she lay.

Within hours she would see Nadine for the first time. She listened to the sounds of approaching dawn and tried to suppress the excitement that suffused her body.

In her life Gilda had not felt love and desire for a great number of women. It had been a daunting experience to learn when one you loved was right for the gift of blood. Mistakes were easy and then paid for over centuries. Gilda brushed away her thoughts, seeking rest. She did not want to think of Nadine.

Dreams of her beginnings had washed over her each dawn on the road when she'd rested. Images as powerful as the Mississippi waters flooded her mind: her mother's authoritative hands, the angle of the sun on the day she'd decided to run away from the plantation, blood scent filling her nostrils when she'd killed the bounty hunter who tried to rape her, the sound of women's voices in the New Orleans bordello where she'd grown into womanhood and been offered the gift of long life.

She chanted the names of those who been her progenitors, hoping to seduce her consciousness into rest. With little effort the darkness in her mind was complete as the sun climbed into the sky.

But late in the day images of a more recent past returned to her. In the dream she stood on a slight hill in the coolness of a bright night, one hundred years before. Aurelia, widow of a colored preacher, stood before her. Her lips were pressed together stiffly, holding tears inside while passion rippled across her skin.

"The past does not lie down and decay like a dead animal. It must be attended to," Gilda had said, by way of explaining her departure from the life they'd shared. Aurelia's bright eyes had looked solemn in her dark, round face. Gilda pulled the young widow's body in close, breathing in the scent of her damp wool cloak and the soap in her hair. A shiver of desire passed between them like an electrical charge as Gilda strained to feel the fullness of Aurelia's breasts against her own. She filled her senses with Aurelia's scent and sound while at the same time she battled the desire inside herself.

She'd pushed Aurelia back, holding her at arm's length, looking into the deep brown eyes for what she knew would be the last time. As she'd packed to leave the town that had been her home for more than a decade, Gilda accepted that life among mortals was the one Aurelia was meant to have. But still Gilda had felt like a betrayer. Aurelia, Nadine's great grandmother, had learned to love for the first time in Gilda's arms. Gilda's abandonment had hurt more than death.

Gilda gasped, suddenly awake. Darkness was complete around her and she lay still to listen, unsure what might have snatched her from rest so abruptly. Her heart was beating fast and memory returned. It was her desire and her loss that had yanked her from rest; and the memory of breaching the rules she'd been so carefully taught. Gilda could hardly bare to think of the letter she'd left behind for Aurelia, the envelope containing the story of her life and the blood.

Gilda lifted the concrete away and took several deep breaths; the night belonged again to her and the past evaporated. Scattering the dirt in the back so the mound would not arouse curiosity, Gilda left the derelict building appearing much as she'd found it. Looking only ahead she set off for the final miles of her journey to Hope.

Nadine knew she planned a visit but Gilda was deliberately vague about the timing. Gilda was a pen pal, a writer Nadine admired, that's all. Gilda's nom de plume was another cloak of invisibility. In the years of correspondence, Gilda had resisted the impulse to try to explain something so inexplicable: how she'd come to know Aurelia, Nadine's long-dead great grandmother. Gilda allowed herself the pleasure of Nadine's letters even when she felt guilty about the secret.

"Kinda like spying, ain't it?" Julius had said once, disapproval ringing the edge of his voice.

"No!" Gilda answered too quickly. "She only knows me as one of probably many people she communicates with. There would be no way to tell her."

"And you still say it was just good fortune that linked you two up?" Julius watched Gilda, the one who'd first given him the blood of long life. He was worried not sure why.

The idealism and activism of the 1960s was quickly fading by the time Julius and Gilda met in the 1970s. The cry "Attica" rang in his ears more loudly than "I'm Black and I'm Proud." Unlike Aurelia, Julius had hungered to leave the past behind; he'd been ready for the life Gilda offered. For 150 years they remained in tune with each other as if truly siblings; lying was not possible between them. So Julius waited, feeling conflict bubbling inside Gilda.

"Isn't it you who taught me not to be ashamed of desire? To keep it like it's a sacred thing?" he asked.

"I'm not ashamed of loving Aurelia. It was so long ago."

Julius said nothing.

"Aurelia has been dead for almost a hundred years!"

"Not so long for us." Wry humor crept back into Julius' voice.

"No," Gilda had reconsidered. "Not so long. But I left her." The despair in her voice was fresh.

"And what about the great granddaughter?"

"I wanted more than just the reports, information."

"She's a standard bearer in the resistance, what else is there?"

"I wanted to know her."

"Would that be in the biblical sense?" Julius had laughed uneasily and watched Gilda trying to smile. They did not speak of Nadine again. Now, standing in the same region where Nadine lived, her conversation with Julius felt like more than an intellectual exercise and one in which she should have paid closer attention.

Soon Gilda would hear, with her own ears, the stories Nadine had to tell. Her letters had been full of news about the loose association to which she belonged and of their fight to keep their area a freetown.

Sitting in her cabin in the New England woods, where the population was minuscule, and usable resources nonexistent the question of incorporation had seemed trivial. But in cities the long arm of business had standardized and controlled in the name of convenience, safety and profit. At first Gilda had been alarmed, but the longer she stayed away from contact with mortals the less urgent their problems were to her.

Ultimately it was Nadine's passion for the fight against incorporation in her town that had finally made the visit inevitable. The seriousness of the struggle was belied by the sign Gilda approached. It read:

HOPE

a freetown

POP.: Any who wish to live here.

Just as Nadine had described, the battered wooden placard was surrounded by twinkling multi-colored lights. Nadine's electronic mail to Gilda described the dangers of maintaining the sign, a job she'd taken on willingly. The bullet holes in it punctuated Nadine's observation that it was not a simple task.

Gilda timed her arrival for twilight. It seemed impolite to appear on a stranger's door, unannounced in the dark of night, especially with the political struggle going on. As soon as she approached the small field that Nadine had described, Gilda knew she'd made a good decision to arrive early. There was a large magnolia tree at the southern end and on a small hillock a small cabin sat shaded by a willow. Nadine had indicated that the path to the house was rigged with traps which would alert her to anyone approaching. She had to be particularly cautious because she was deaf, because she lived alone and because of the organizing work she did.

Gilda stood in the heart of the resistance movement for this area and wondered, for the first time, how much danger might surround Nadine.

Moving cautiously across the field toward the cabin, Gilda could feel the presence of more than one person inside. She easily skirted the warning devices and circled the house to examine it more closely. The root cellar and rear doors were locked tight and brightly colored fabric hung at all the windows.

The back porch overflowed with barrels, boxes, gardening tools and other implements. Her stillness made Gilda almost invisible as she leaned in toward a window and listened to the voices muffled by the window. It was an oddly shaped conversation, with great pauses and anger. A man spoke so sarcastically that Gilda felt her stomach tighten. His words hung in the air, accusing and taunting, and Gilda waited for the response. There was no voice but she could hear rustling sounds.

Gilda circled silently around, back to the front of the cabin and stood at the screen door. As she reached out to press the buzzer she wondered for a moment how effective that would be. But at her touch the lights in the house dimmed and rose again.

Nadine hurried toward the front door as if she were eager to leave the hard voice behind. She stood at the screen for a moment looking puzzled, then she reached out to unlock it. Her eyes blazed and her mouth opened, revealing glistening teeth behind full lips which turned up in a wide smile.

Her hands, poised in front of her, were delicate, their light brown palms crossed by dark lines. She was very still, fingertips poised. Then her hands moved through the air smoothly like banners rippling in the wind.

"You're here! You look like your letters." Nadine smiled as her hands spoke the signs known by many who did not hear. Gilda had prepared herself—-her response was no less expert: "And you are Nadine!"

She was grateful she didn't have to use her voice because she was certain she would not find it. Gilda held her breath for a moment as she stared at Nadine, who was the living image of Aurelia.

Nadine's hands rested lightly in the air before her, waiting to speak again. Her thick dark hair was braided in symmetrical rows over the crown of her head and down the nape of her neck just as Aurelia's had been. Gilda looked past her to see two young men step into the room. It was a small living room with a worn couch and chair surrounded by bookcases. Everything was immaculately clean and orderly, which made the men seem especially out of place.

They appeared to be in their late twenties, one black, one white. The white one's dark hair was lank with dirt and he affected the paramilitary garb favored by all young revolutionaries in the past century. The other young man was dark, with an unkempt beard and filthy nails. He wore dirty work clothes; a large patch with a clenched fist decorated the stained shirt. They stood in the doorway, clearly angry that they'd been interrupted.

The disagreement had melted out of Nadine's thoughts. Her hands leapt and danced as she explained her visitor. She introduced them—Carl, the white one, seemed adept at signing while the other, Andrew, was full of disdain. He barely looked at Nadine as she signed. Before she could finish the introduction they said an abrupt goodbye and left, not bothering to close the door behind them.

Nadine gave Gilda apologies. "Many things happen now. They have no manners and trouble makes them lazy not smart."

Gilda laughed. "I'm sorry to interrupt."

"No, enough of them. This is one time I wish I could speak out loud. I would swear so loud they would wish to be deaf."

She laughed a crackling sound as she signed and Gilda felt her skin come alive, as if Aurelia had walked into the room.

"Trouble?" Gilda spoke in order to touch the reality in front of her.

"More and more the same trouble. I organize. We meet with each other and they want only to fight. They don't know the others who want to help. They don't care about anyone else or our ideas. They want to blow things up."

Gilda was surprised that the resistance was so strong and so close to violence.

"What do you want?"

"Forget them and visit you. But I don't have my manners, what can I offer—-wine, water?

"Water. In a shower, if possible."

"Oh! Yes. Through here. I'll give you towels."

"I walked for a good part of the trip," Gilda said.

Nadine actually looked at Gilda's clothes and realized what she said was true.

"Give them to me; they can wash at the same time."

Gilda closed herself in the small bathroom and set the shower. She tossed her clothes back outside the door, into Nadine's bedroom and stepped into the water, bracing for the shock. The movement of water was always unsettling at first for those like her; it pulsed with her blood making her sluggish. But she soon became accustomed to it and hurriedly washed, anxious to return to Nadine. She didn't know what she would say. She had thought she would have a casual visit and be on her way. But once she stepped through the door she wasn't sure it would be easy to be so close to the past.

When she emerged, Gilda felt a fluttering in her stomach that she didn't understand. She unrolled her pack and removed a light blue one piece suit that always made her feel somewhat festive and relaxed at the same time. The fabric clung to her muscular frame. In the shower she'd unbraided and washed her brown hair. She now pulled it back and twisted it into one long braid from the crown of her head down to her neck. She pulled aside the curtain at the window and saw that full darkness was almost upon them. She would go out for her share of the blood soon.

In the living room Nadine had set out a bottle of red wine and glasses. She stood by the chair as if awaiting Gilda's approval. Gilda sat on the couch and gestured for Nadine to sit beside her. Nadine poured a glass of wine for each of them. Gilda decline the cheese, but sipped eagerly at the wine. The thick taste was warm in her mouth but not nearly as rich as the taste of blood.

"Good now?" Nadine asked. As she sat her signing became smaller, almost as if she were whispering.

"Much. I'm sorry I surprised you. I hope this is OK. I don't want to interfere with your plans."

"No plans. I was worried."

"Why?"

"I was afraid you wouldn't come, or something would happen. Travel is not easy now."

"Yes, I saw that."

"You are just as I imagined. I mean you shine just like your words."

Gilda laughed as she watched the large hands come to rest. She made herself look away. Across the room Nadine had a reading lamp sitting beside her overstuffed chair in the exact same position that Aurelia had. A book lay facedown in the seat cushion.

"You carry secrets more easily than I do."

Gilda was startled. "What do you mean?"

"When you wrote to me I knew you didn't use your real name. It made sense, but now I wonder if you'll tell me."

"Of course." A small tremor rippled through Gilda's body. Trust was one thing she could not afford and one thing she needed.

"Gilda," she said. "I'm sorry. I've traveled with that nom de plume for quite a while. I almost forgot it wasn't mine."

Nadine's eyes glistened as if she were going to cry. Gilda stood abruptly, the force of the young woman's emotions unnerved her.

"I'm going out. I want to walk for a little while." Gilda needed to escape the sensations roiling inside the room.

Although her eyes clearly indicated she wanted to convey something, Nadine said nothing. She held the door open and Gilda slipped out to the night.

She walked back out on the path where she'd entered, trying to focus on the warm, damp air around her, not on her twisting emotions. She turned west at the end of the road and went several meters toward what she assumed would be the town.

She passed a block of apartments that looked disheveled like discarded clothes, and were surrounded by even more ragged patches of grass. Further west a circular exit dropped down behind the road and led into the town of Hope. A small grocery store, a coffee shop/bus depot, a shuttered post office and abandoned car dealership made up one side of the town square. Another held a few other boarded up buildings, none more than two stories. A third side was completely flattened. Gilda approached curiously; the oddity of an empty lot in the middle of a small town was puzzling. A wire link fence circled the plot of land which showed the rubble of a destroyed building. A small sign attached to the fence read: "Former site of USA Department Store." Someone had scrawled across the metal sign: "Pigs."

Gilda looked back across the square. Despite the moderate weather and starry sky, no one strolled the street; no cars were parked by the curb, and no neon lit the night. The silence implied more than simply a quiet town. Gilda walked several streets that led off of the square and found the same unnatural quiet. One or two homes seemed to hide activity, but all shades were drawn and the evening was full of whispers.

She circled back to the highway and stood, again, before the stack of apartments, listening to the evening sounds, searching. She stood at the edge of one of the buildings and sifted through the noises until she heard what she wanted. She focused easily, cutting through the noise of people living in close quarters. She held her line of focus, drawing Andrew outside on the far side of the block of buildings.

He looked around with a puzzled expression on his face. He'd changed from the work clothes she'd seen earlier and now wore an old tee shirt and shorts. When he saw Gilda he walked purposefully toward her.

"What're you doing here?" Andrew's anger was thick like the grime that he'd washed away from his hands.

"Talk." Gilda signed as she spoke, as if he were deaf.

"I don't need signs."

"We all need signs, Andrew. Something telling us what's ahead."

"I can hear as good as anybody."

"Now that's where I think you're wrong. You don't hear at all. Or I'd say you don't listen. Your friend, Carl, he listens. But he's scared to contradict you because you'll call him a racist. You, on the other hand do not listen. You're only waiting for your turn to talk. To prove how much you know."

"Bitch, I get enough bullshit from that other one so don't start . . . "

"If you use the word bitch again you had better be talking about a dog."

Andrew sucked air in through his teeth dismissively and turned to walk away. Gilda caught his sleeve easily. He wrenched away.

"Don't make me act out on your ass," Andrew said, the

eagerness barely hidden in his voice.

"What is it that makes you need to hurt me? To hurt Nadine?"

"Don't go psycho-babe on me, please." He backed away, smirking.

"But there is something, in the back of your head, or here in the town culture that gives you some kind of hunger. That's not where the power is, Andrew."

"Bitch, I told you . . . "

Before he perceived her movement Gilda stepped in close to him. Her left fist was a flash that left him lying on the ground. Andrew looked up at her in shock but sprang to his feet with the facility of youth. He raised his hand to return the blow but Gilda caught his wrist and pulled his arm around behind his back.

"Is this what you want to do to me? Is this what you want to do to anybody who doesn't follow you?"

"Who the hell are you?" Bravado and fear mingled in Andrew's rasping voice. The pain of Gilda's grip shot through his arm, taking his breath away.

"You know what kind of impulse that's called, Andrew? Fascism. Is that who you want to be? I thought that was what you're fighting against?"

Gripping his arm and his collar, Gilda pulled Andrew backward into the shadow of one of the buildings that held maintenance equipment. She kicked in the door to a utility room behind her and pulled Andrew into the darkness.

"What are you doing?" he gasped when she thrust him further into the room. He backed away until he felt the edge of a table stop his retreat. Not able to turn from her silhouette in the doorway, he reached behind him, desperately feeling for a weapon. He stopped reaching when he saw the orange swirl of light where he thought her eyes were.

"Um," Gilda said and locked him in her gaze. She listened to his thoughts. He was full of arrogance that only slightly wilted with his confusion. She could feel his dedication to preserving their town but it was in danger of being subverted by his impatience. She recognized the infection of ego and prejudices that pulsed through him, giving him a sense of righteousness— who else could know what was right? Gilda wanted to shake him out of his stupidity, but instead reached over and, using the sharp nail of her smallest finger, sliced neatly across the flesh of his neck. Andrew, locked in her gaze, felt nothing. She took his blood and continued to listen inside. He was certain he and the other men knew the only way their fight should be waged. He thought Nadine and all women were like children to be led.

A fascist, just as she'd sensed. Gilda thought it might feel good to wipe his mind completely, to leave him like a babbling child with no memories or ambitions. Let his mother start to raise him all over again and see if she did better this time.

Instead she simply introduced doubt and a need to listen. She took the blood she required and left him with an opening to the idea that he could be wrong. All the years of television, movies, brothers, fathers and some women could be completely wrong. Gilda drew his blood out and tried to keep her thoughts on the seed she was planting and not on how angry his ignorance made her. She could see their fight for the freetown disintegrating under the stunted ideas he and Carl threw out like a caustic solution of quicklime. They were leaders as much as Nadine and their influence could foster cooperation or create dissension. Gilda tried to plant inside him the capacity to build, not just destroy.

She left Andrew slumped across the table, his eyes unfocussed, and walked away unhurriedly. When he came to himself he would remember nothing of their encounter, but he would wonder if he really knew as much as he always thought he did. As she turned back to the road that led to Nadine's house she hoped the seed would grow before the movement was destroyed.

She turned back to the highway, studded with gouges and weeds, making her way back to Nadine in minutes. Once at the door her hand trembled, hovering over the bell, not certain what the next moment would hold.

Nadine opened the door before the button was pushed, as if Gilda came home to her every day.

"Did you see the town?"

"Yes. The empty lot on the north side of the square?"

A deep sigh rippled through Nadine's body before she unfolded her hands.

"Horrible. When the town voted to refuse incorporation . . . ten years ago . . . they

closed the gas station first."

"Who?"

"Bell Oil, which is a subsidiary of Ford Industries, which is owned by Shoshida International, all of which belongs to the U.S. government."

Gilda watched the softness in Nadine harden as she explained how the takeover of her town had stumbled. "Then the National Guard installation was relocated, and the one factory in town was closed down." The confusion in Gilda's eyes grew.

"It happens all over." Having seen the words formed in the air, Nadine ran out of energy. She dug her hands into her lap as she sat down.

Gilda tried to find the words, not so much with her hands, but in her mind. "What did people do?"

"First they fought with each other, of course. All the black folks blamed the white folks and for once the white folks couldn't blame us!" Nadine's grim chuckle filled the room. "We created a coalition. We got people to speak Vietnamese and Spanish so everybody came in. It worked. We lived together here for years. Everybody suspects somebody of something but we all love the land. People committed to stick together and we did. Then the government closed the department store. Okay," Nadine said with a stiff shrug. "Then they blew it up."

"What!"

"Somebody planted bombs and boom! It had to be them, the government, because right after that we started hearing news reports that the coalition was responsible for the bomb. People in town got mad . . . they hoped the department store would open up again, with jobs. When everything settled. They didn't understand that the government was not going to do anything in this town until we agreed to incorporate. We have to agree to take on all the stores they have and work for them."

"What about the movement?"

"You saw. Andrew and Carl are trying to break off. They think we should blow things up."

"And what do you think."

"We try to hold together. They say we're cowards. Most of the women resisting the bomb for a bomb idea, so they dismiss us. I talked to Carl and Andrew because we grew up together. We went to the same schools, everything."

Nadine got up from the couch as Gilda finally sat down. She walked around the small living room trying to orient herself.

"But I don't know them anymore. Andrew acts like he's in an old war movie. The two of them are still boys on the playground, except it's our town."

The silence around them felt as dark as the night outside the window. Nadine spoke as if to dispel it. "Sometimes he listens. He listens to Carl when no one can see them."

"Can I do anything?" Gilda asked, uncertain what that might be.

"Can you?" The edge of Nadine's voice was hard but her eyes again glistened with tears.

Gilda pulled back and tried not to listen to Nadine's thoughts; she did not want to betray their friendship with that secret intrusion. She waited for Nadine to speak.

Nadine raised her hand to her head as if she could push some information forward then said: "I know."

"What is it you know?"

"I know you are Gilda." She walked over to the large chair and picked up the book that had been open in its seat. She pulled out an envelope, brown with age, holding it tenderly as if the words spoke through the paper into her hands.

"I know you were probably laughing when I offered you food."

Gilda didn't take the letter. She recognized her own handwriting and still remembered almost every word. The letter she'd written to Aurelia before she left her decades ago described Gilda's beginnings in slavery, and how she learned to take the blood. It was a chronicle of a hundred years of life that could be explained in no real way.

"I would never laugh at an offer made in kindness."

"She told me about you before she died. I thought at first it was some kind of dream she imagined as she drifted into the other world. Then she gave me the letter and said if I ever need you, if there was deep trouble I hold onto the letter and think of her as hard as I could and think of you and you would come.

Gilda wasn't certain she actually understood the signs Nadine was making. She wondered if she'd lost her facility and this was all a mistake.

"At first I just kept the letter in the back of my drawer. I'd look at it sometimes and think of her. It made me sad. Then I decided to see what would happen. I studied it every night for weeks. And then I found your books. Even with the pen name I knew it was you. I wrote to you. And here you are."

Gilda stood abruptly and moved away from Nadine. She had never been in this place before. No mortal was ever so close to her knowing who and what she was. Except Aurelia.

This time she did listen. It was as she thought it would be. Nadine's mind was suffused with curiosity, sadness and other feelings Gilda had not been ready for. There were no tricks, no malevolence. But the shock of Nadine's knowing made Gilda's body come alive with electricity.

Gilda pulled back and tried to defuse the fires that swirled inside of her. The dissension within the resistance movement was one problem she might be able to help Nadine with, but she was completely unsure of what to do about the knowledge between them. Nadine sat silently, her hands folded in her lap, the letter between them. Tears stood in her eyes but she did not seem afraid.

Gilda moved so close to Nadine, the young woman leaned back to meet her gaze. Gilda gripped her shoulders and pulled Nadine up from the chair. Still she showed no fear. Gilda imagined Aurelia standing before her as she had a hundred years before. The soft crinkle of hair braided back away from her face, the curve of her breasts against Gilda's, even the slightly cinnamon scent was familiar.

Nadine opened her mouth as if she might speak. Gilda pulled her in close and covered Nadine's mouth with her own. Gilda encircled her in her arms until Nadine responded. Gilda remembered the press of their bodies well. She held the woman she'd loved so long ago. Her kisses were demanding, yet Nadine matched her urgency, holding on with well-muscled arms and strong hands.

Gilda pressed her back into the chair, her mouth like a velvet weight that would not let her go. Gilda's breath came more quickly but this time she listened to Nadine's thoughts. What she heard was: "I knew this would be."

Gilda wanted to lift her and take her to the bedroom she glimpsed earlier, but she couldn't bear to pull her mouth from the soft fullness of Nadine. She knelt on the outer edge of the huge armchair's seat and leaned down farther so they almost stretched out fully. Nadine raised one leg over the edge of the arm of the chair opening herself. Gilda slid her body in close, locking them together as Nadine moved against the hard muscle of Gilda's thigh. Gilda had many years of waiting and moving. Tonight she did both—-holding still until Nadine arched her back to meet her in supplication for more of her touch. Then she thrust forward with the stony heat she'd been holding inside for a hundred years.

Her mouth bruised Nadine's and a drop of blood surfaced on her lip. Gilda stopped in shock. Nadine opened her mouth wider and pressed her lips to Gilda's. Inside Nadine's head questions swirled—what did this loving mean? Would she have to leave her world to follow this desire? But the rush of hunger drowned out the whispering questions. Gilda heard them echo faintly through their jagged breathing as she sucked at the small wound on Nadine's lip, knowing she might make it bigger or slice the flesh at Nadine's neck when she wanted more. The rhythm of their bodies built, shaking the chair and rattling the glass of wine sitting on the side table. Gilda drew the blood out slowly, savoring the ferrous warmth. In her head were the images of Aurelia, the smell of damp wool and motor oil, so she opened her eyes to stare into the face of Aurelia's great granddaughter. The face was the same, the body was full as Aurelia's had been. Nadine met Gilda's gaze. But where Aurelia had been tentative and afraid, Nadine was hungry and insistent.

Gilda could feel the pressure as it built inside Nadine

matching her own. Gilda slid her hand out from under Nadine just as her back arched. She thrust against the hard muscle of Gilda's leg, and her body convulsed with pleasure. Gilda used the long nail of her smallest finger to open a tiny wound at the side of Nadine's neck. The shock stopped Nadine's movement at its height. She gasped. Gilda pressed her lips to the place where the blood flowed and once more Nadine felt fire build inside her. But this time it came with fear. But Gilda would not move away. She felt the fear but could not let go. She pinned Nadine to the chair, sucking the blood from her and letting her own body beat its rhythm against the girl. Gilda could feel the life leaving Nadine and entering her—-through the blood and through the burning center where their bodies met. The wetness flooded Nadine and Gilda as the sound of blood filled the room. Desire burst from Gilda as she met each of Nadine's frightened and passionate thrusts. Now was the moment for Nadine to taste her blood.

Their bodies ignited but an explosion knocked Gilda to the floor. Dazed, she looked up at Nadine, who was barely conscious. Confusion and rage replaced the desire inside her. She knew she had to protect Nadine from whatever had intervened. Hurriedly she held her hand to Nadine's wound to seal it and keep her in sleep, then carried her into the bedroom. Her need for Nadine had drained Gilda, and the shock of what she'd almost done left her weak. Gilda focused inside herself, slowed her breathing and looked around the bedroom as if she wasn't certain where she was. Once she'd spread a blanket up over Nadine's chilled form, Gilda gathered her strength so she could push her thoughts out into the night to understand what had happened.

Her body, already alert, was a fiber absorbing all that surrounded the cabin. There was someone there, cloaked in darkness and silence, keeping her at bay yet drawing her out. She scanned the field with her mind. The rustle of trees was softly enticing. In the shadow of one draped with kudzu she felt the cloaking drop and in her mind's eye she saw Julius. Gilda rocked backward in relief and shock.

Gilda touched the side of Nadine's sleeping face and her lips tenderly with her fingertips: "Rest, trust, home." Gilda sent the thought to Nadine. She stepped outside the cabin, moving through the traps that circled Nadine's house quickly. Julius leaned against the tree as if he were just waiting for a bus, not calling out telepathically to his old friend and sister.

As she approached he moved out of the shadow and she could see his anger.

Nearly six feet tall, Julius towered over Gilda, looking exactly as he had when she'd brought him into the family more than fifty years before. Trim and agile, his reddish brown skin was sprinkled with freckles. His dark nappy hair was cut close, just as it had been in the days of Black Power.

"How long?" he asked as he always did.

"What's long? Gilda responded, barely able to find her voice for the familiar greeting. What was long in a life that lasts several lifetimes? To not see your loved ones in a year or a decade was nothing. She couldn't manage the casual shrug that usually went with her answer.

"So," Julius said, never one to delay.

"She's Aurelia's great granddaughter."

"I got that four-one-one already, my sweet. I'm awaiting more up-to-date data."

"No, I mean really her offspring. She's organized such a cadre of activists, it's amazing."

"Got that already. I'm in with the grassroots folks, remember."

Gilda heard an edge in Julius' voice she was not used to. And Julius was not accustomed to seeing Gilda walk around her thoughts.

"Let's go in. I don't want her to worry."

"You should have been thinking about that a moment ago."

Julius had never spoken to her harshly.

"She was waiting for me."

"She was waiting for a dream her great grandmother had. She wasn't expecting to die."

"I would never let her die."

"And what about her work here? Is that just a bump in your road on the way to getting what you want?"

"What about what I want?"

"You wanted Aurelia. This is not Aurelia!"

"She was waiting for me."

"Like I was waiting for you?" The sound of the question sent shivers of anger through Gilda. They never spoke of the time before, when he was a mortal and had wanted her, just as Gilda wanted Aurelia so long ago and wanted Nadine now. He had left the desire behind, or at least put it in a private compartment in exchange for being close to her through time. He hadn't meant the bitterness to color the words so brightly.

"No, she was not waiting for you," he said more gently. She was reading a letter her great grandmamma left her and thinking Wonder Woman or Xena was going to come along and help her fix up this mess that's turned into Corporatamerica."

"I . . . " Gilda couldn't answer. The blood, Aurelia's blood, was moving too quickly through her, making her brain feel like it was burning just as the rest of her body had been doing moments before.

"You saw Aurelia for who she was then," Julius broke into her thoughts more gently. "She needed to be right where she was, doing the work she was doing. She was meant to remain mortal, to hold onto those bonds. She made life better for the colored folks in Rosebud, Missouri, Gilda!"

Julius' urgent words brought back the enthralling scent of

Aurelia's hair on that final night. Gilda drew a sharp breath as if she were drowning.

"You knew then our life of wandering would drain the spirit from her. You knew it," Julius said softly.

Gilda understood the bonds never so clearly as when she stood holding Aurelia in her arms, wanting desperately to sever all those connections; wanting to deliver to her the gift of long life.

"Don't do this, my sister."

"She . . . "

"She's the girl, the one you used to be when you escaped the plantation. Alone, tough, and needing help. If you take her now, before she knows what she really must know, you're no better than those other vampyres we despise. You're be no better than the corporation leveling this town and making the citizens obey."

Gilda stared at Julius and clutched her hands in front of her, wanting to slap him. More than that she wanted to rip a branch from one of the trees behind him and thrust it through his heart and watch him turn to dust. He was doing that to her with his words.

"Not her, Gilda. Just not her. Not now."

"We'll see." The ice in her voice frosted the air as she turned on her heel and walked back toward the cabin. Then said over her shoulder: "How's your ASL?"

"Right on the money."

"Watch your step."

"I plan to, sister love," Julius said anxiously, not certain what Gilda meant.

Inside, Nadine lay deep in sleep, unaware of Gilda and Julius as they checked her breathing.

Julius walked around the neat cabin rooms, admiring the thorough way everything was organized.

"She knows what she's doing," Julius said softly, although Nadine wouldn't wake before morning.

She couldn't hear them gather Gilda's clean clothes, then open the doors to the shallow root cellar beneath her house and spread their pallets side by side. Julius took a rusty chain from Nadine's tool shed and wound it through the inner handles. Gilda held the links together until she generated enough heat to fuse them. They lay in the darkness while Gilda told Julius of the disputes, her encounter with Andrew and the danger that Hope was going to have a split leadership which would surely lead to losing their battle.

"You're ready to take her away from the struggle, to leave it to Andrew and Carl?" Julius asked.

Gilda said nothing but jumped up and walked around the small, dark cellar, five steps in one direction another five back. Finally she lay down next to Julius. They cast a circle of reflection around themselves, repelling the curious, and then rested uneasily when the morning sun began to rise.

When Nadine awoke in the afternoon she wondered if she'd dreamed everything that had happened between her and Gilda. But the feeling in her body told her that wasn't true. She rushed from the bedroom and looked quickly through the living room and kitchen and had a moment of panic when she didn't find any evidence that Gilda had been there.

She stepped outside and looked around the property. The old tree stood alone and impressive and Nadine imagined she could hear the leaves she saw moving in the breeze. Nothing looked disturbed from her porch to the distant horizon so she turned to go back in the house. She then noticed the door to the root cellar. She hadn't gone down there in a couple of weeks, the day she'd made sweet potatoes for a meeting. She stood over the door for a moment looking down at it as if it were glass, then backed away. She felt puzzled; her mind couldn't quite focus there so she went back inside the cabin. She spent the day strategizing for a meeting with a group that did not want Andrew to take over and then strategizing about how to get all the groups together.

Picking through her cooking utensils Nadine gathered the hidden parts of her specially built Morse equipment and reassembled them hurriedly so she could communicate with others she knew would be coming to the meeting tonight. She picked at some food and sat in her chair re-reading the letter Gilda had written to Aurelia then she slipped it into the cushion of the chair out of sight. For some reason tonight it made her feel sad and her energy was so low she fell asleep.

She awoke when she dreamed that the door to the root cellar slammed shut. Then the lights dimmed and Nadine leapt from the chair. She yanked the door open and threw herself into Gilda's arms.

"I thought I dreamed you were here."

Gilda took a deep breath that carried the scent of Nadine's body deeply into her brain, then pushed her back. Nadine then noticed Julius standing behind Gilda.

"Oh . . . I . . . "

"This is my brother, Julius. He's come to give us his wisdom." The ironic edge in Gilda's voice was not subtle.

"My sister, I've heard so much about you. Back in Wisconsin you're a legend. I can hardly believe I'm finally meeting you." His hands moved as easily as Gilda's had.

"You work with grass roots organizations?" Nadine asked, puzzled. He was clearly like Gilda, a vampire. But something about him seemed so mortal she found it hard to believe.

"I've been with workers in Wisconsin and Illinois territories."

Nadine stepped back into the cabin.

"We have a meeting tonight."

"That's why I'm here," Julius signed smoothly.

"I'm not feeling well. I may cancel it."

"No!" Julius responded quickly. "You just need a little rest." His hands were no longer moving; it was his voice inside her head that Nadine heard.

"Why don't you sit for a while and finish your nap."

Nadine sat back in her chair and slipped her hand down between the cushion to feel the comfort of the letter.

"Do it," Julius said to Gilda with no emphasis.

"To leave her, like I left Aurelia . . . I can't." There were no longer tears for Gilda and those like her but her voice was full of the sound of crying. They both knew Julius was right.

"If you ever loved Aurelia you'll make the break complete," Julius whispered. Then, the edge of his voice hardened: "You've taken her blood and left nothing in exchange."

They stood above Nadine. Gilda took slow, steady breaths, until they matched Nadine who relaxed into the chair as if she would sleep for many days. Julius listened as Gilda probed Nadine's mind, slowly moving through the details that filled it—what time the others would be arriving, if she'd set out enough to eat, how would the meeting go, would she lose to Andrew's easy violence.

Julius heard the thoughts and ideas being pealed away and set aside and marveled at Gilda's skill. She felt for the rhythm of Nadine's thoughts and slipped in among them, then sectioned them off like a surgeon. Memory of the letter, the story Aurelia had shared with her were neatly packaged and withdrawn. In the place where Gilda found Nadine's desire Julius refused to turn away. The intensity of the feelings washed over him as Gilda took a deep breath, sucking the desire for her out of Nadine's mind and body.

Gilda continued more deeply to the place that was more dangerous, the soft folds where Nadine held onto the knowledge of Gilda's desire for her. This was the most important memory to remove. Left there it could rekindle the love Nadine felt, and once Gilda was gone Nadine would be alone with a heart that was inexplicably broken. Gilda let her mind touch those places where her love had settled inside; she drew them away, keeping her breath steady and her attention firm. Nadine would remember nothing of the desire they'd shared the day before or Gilda's relationship to Aurelia. The bonds of the past would be broken completely.

The silent words she used to ease the feelings free from Nadine were like silken things slithering inside Nadine's memory. They retrieved all and returned them to Gilda. She took them in until her heart was so full she felt she would bend under the weight.

In the empty places she left suggestions of full conversations about the landscape around them, the writing Nadine knew was Gilda's life and fresh approaches to the questions raised by Andrew and other dissenters. Gilda touched small places where Nadine had hidden her doubts about leaving the movement and the primal fear she'd suppressed when she felt the blood leaving her body. She pulled those things closer to the surface and made Nadine's connection to life and the movement more primary. In place of the desire they had shared, Gilda left Nadine knowledge that such desire could be hers—sometime.

When it was done Julius stepped back and sat on the couch just as Nadine opened her eyes.

"I'm sorry. I dropped off."

"You needed your rest for the meeting tonight."

"Where are my manners? Can I get you and Julius something to eat before the others arrive?"

"No, thank you. We've already eaten," Gilda said.

"I'm so thirsty. Excuse me." Nadine rose from the chair

and walked a little unsteadily from the living room. "We have plenty to eat so if you change your minds . . . " she turned and signed just before disappearing into the kitchen.

Gilda reached between the cushions of the chair, removed the old letter and handed it to Julius who slipped it inside his jacket.

"I can't believe you actually came all this way to visit me. I feel so honored," Nadine signed when she came back.

"Well it was Julius, who convinced me. He thought we might be able to help. He's had some experience with the things you wrote to me about."

"We won't interfere . . . " Julius started

"No, please. Our movement is connected to all the movements. We'll need all the brains we can get."

"Not sure about the brains, sisterlove. But I got enough attitude for any revolution."

They laughed as Julius' signing settled into the sly rhythms of his speaking voice.

Nadine looked around the room, checking that everything was set up.

"I'll just put your packs in my bedroom until after the meeting, if that's all right."

"Of course." Here, I'll get them," Julius said as he leapt form the couch and carried them away.

"I really did love our conversation this afternoon. I can't say that enough. How often do you get to meet your favorite writer?"

Gilda ached as she watched Nadine's hands move in their fullness. The hands that Gilda had felt on her back only hours before, signed her words so dispassionately. She was still Aurelia's mirror image but now she had no memory of who Gilda really was.

"Having your brother come with you to help us figure out

what to do next is so kind. We're going to win this. But I'm happy for any help I can get."

"I couldn't have kept him away."

Nadine was quiet as she looked around the room and then back at Gilda. This time her eyes were filled with a mixture of happiness and distraction. The pull of the meeting already took her away from Gilda.

"Before the meeting starts . . . I know this is silly but . . . " Nadine stopped, shy.

"But what?"

"I often wonder about writers . . . "

"What do you wonder, Nadine?" Gilda asked cautiously.

"Is that your real name that you use or is Abby Bird a pen name?"

"It's my real name."

Gilda pulled her gaze away from the open pleasure on Nadine's face, looking toward the bedroom as Julius emerged. He was relieved to see the sharp edge of loss surge over Gilda like relentless tide.

Jackson Square

M. J. WILLIAMZ

she was so damned hot and so damned moist. Just like she is every time I visit her. Anyone who's ever been to New Orleans in the summer will agree. Hot and muggy, that's how she is. Creatures like myself don't sweat, so it's not as uncomfortable for us. Add to that the fact that tourists don't do so well in humidity, so the beautiful women are all scantily clad, and what vampire could resist the streets of the French Quarter in June?

I awoke that evening in my casket, relishing the feel of the soft satin against my naked skin. In the first few moments after waking, my hands slid down my flat, taut stomach into the curls of hair where my legs met. Even after all this time, the feel of fingertips, even my own, sliding lower cause my clit to swell. I moved my fingers just past the throbbing nerve center and slipped them between my swollen lips. Not surprisingly, I was greeted with slick, smooth, wet heat. Teasing myself, I slowly dragged my fingers back and forth along the length of my opening. All the way down and then back to surround my clit. Needing more, I plunged my fingers deep inside myself, as deep as they would go, and began to move them in and out. With a mind of their own, my hips moved with them, urging them deeper.

Coated with my juices, I moved my fingers back to my engorged clitoris, rubbing it hard, pressing it into my pubis. Needing, *craving* release, I pressed harder, just under my clit, where the pressure can take me over the edge. But nothing was working. I was teetering on the edge but couldn't catapult myself over.

Frustrated, I realized that I didn't have enough blood in me to take myself to a climax. I quit torturing myself and just lay there, waiting for my breathing to return to normal.

Climbing out of my coffin, I quickly threw on a pair of faded jeans and a plain white T-shirt. My clothes were lose enough not to impede my mobility but not so baggy that they would hide my muscular frame.

I cracked open the shutters on the third floor of the Old Ursaline Convent. The night air was still, with the scent of the centuries-old city heavy upon it. Along with the smells came the sounds: the shuffling of feet along the cobblestone, the voices of revelers who had happened off the beaten path and ended up on Chartres Street, trying to find their way back to Bourbon.

Early though it was, I felt the strong need to feed. Careful that no one was looking, I jumped the three stories to the ground and made my way to Jackson Square, home of the homeless, meeting place for those with nowhere to go. The stench of the occupants of the square hit me blocks before I arrived. Unwashed and unclaimed, these outcasts of society were, for the most part, disposable. And, while not my favorite flavor, I knew I could find someone to feed off, certain no one would ever notice them gone.

The trick was taking them without being noticed. Not an easy task but one I had mastered over the centuries. Walking past the cathedral, I kept my eyes open for anyone who had drifted away from the different groups and ended up by him- or herself. Almost at the other end of the square, just past the last of the palm readers, lay a solitary figure. Checking to be sure I was unobserved, I quickly grabbed the figure and, holding it next to me, I leapt over the fence and into the portion of the park that was locked every evening to keep indigents and criminals out. The whole process took less than two seconds.

When I have my victims down, I slip into robotic mode. There is no thinking or feeling, only feeding. The need to feed supersedes all other emotions and all reason. As I bent my head to my victim's neck, all my focus was on that neck. The blood pulsing through it called to me. Suddenly the crowds didn't exist. Nothing did, except my need.

My fangs were just about to break the skin, when my victim pushed hard against me, catching me off guard, since I had assumed the bum was unconscious in an alcoholic stupor. I ended up on my ass a few feet away from my meal.

Forcing myself to focus on something besides my hunger, I looked over at my victim, surprised to see a very conscious, very beautiful, and very angry brown-eyed woman.

"What the hell do you think you're doin'?" She demanded.

I was speechless. She was the most beautiful woman I'd ever seen. Looking away from her eyes, I admired her high cheekbones, her full yet petulant lips. Looking lower, I saw full, firm breasts straining against a tight white tank top, the white shirt contrasting nicely with her mahogany skin. How did I not notice her beauty before?

"What the hell are you lookin' at?" she asked, standing up and crossing her arms, effectively impeding my view.

Quickly, I jumped up and stood beside her, trying to think of something to say to explain my actions.

"I thought you were hurt," I lied lamely. I couldn't stop looking at her. My hands itched to run through her black hair.

My lips longed to taste hers. And between my legs, the activity had resumed.

"Yeah, right," she threw back at me. "If you thought I was hurt, why didn't you check on me over there?" She nodded her chin toward the other side of the fence. The movement stretched her neck and reminded me once again that I had yet to feed. But I had other needs, other needs I thought she could meet.

"And what the hell was that jump over the fence? How'd you do that?"

I had to think and think fast. I needed to divert her attention from things that she didn't need to know. Like any good butch, I knew the way to get her on a different subject was to get her to talk about herself. It never fails.

"What were you doin' lyin' on that bench?" I began. "You don't look like the typical street person."

"I'm not a typical street person, thank you very much! I got in a fight with my girlfriend and needed to get some air."

"And you fell asleep in Jackson Square?" I asked incredulously.

"If you must know, I was layin' there, not sleeping, minding my own business when you grabbed me and did your little high jump routine. Which you have yet to explain," she added.

"What did you and your girlfriend fight about?"

"That's none of your damned business. Now, you better get the hell away from me or I'm gonna scream as loud as I can. I don't know who you are or what you want, but you're creepin' me out."

"I'm sorry. I don't mean to creep you out. Let me get us back over the fence and I'll be on my way."

"You think I'm gonna let *you* near me again? I don't know what your game is, but I don't want any part of it."

"Look," I tried to sound as earnest as possible. "I really

thought you were dead. All I was doin' was checkin' you for a pulse when you pushed me away."

"Yeah? Well, it seems to me that most people would check for a pulse with their hand, not their mouths! It looked to me like you were going to *bite* me. What are you? Some kind of freak?"

Looking down, I ran my fingers through my short dark hair, down to my neck, which was suddenly very tight with frustration. Recognizing there was no way to logically explain my actions, I decided to just give up and leave her alone. I needed to get some blood, and when that need was met, my mind would be cleared. The need to take this woman as my own would dissipate. The fact that she had nectar much sweeter than blood that would nourish me for much longer was something I couldn't dwell on.

"Look. I'm sorry," I told her. "I'm gonna go now. Good luck with your girlfriend."

Her hand shot out and grabbed my arm as I turned away.

"So you're just gonna leave me here? How the hell am I supposed to get out of this area?" she asked, her hand motioning to the fence.

My heart was racing, my resolve weakening. If I didn't get away from this woman soon, I'd do something rash. A vampire can only go so long between feedings and still stay rational. I knew I was approaching my breaking point.

Pulling my arm free, I turned on her, backing her into a tree. My gaze never left her eyes as I closed the distance between us. There was barely an inch separating us. I could feel the heat radiating from her; could sense her nipples so close to brushing against me.

"You don't know who you're messing with," I managed huskily. "Unless you're willing to face the consequences, I suggest you let me walk away."

The fear that I'd seen in her eyes seemed to dissipate. I saw the hard onyx lighten to soft chocolate. She didn't say anything for a moment as she locked her eyes on mine.

"You've got some nice eyes," she broke her silence. "They're almost purple they're so dark, but they don't look scary. I'm not afraid of you, really. Actually, I think you're kind of cute."

"Then you'll let me help you out of here?"

"Will you tell me your story first?"

"Look. Either I get you out of here, or I leave you here. But trust me, either way, it's gotta happen now."

She moved her hands up my arms, letting out an appreciative sigh as she lightly squeezed my tight biceps.

"I'm serious," I whispered.

"Mmm? What's the hurry?" She asked as her hands moved up to my shoulders, then slid to my chest, resting just above my small breasts. I felt the tightness as my nipples puckered. I knew without looking that they were poking through my shirt. Her hands slid lower, and I grabbed her wrists, harder than intended.

"Ouch!" She cried, but didn't try to pull her hands away. "You're quite the tough butch, aren't you? So big and strong. Are you too tough to have a girl touch your titties?"

I tried to think; to come up with a decent response. Preferably something quick and witty, but my needs had reached a boiling point. Too many needs at once. I couldn't think. I could only act. Placing her hands squarely on my breasts, I leaned in and claimed her mouth hard with mine.

Her full lips parted immediately, allowing my tongue inside to tangle with hers. My arms went around her, pulling her tight against me as we kissed. She moved her hands away from my breasts and slid them around my neck, pulling my mouth closer, driving her tongue deeper into my mouth.

My tongue worked madly in her mouth, licking every

surface, wanting to lick elsewhere but relishing the feel of the inside of her mouth. Her hands began moving down my back, up my sides. She wedged them in between us and grabbed my breasts, squeezing them hard. I arched my back, pressing them harder into her hands, while my mouth relinquished its hold on hers and I began to kiss down her cheek to her neck. Blood rushed just under the skin, rushing harder with her arousal. I playfully nipped her neck, teasingly at first but then enough to break the skin. Just a taste, I told myself. I sucked hard through the microscopic holes, drawing her blood into my mouth, savoring her unique flavor while I gained strength for what was to come.

I sucked hard one last time, and she moaned loudly, releasing her grip on my breasts while her hands slid lower, working to unbutton my jeans.

"Baby," I whispered. "Baby, we need to move away from here."

Stopping her hands, I held her still until she looked at me. When our eyes met and she nodded, I took her hand and led her deeper into the garden, away from the milling crowds and their curious eyes.

Stopping in a grassy area surrounded by shrubs, I sat down and pulled her down with me. Kissing her again, I rolled her over onto her back and moved my hands over her breasts. They were full, her nipples taut with arousal. I kneaded them, squeezing them together, and was rewarded by the frantic motion of her tongue in my mouth. She broke the kiss briefly to take her shirt over her head. The beautiful brown mounds mesmerized me. Immediately squeezing them together, I sucked both nipples as one, as hard as I could. Her death grip on my head told me I was right where she wanted me.

I took her hands away from my head and placed them around her breasts, so my hands were free to move south.

My left hand played just under the waistband of her shorts while my right hand slid between her legs. I could feel the heat through the denim and the wetness seeping through as I stroked along the seam.

She let go of her breasts and quickly undid her shorts; sliding out of them and spreading her legs to grant me access. I began kissing her mouth again while my hand moved lightly up and down her soft inner thigh. Apparently, she'd waited long enough as she grabbed my hand and placed it between her legs. My palm rested on her clitoris, erect and poking into me. I pressed against it, moving in circles over it while my fingers slid over her folds, pulling and pinching, but not venturing between.

Her tongue was frantic in my mouth. The hand behind my head had me pressed hard into her. Her other hand slid between her legs and pressed my fingers inside her. The feel of her fingers on mine sent my senses reeling. Our fingers were slick, sliding over each other as we pressed deeper, exploring the very depths of her.

She released my hand and moved to unbutton my jeans. Grabbing her wrist, I caught her hand and brought it to my mouth. One by one I sucked her fingers, tasting her offering, getting stronger with every lick, every suck. The only substance that gives a vampire more strength than blood is the milk of love that flows so freely from an aroused woman.

When her fingers were clean and my strength had grown, I placed her hand back on my jeans and helped her unbutton them. With no underwear to impede her, her fingers immediately entered my wetness, which engulfed them greedily. I had three fingers moving in and out of her as her fingers delved deep inside me. Our tongues moved more wildly inside each other's mouths as we urged each other on.

Her hips were moving up and down against me at a faster

and faster pace. She was bucking hard, driving herself onto me, driving me deeper inside her. Her fingers were still inside my jeans but had grown still, and I knew all her energy was focused on her impending climax. My hips moved against her, but my focus was on the soft spot I'd found inside her. I rubbed it with my fingers as my hand moved in and out.

Our mouths separated as she panted and moaned, and I knew she was close. I wanted to feel her climax on me, to feel her orgasm flow down my hand. Just as I felt her whole body tighten for the final release, she finally moved her hand inside my jeans. She pinched my clitoris between her fingers, causing me to cry out. Next she pulled at it and then pressed it hard into my pubis. As she got closer and closer, she rubbed me harder and harder. It didn't take long for me to join her. Together we sailed over the edge and tumbled into orgasmic bliss, floating back to earth while our fingers continued to work each other.

When I could think again, I moved between her legs and lapped up all that had poured from her.

"So, who exactly are you?" She asked, propped on her elbows and looking down at me.

"I guess I'm your date for the night," I answered, moving up to kiss her hard on her mouth. When I pulled away I asked, "Do you have someplace a little more comfortable where we can continue?"

"Mmmm," she murmured, sliding her hand between my legs again. "Right here seems to work just fine."

My hand cupped her clitoris again and the last coherent thought I had was that she was so damned hot and so damned moist.

The Lady Is a Vamp

KRISTINA WRIGHT

Her voice enthralled. There was no other word for it. When Angelica sang, her voice reached inside you and pulled out emotions you'd never felt before. I'd been the bartender at The Blue Note for five years, and I'd seen singers come and go, but I'd never heard anyone like Angelica, and I never tired of listening to her magic voice. She had Cassandra Wilson's sensuality and Nina Simone's melancholy, but there was something more, something that was pure Angelica. When she sang "Someone to Watch Over Me," I ached to be the one to protect her. The funny thing was, Angelica didn't need a guardian. She was the strongest, toughest bitch I'd ever met, and I hated her. I also loved her and hated myself for it.

Angelica was in rare form this night. It was nearly two a.m. on a Friday night, The Blue Note was packed to the rafters, and I was making money hand over fist. Angelica was wooing her audience with an obscure tune I recognized as Billie Holiday only because I knew her tastes. Her band, an unlikely ragtag trio named Bubba Chryst, backed up Angelica's vocals as if their music was merely an extension of her voice. It's a hell of an experience, listening to something so pure, so natural. Angelica's gift was as much in reading the audience as it was in singing, and she didn't disappoint.

The audience went wild as she finished the set. Angelica

closed her eyes and threw back her head, accepting their adulation as if she were being touched physically. Her dark skin, amply exposed by a white silk gown slit up to her hip, glistened with perspiration. Angelica gave her all to her audience, and they responded in kind. The energy in the room was palpable, almost suffocating.

"Thank you," she murmured into her microphone, her voice the sound of ice in a whiskey glass. "You've been wonderful. I don't deserve this."

Humility and musicians go together about as well as cowardice and soldiers. I smirked at Angelica over the heads of the crowd, but she only stared me down. Bitch. I'd never made much of an effort to get to know her because she'd made it perfectly clear the talent didn't mingle with the help. She'd been playing The Blue Note for nearly a year, and I'd been obsessing over her since day one, but I would have slit my own wrists if she'd ever found out how I felt about her. Angelica was trouble, and I knew enough to leave trouble alone.

The audience wanted her as much as I did, and their applause didn't fade until Angelica disappeared backstage with a haughty toss of her head. The crowd dispersed, but a few of my regulars lingered until I announced last call, then they slowly made their way out into the dark and silent streets. I stayed after the rest of the staff left, cleaning and setting up for the next night.

"I'm heading home," Rick, the manager, called from the back of the bar. "Want me to walk you out?"

"Nah, I've got a few more things to do."

"All right. Be careful and don't forget to lock up."

I laughed. Rick always said the same thing. "I will. G'night."

I like being in the bar by myself. There's something about the silence after so much noise, the lingering smell of beer and sweat in the wide empty space that soothes me and helps me unwind. I wouldn't get home until after four, but I'd sleep like the dead until noon. It wasn't for everyone, but I loved being a bartender.

I had just finished inventorying the liquor and making a list for Rick when I heard a sound from the back room. I listened, my pulse quickening just a bit.

"Rick?"

There was no response. I kept a baseball bat under the bar, but it was more for tradition than anything else, because I'd never needed it. I'm no little girl; I've got a few pounds on my ass and enough kickboxing sessions under my belt to be able to hold my own with all but the biggest, meanest drunks. Tonight, though, something about the way the hair on the back of my neck was standing up made me grab the bat on my way to the back of the bar.

"Hello?" I called again.

There was still no answer, and every sense was on alert as I stepped through the doorway that lead to Rick's office and the backstage area.

I gave up on playing nice. "I'd suggest you say something, motherfucker, or I'm going to bust your head open and then call the police to collect what's left of you."

"Would you please shut the hell up? You're making enough noise to wake the dead."

I jumped, nearly taking Angelica's head off with the bat as I jerked back. "Jesus, Angelica. Why the hell didn't you say something?"

She stepped out of the shadows, her face eerie and hollow in the dim red light cast by the exit sign over the back door. She had changed out of her white gown and into a dark dressing gown, which is why I hadn't seen her at first. She looked like an apparition and, for some reason, I tightened my grip on the bat.

"I thought you left," I said, hating the quiver in my voice. "Why didn't you say something?"

"I didn't think you'd try to kill me, or I would have." Her laughter was as musical as her voice, but it was tinged with bitterness. "I didn't want to go home."

"Why?"

She stepped toward me, but I didn't feel threatened any longer. "Because I'm so tired of being alone."

I'd never thought much about what Angelica did when she wasn't at The Blue Note. She performed two sets a night, Thursday through Saturday. The rest of the week we had a rotating list of singers and bands, none of them as good as Angelica. She was our headliner, and she pulled in the crowds. It never occurred to me to wonder how she spent her days, or the nights she wasn't at the club. Funny, since I had obsessed over her for months, that I'd never once imagined where she lived, what she did for fun. My secret fantasies of Angelica always took place in The Blue Note. I don't know why that realization startled me, but it did.

"You don't have anyone?" I asked finally.

She shook her head. "No one."

"Not even a cat?"

She laughed again. "Hate the damn things."

The conversation was too fucking surreal for me. "Well, I'm exhausted, so I'm going to finish up and head home. Try not to scare the shit out of me again, okay?"

"Wait," she said softly. "Please."

I don't know if it was her tone or the *please*, but I stopped in my tracks. "What, Angelica?"

"Don't go. Stay for a while. Let's . . . talk."

I was annoyed with her for no good reason. "I can't. I need to get some sleep."

"Me, too. The sun will be up soon."

"Right. So, why don't you hang out for a few minutes and I'll walk out with you," I said. Feeling a little guilty, I added, "We can talk tomorrow night."

Her smile was wistful. "Please, Shannon. Stay with me. Just for bit."

I sighed. I wanted to resist, but I couldn't. Angelica's voice did things to me. I was no different from anyone who came to hear her perform; I was enthralled. Correction: I *was* different. I knew better than to fall under her spell, but I had fallen anyway.

"Fine. Just for a little while."

She reached out to me and took my hand. It was the first time in all the months I'd known her that we had ever touched, and it felt strange. Her skin was cool, almost icy. Her fingers wrapped around my hand like a mother's around a young child's as she led me toward the stage. The club was nearly pitch black, with the exception of a couple of lights over the bar, and I had to step carefully to make sure I didn't trip over anything. Angelica had no such problems.

"We can sit in Rick's office," I said, reluctant to sit in the darkness with her. "I have a key."

"Let's sit here." She lowered herself gracefully onto the edge of the stage, her feet not quite touching the ground. "It feels odd being anyplace else."

That didn't surprise me. Even with the stage lights off, Angelica seemed completely at home sitting on the dark stage. I sat down next to her, plopped down was more like it, and tried to think of something to say. We sat like that, side by side, looking out toward the bar and the tables scattered around the floor, for several minutes. Finally, it was Angelica who broke the silence.

"You don't like me, do you?" I started to protest and then figured there was no point in lying. Whatever this was, whatever Angelica's sudden desire to be my best buddy, I wouldn't lie to her. Besides, I figured she already knew. I turned sideways so that I could look at her, tucking one leg under me. "I think you're one of the coldest, most arrogant people I've ever met."

She nodded. "I am."

"But I think there's a lot more to you than what you show other people," I added, not sure where it came from. It was true, but until I spoke the words, I hadn't realized it.

She looked over at me, her expression unreadable. "More than you could possibly know."

I am not an impulsive person by nature. I don't gamble money I can't afford to lose; I don't take risks if the consequences outweigh the rewards. I've seen enough bad stuff in the world to know better than to believe in the good of mankind. But right then, in that moment, sitting on that stage, I believed Angelica needed something—needed me—and that was enough to make me lean forward and kiss her.

If her hand had been cool, her lips were as icy as her personality. She didn't resist me, but she didn't exactly meet me halfway. She made me work for the kiss, holding her body still and away from me as I insistently stroked her lips with my tongue, willing her to part them. When she finally opened her mouth and let my tongue slip inside, it felt like an incredible gift. I put my hand on the back of her neck, pulling her closer, afraid if I hesitated, she would move away.

Angelica relaxed then and began kissing me in earnest. She put her hands around my waist, sliding them under my T-shirt. I moaned into her mouth at the simple touch of her hands on my bare back and felt a tremor go through her, as if she'd gotten a chill. I hauled her closer, until she was practically sitting on my lap, and kissed her hard. Her robe was thin and silky, and I could feel her slender body beneath it. I felt feverish with the desire to strip the robe off her and touch her everywhere, touch every inch of skin I'd imagined in my fantasies.

I moaned again, the power of my imagination combined with the reality of kissing Angelica almost enough to bring me to orgasm. It was amazing, incredible. *Wrong.* I pulled away and looked at Angelica. My breath was coming in ragged pants, but she looked as cool and calm as if she'd been taking a nap. "What the *hell* is going on?"

She stroked my cheek with one chilly fingertip and smiled. It wasn't a friendly smile. It was predatory, her teeth flashing white and bright even though there was hardly any light to see by. "What do you mean? You kissed me."

I shook my head, trying to clear the fog of lust that had settled over me. "I know. But . . . this is . . . God, I don't know what this is."

I couldn't even think straight. All I wanted to do was keep kissing Angelica. It was more than just lust; it was a driving force. Even while I tried to make sense of what was happening, I felt compelled to kiss her again. I felt stoned, so high I was hallucinating that Angelica was glowing in the dark. My skin was hypersensitive to her touch, and I alternated between wanting to pull her closer and wanting to push her away. I tried to remember what I'd had to drink that night, wondering if someone had slipped me something. I shook my head. I couldn't seem to remember anything past Angelica scaring the shit out of me backstage.

Angelica leaned forward, nipping my ear with her teeth. "It's passion, *mon ami,*" she whispered. "Don't you feel it?" I *did* feel it, and it felt out of control. My cautious nature said to get up, grab my keys, and get the hell out of there, but my passion was overpowering all rationale. "I'm not a fucking groupie," I said, even while my hands were parting Angelica's robe. "Stop playing games with me."

She leaned back to let her robe slide from her shoulders. Her breasts were small and firm, her nipples as dark as the mahogany bar. I forgot what I had been saying, feeling a rush of wetness between my legs. I lowered my face between Angelica's breasts and breathed in her spicy, perfumed scent. She shuddered in my arms, holding me to her chest.

I nuzzled her breasts and then sucked one small nipple into my mouth. She wrapped my hair around her hand and pulled it taut, and I whimpered from the combination of sensations. I sucked her nipples in turn until they were slick and wet with my saliva, standing up from her chest like stones.

She pushed me away. "Take off your clothes," she said. Her voice was still even, unaffected, but there was an urgency to her words.

"There's a couch in Rick's office," I offered again. It didn't really matter to me where we were as long as I was with Angelica. I was thinking of her comfort, the hard wood floor would hurt her thin body.

Angelica shook her head. "No. Here. *Now*."

I didn't protest as she reached for my T-shirt and pulled it over my head. My breasts were bigger, heavier than hers, and I moaned as she lifted them from the cups of my sports bra.

"So pretty," she said, hefting them in her hands and running her thumbs across my already hard nipples. "So responsive."

"Touch me," I said, not even recognizing my own voice. "Please."

She leaned forward, her short hair feeling rough and nubby against my skin, and trailed gentle kisses across my breasts. Looking up at me with dark, kohl-lined eyes, she said, "Like that?"

I growled, wanting more, needing it. "Harder."

She sucked the swell of my breast into her mouth, and I felt the hard edge of her teeth. A tremor ran through me, and

I whimpered.

"More," I whispered.

She sucked and nibbled my breasts, using her teeth and tongue to tease my nipples until they ached. I clung to her, digging my fingers into her bony shoulders as she tormented me with her mouth. I could feel the tension building in my body, the need. My response to Angelica's touch was overwhelming, unnerving.

"Oh, *fuck*," I gasped as she bit down on my nipple. An exquisite feeling of pleasure followed the sharp sting of pain. "More," I urged.

She bit me again, and again I felt pain followed by pleasure. I wasn't a masochist by any stretch of the imagination, but Angelica was making a believer out of me. When she finally pulled away and looked at me, I was trembling and panting.

"Take off your jeans," she said. "I need you."

I didn't argue that I needed her more than she needed me. My fingers felt numb and clumsy as I fumbled with my belt, never looking away from Angelica's serene face. If she hadn't said she needed me, I wouldn't have believed I had affected her at all. As it was, I felt a nagging doubt in the back of my mind that she was playing me, that this was some sort of game I would live to regret. Whatever misgivings I had paled in comparison to the desire coursing through my veins. Angelica said she needed me, and I would give her whatever she wanted. Anything she wanted.

I kicked off my shoes and wriggled out of my jeans and panties without ever standing up. It wasn't the most graceful presentation, but it didn't seem to matter right then. All that mattered was getting my clothes off as quickly as possible.

Angelica slipped her robe the rest of the way off, her thin, dark body seeming to absorb what little light there was. Without a word, she pushed me backward on the stage and stretched out on top of me. She was all sharp angles and cool flesh, feeling as weightless as a baby bird I'd once held when I was a child. She braced her hands on either side of my head and looked into my eyes.

"I need you, Shannon," she said again. Her teeth flashed in the darkness, but it was a grimace, not a smile. "I need you like I haven't needed anyone in a long time.""Shut up and fuck me." She laughed against my mouth. "What a strange girl you are."

I kissed her fiercely, angry at her laughter, angry at my body's betrayal. I wanted Angelica so desperately I throbbed with my need. Fearful she would leave me wanting, I clung to her, running my hands down her naked back to her narrow hips. I spread my legs, and she settled between them, her pelvic mound pressing tightly against my crotch.

"You want me," she said. "You need this."

"Yes, yes." I whimpered, rubbing my cunt against her, feeling the delicious friction of her body against mine.

Angelica thrust downward, pinning me to the floor. She nibbled at my neck and shoulders, her teeth sharp and biting. The floor was cold and hard, but I didn't care. I arched my back and guided her head to my breasts. My nipples felt tender, raw, but I needed her mouth on them again.

My soft cries echoed through the bar, an appreciative audience of one. I bucked under Angelica's thrusts, driving my cunt up against her and wanting more. "Please, please," I moaned. "Please, Angelica."

With excruciating slowness, she worked her way down my body. Her bites were harder, rougher, as if her own need had finally overtaken her cool control. I was trembling uncontrollably by the time she was kneeling between my spread thighs. I raised my hips, offering myself to her like a pagan sacrifice. She blew cool air across my engorged cunt, and I whimpered. She parted my lips with her nails and I moaned. She bit my clit, and I screamed.

The pain was like nothing I'd ever felt: awful and beautiful, frightening and precious. I thrashed under her mouth, driving my cunt upward, demanding more of the exquisite pain only Angelica could give me. She ravaged my tender flesh, slurping and sucking me like an overripe mango. An image of her licking my blood flashed through my fevered brain, though I knew it was only my own arousal that was causing so much wetness.

"Yes, yes, yes," I gasped, holding her head tightly and anchoring her to me. "Fuck me."

My orgasm swept over me without warning, my body going rigid with my release. I wrapped my legs around Angelica's shoulders and fucked her mouth with such force I expected her to pull away. She didn't. She dug her nails into my ass and kept eating me. I couldn't stop coming, screaming out in near agony as she devoured me with her lips and tongue and teeth.

"Enough," I whimpered finally. "Stop. Please."

She didn't seem to hear me, and if she did, she didn't respond. I reached down to push her away, but she was unyielding.

"Please, Angelica, enough," I gasped, still coming in waves. "Let me fuck you."

I felt her tongue go still on my clit, but the relief was momentary. She shifted her weight, never raising her mouth from my tender cunt, and turned so that her knees were on either side of my head. I stared up into the darkness between her legs, inhaling her musky scent. I leaned up and gently tongued her cunt, feeling her body quiver above me. She was still sucking me, and I was helpless beneath the onslaught. I wrapped my arms around her narrow thighs and pulled her down to my mouth, intent on distracting her.

Angelica's cunt was cool and moist. I stroked the flat of my tongue from the firm ridge of her clit up to the smooth skin of her perineum, again and again until I coaxed the softest of moans from her. Thus rewarded, I sucked each of her thin, hairless cunt lips into my mouth, nibbling until she squirmed above me. She murmured something, but her words were lost between my thighs.

"What?"

"Don't hurt me," she repeated.

I nearly laughed. I felt like a raw bar open for her dining pleasure, and she was telling me not to hurt her. Still, I obliged, using soft, gentle strokes to tease her. I felt her grow wetter as I licked, and though she was still devouring my cunt like a hungry animal, I focused on making her come. Over and over, I licked and sucked her, until her cunt felt like the fattest, plumpest part of her body. I could feel the tension in her limbs, could tell by the way she'd slowed her ministrations on my abused crotch that she was close to orgasm. I took a chance and sucked her clit between my lips, not quite as hard as she had mine but hard enough for her to know I was serious. It worked. Angelica came.

Her orgasm was a thing of terrible beauty. She went stiff above me, biting down on the inside of my thigh so hard I screamed, my pain reverberating up into her open cunt. It wasn't until I took a breath that I realized she was screaming, too. Her voice was a high-pitched wail of agony, and it scared me because I had caused it. On and on it went, and I kept sucking her clit as she screamed. Finally, and after what seemed like a long, long time, her voice faded away into the darkness. Her body shuddered above me and I thought she was crying.

I let her clit slide from between my lips, remorse settling in my chest like a rock. "I'm sorry. I didn't mean to hurt you."

She slid off my sweat-slick body, and as she lay beside me on the stage, I realized she was laughing. "Oh, Shannon," she gasped. "Thank you, thank you."

I sat up, hesitating to touch her. It was ridiculous, given that I'd just had her clit in a vice grip between my teeth, but I suddenly didn't feel like she would welcome my touch. "For what?"

"For *that*," she said, gesturing up into the air. "For making me *feel* what you felt. It was . . . startling. Even on my best nights, I don't get to feel *that*. I may have to give up singing for whoring."

I was lost. I had no idea what she was talking about. My body was damp, slick. I was so incredibly wet, like I'd never been before. Wetness trickled between my thighs, and it felt like there was a puddle beneath me.

Angelica was still laughing, and it wasn't a pleasant sound. She didn't seem like herself. She seemed . . . manic. I edged away from her, slipping easily on the wetness beneath me.

I wrinkled my nose. The scent of sex was heavy in the still air. Sex and something else, something metallic. I thought my period might have started, which would explain why I had been so unbelievably horny.

"I'm going to clean up," I said. "Rick will know what we were up to if he gets a whiff of this place."

I left Angelica there on the dark stage and fumbled my way to the bathroom next to Rick's office. I flipped on the light and caught a glimpse of myself in the mirror above the sink. "What the fuck?"

I froze as realization sank in, my mouth open in a silent scream.

My neck and chest were streaked with blood. I looked down and saw that my breasts, belly, and thighs were also covered in blood. My knees felt weak. I sat on the closed lid of

the toilet and looked between my legs. My cunt was swollen
and red, and blood was still flowing from the bite mark in my
thigh. Except for that one deep bite, the rest of my injuries
seemed superficial, but that was cold comfort when looking
at so much blood.

I wiped off what I could with a wad of wet paper towels,
wincing at the roughness on my damaged flesh. I was almost
scared to touch myself between my legs, but thankfully—
perhaps because I was in shock—the pain wasn't so bad.

When I'd done the best I could without a first aid kit, I
slammed open the bathroom door. I was angry, furious. My
rage was as overwhelming as my passion had been, and I
trembled with barely controlled emotion. My night vision was
gone after spending so long in the bathroom, so I threw the
main switch to illuminate the stage.

"You fucking bitch. Do you see what you did to me?"

I was talking to myself. Other than a drying puddle of my
blood, the stage was empty. Angelica was gone.

The Price

J. T. LANGDON

I was sitting in the office of Nori Aretz, editor-in-chief of *Trends* magazine, when she dropped this little bombshell on me: "Francesca DeStasio has agreed to an exclusive interview."

DeStasio was the hottest name in fashion at that moment. Her designs were seen on movie stars at the Academy Awards. I peeled an original DeStasio off a French actress when I was at Cannes last year. The Italian fashion designer had become an icon in our little universe. But she did not give interviews.

Francesca DeStasio had never appeared on television. She did not speak to reporters, not even to snap out a terse "No comment." The most one could hope for was a brief statement issued through her personal assistant, but even that was a rarity.

I finally managed to yank my jaw off the floor. "How on earth did you swing that?"

"I'm not sure," Nori said. "God knows I make requests all the time, and the answer is always a flat 'no.' Then her assistant calls me at home this morning and tells me Signora DeStasio wishes to speak on the record. Apparently she is spending the winter in California, location undisclosed."

"So this will be a phone interview?" I asked, a little disappointed.

Nori shook her head and smiled. "Signora DeStasio wants you to be her guest for the weekend. And she requested you, specifically. I've got you booked on the first plane to Los Angeles. Her car will pick you up at the airport. So go home and pack a bag as fast as you can."

I sat there, numb. This was too good to be true. She had asked for me by name? Why? Who cared! I was going to spend the weekend with Francesca DeStasio.

I was jolted from a semirestful nap when my plane began its descent into Los Angeles. The plane touched down, then taxied to the gate farthest from the baggage claim. I decided to do something naughty and unfastened my seat belt before the light came on. Sometimes little acts of rebellion are all that keep me from taking out my fellow passengers. As soon as the plane rolled to a stop I got my bag out of the overhead compartment.

I emerged from the tunnel and looked around, expecting to find a driver in black livery holding up a sign with my name on it. What I got was even better: The woman who approached me looked to be about my age, which is to say early thirties, though she may have been a few years older. She was dressed to kill in a tight black skirt and aqua blouse. From a distance she seemed a little taller than me and slimmer, too, with a short crop of blonde hair that looked too good to be natural but probably was. Amazing blue eyes sought me out once I deplaned.

"Alyssa Kerrey?"

I nodded. "Yes?"

"I'm Jillian Melbourne, Ms. DeStasio's personal assistant. Please, call me Jillian."

I took the hand offered me and squeezed it. The skin was soft and warm. I held on longer than I should have and held her gaze. "Nice to meet you, Jillian. How did you know who I was?"

Jillian smiled, and we started walking. "You don't remember me, I take it."

I admit, I didn't remember her. Dear God, please don't let me have slept with her and forgotten. No. I would remember making love to this woman. Hell, I'd still be getting off in the shower to the memory of it. "Have we met?"

"In Milan, last year," Jillian said. "You were covering the release of Ms. DeStasio's new line."

"Yes, of course." I remembered now. That had been a great trip. The new line had been brilliant, Francesca DeStasio's best work to date. And the more I thought about it, the more I remembered Jillian in particular. She'd made a brief statement on behalf of Ms. DeStasio, then took a few questions, including one from me. And she remembered me from that brief exchange?

It didn't take as long as I thought for us to reach the baggage claim. Or maybe it did, and I was just too busy looking at Jillian's legs to notice. You don't see a lot of suntanned legs in Chicago in winter, nor do they look as good Jillian's did. I'm lucky I didn't bump into someone. Jillian had been talking to me while we walked, and I had made the appropriate grunting sounds to keep the conversation rolling along while I drooled over her long, tan legs. When we reached the baggage claim I realized, sheepishly, that Jillian was looking right at me.

"Did you check any luggage?"

"No," I said, hefting my gym bag. "I prefer to travel light."

"Wonderful," Jillian said. She made the word sound kinky.

There was a black stretch limousine waiting for us outside. I got in and Jillian took the seat opposite me. She crossed her legs, then started rubbing them together like a cricket. I couldn't tell if it was a natural thing or if she was coming on to me. It might have been both. Raw sexuality oozed from her like sap from a tree. I'm not much for small talk but I needed something to relieve the tension. Changing seats so I could kiss her didn't seem like a bright idea. I went with idle chitchat.

"So how long have you worked for Ms. DeStasio?" I asked.

Jillian laughed. "Seems like forever."

I'm glad this wasn't an actual interview. Answers like that are the reason I drink. But she had the cutest twinkle in her eyes, and I was quick to forgive. So I pressed on. "I am looking forward to meeting her."

"And she is looking forward to meeting you," Jillian said.

Unusually dark tinted windows prevented me from seeing where we were headed. I passed the time engaging Jillian in casual conversation about nothing in particular and ogling her long, tan legs. Yes, I keep repeating that—long, tan legs—but they were. The two of us exchanged a couple of suggestive glances and traded some double entendres that raised my hopes for sharing Jillian's bed that night. I love assignments where I get laid.

I think the car finally rolled to stop an hour outside of Los Angeles, but I wouldn't swear to it. Between flirting with Jillian and jet lag, I lost all track of time. The truth was, we could have been driving around in circles the whole time, and I wouldn't have known the difference. But why all the mystery?

Jillian climbed out of the car, and I followed after her. I had been driven to an impressive mansion set so far back that I could not see the main road it was on. I'd been to houses like it before. It was the kind of place rock stars lived in after making it big, then were forced to sell five years later when their latest record bombed and it was time to pay off creditors. Ah, the ups and downs of show business. I'll stick to being a reporter, thank you. I might not live in places like this, but I get to visit them now and again. In my opinion, drifting in and out of that circle is much better than living in it, and much more stable.

I followed Jillian into the foyer. It was done up in marble. There was a spiral staircase leading upstairs and corridors to either side of me. The house looked more like a museum than a residence. It was spotless. I have enough trouble keeping dust bunnies out of my two-bedroom apartment back in Chicago. How do you maintain a place like this? It boggles the mind.

"Like it?"

I turned. Jillian was standing at the foot of the steps. Light pouring through a stained-glass window caught her just right and made her look like a goddess. I hoped I hadn't read her wrong in the car.

"It's incredible," I said. Now you can see how I became a respected fashion reporter. I have such a flair for language.

"Yes," Jillian said. "Ms. DeStasio is quite pleased with it. Though she much prefers her villa in Tuscany. You will have to join her there some time."

"I'd love that," I said.

Jillian smiled. "Come. I'll show you to your room."

The room was bigger than my apartment. I could've gotten lost in it. Plush red carpeting so deep that I sank into it stretched from wall to wall. The furniture, solid mahogany, was a hundred years old if it was a day. In the center of the room was a four-poster covered with pillows in a variety of sizes. I flashed on the image of Jillian spread-eagled on the bed, wrists and ankles tied to the posts. Bad me, thinking naughty thoughts like that.

"I hope this will do," Jillian said.

I laughed. "Yes, it will do. Thanks."

"You're welcome," Jillian said. "Well, I'm sure you must be

exhausted after that ghastly flight from Chicago. And since Ms. DeStasio is otherwise occupied at the moment I will leave you to a short nap. Is that all right?"

"More than all right," I said. And then I took complete leave of my senses and threw caution to the wind. "Would you like to join me?"

Jillian didn't so much as blink an eye. She moved closer and touched the tip of her finger to my lips. "Nothing would please me more, Alyssa. Believe me. However I must see to other matters before Ms. DeStasio . . . becomes available. But we have the entire weekend to get better acquainted. Rest assured we will."

I pursed my lips, kissing the tip of her finger. Jillian kept it there for a long moment, then left me to consider the possibilities the weekend had to offer.

I rolled over and stared at the empty space next to me with a sigh. The promise Jillian had made echoed in my mind, and though I was looking forward to the moment she would make good on it, I was still frustrated. I wanted to get off. My hand was already between my legs, stroking lightly, but with the prospect of humping a gorgeous blonde looming over me, I knew masturbating just wouldn't be that satisfying.

Better to wait. What time was it, anyway?

I looked around but couldn't find a clock. Great. Someone should have come for me, I thought, but with my luck I was keeping Francesca DeStasio waiting.

I got out of bed and ambled into the connecting bathroom. There were no mirrors. What kind of house was this? I stripped off the T-shirt and panties I called pajamas and washed up at the sink. A shower would have been more refreshing—a nice hot bath, heaven—but if I was late for something, I didn't want to make things worse. I cleaned up with a damp washcloth, lingering over certain places more than others, then returned to the bedroom.

There was no chance little ol' me could ever impress Francesca DeStasio with my fashion sense, so I kept things simple: a peasant blouse, khaki trousers, and loafers. The casual look never had failed me in the past. I ran a brush through my hair and headed downstairs.

The stillness of the house unnerved me. Had everyone slipped out while I was sleeping? I was more than a little confused at the turn the assignment was taking. Ms. DeStasio had invited me, right? I moved through the house, searching for signs of life. What I ended up getting was an unescorted tour. I stumbled upon an impressive library, a conservatory, and a kitchen that didn't look like it had ever been used. There were no servants around to direct me, no maid, no butler, no cook, nobody.

I found myself walking down a long, narrow corridor and was just about to call out for Jillian when I heard a faint noise up ahead. It sounded like a puppy whimpering for attention. I followed the sound to a pair of massive oak doors at the end of the hall, doors open just far enough to let me peer inside.

There are lots of clichés I could toss out now. I'm not sure which of them is the most applicable. Curiosity killed the cat? Nah. Mind your own beeswax? Never did understand that one. I think what it comes down to is this: Never open a door unless you are prepared to see what is on the other side. In this case, those doors were open to me when I got there. But you get the idea. I shouldn't have looked. I realized that much too late. I was not prepared to see what was on the other side of those doors. Looking back, I realize, not without a sense of resignation, that that single glance changed my life for an eternity. At the time I just felt like someone at the scene of a car wreck: I knew I should look away, but I just couldn't.

A young woman I had never seen in my life was naked and shackled to the wall. Her red hair swished from side to side because the frightened thing was shaking her head in protest. She had welts over her back, buttocks, and thighs. The welts had been administered by a whip. The whip was in the hands of the older woman standing behind her. The woman with the whip in hand held my attention for the longest time. I might have groaned involuntarily. I'm sure I got a little damp between the legs.

Though I had never met her, never even seen her, I had no doubt that I was now looking at Francesca DeStasio. I cannot think of enough adjectives to describe her beauty. I could fill page after page with elegant prose and never do the woman justice. How do you describe perfection? The task is too daunting, and I will not attempt it here. So I'll be practical.

Francesca DeStasio looked to be in her forties. She had full-bodied raven-black shoulder-length hair that bounced when she moved. Her figure, of which I had just a tantalizing glimpse, was curvaceous and firm. She was dressed in a black silk kimono, nothing more, the sash undone so it billowed around her when she brought the whip down on the redhead's bottom.

"Oh!" the redhead cried. "Mistress! Please have mercy!"

Mistress DeStasio answered with three lashes that made me wince. Each time the whip came down, the redhead cried out. She fought against the restraints around her wrists and ankles, bucking like a wild animal. Her body glistened with a fine patina of sweat. From where I stood I could see evidence of her arousal, too.

"You beg for mercy, wench?" Mistress DeStasio sneered. "You deserve none!"

I shuddered. The power in her voice left me aching and out of breath. I could not imagine crossing this woman. She would have me for lunch. I watched her bring the whip down again and again as the redhead howled in agony.

"Please! I swear I won't do it again!"

"I'll make sure of that," Mistress DeStasio said. "How dare you leave without permission! Have you no sense, child? You risk exposing us all! And for what? Mixing with commoners at some dance club! Do I not satisfy your needs?"

"Yes, Mistress!"

"Then why have you defied me?"

"Mistress, I—"

Mistress DeStasio brought the whip down before the redhead could finish. She flogged the poor woman within an inch of her life. I wanted to rush in and put a stop to it, but something prevented me. I'm not sure if I feared what might happen to me or I just wanted it to go on. Whatever the reason, I was frozen in place, watching in a mixture of horror and arousal as Francesca DeStasio brought the whip down again and again. She seemed possessed, as unable to stop as I was to intervene. Something had its hooks in her, and she kept at it without flinching, whipping the shackled woman over and over.

The redhead let out a piercing scream that forced Mistress DeStasio to stop. Looking harder, I saw the mistress had drawn blood with that last sting of the whip. She reached down and wiped the blood away with the tips of her fingers, then, raising those fingers to her lips, licked it off. The smile that spread over her face could only be described as blissful. I've seen drunks get that look taking their first sip of gin for the night. I think I get that look eating chocolate-chip cheesecake. Mistress DeStasio cleaned the blood off her fingers, then leaned closer and licked more blood from the redhead's bottom. I heard the red-haired woman moan.

Mistress DeStasio lapped up the last few drops of blood, then stood up and swept the redhead's mane aside to bare a long, creamy neck. "You taste wonderful, child."

I thought Mistress DeStasio meant to kiss her, but when she opened her mouth I saw the fangs, and for the first time I knew real fear. It washed over me in waves. I backed away from the door, knowing I had to get the hell out of there as soon as possible. But when I turned around it became clear I would not be going anywhere for a while.

Jillian smiled at me. I have no idea how long she had been standing there, but what mattered was that she was standing there now, looking just as gorgeous as she had before. She dipped her head in a slight nod.

"I went upstairs to get you," Jillian said, "but you were gone."

"I . . . I came down looking for you," I managed to blurt out.

"Mmmm. Found more than you bargained for, eh?"

I started to respond, but no sound came out. Then I tried to move but could not. Jillian was closer now. When had she done that? I don't remember seeing her move, but there she was right in front of me, so close our lips were practically touching. Then our lips were touching, and I felt a hand come up to cup the back of my head.

The kiss seemed to go on forever, and I was swimming in delight. I felt lightheaded, disoriented, and scared. I was so scared. What was happening to me? The room began to spin around me. Part of me didn't care, wanting to savor the lushness of those lips. The other part of me gained control long enough to pull back.

"Jillian, . . . what . . ." As if through a dense fog I watched her pull a syringe from my arm.

"Sweet dreams," Jillian murmured over my lips.

Sleeping seemed like such a wonderful idea that when a dark pool opened at my feet I put up no protest, sinking into the abyss and the peace it had to offer.

I awoke to the sounds of lovemaking. At first I thought I was dreaming. I felt hungover and sluggish. There was a chill to the air I hadn't noticed before, then I realized I had been stripped naked. Still lost in a sea of darkness I listened to the erotic chorus that filled the room. There is no mistaking the sounds of a woman being pleasured, the soft little moans, the sudden sharp intakes of air, and the sighs of relief that follow. I loved hearing it. I loved making a woman make those sounds even more.

It took a few moments, but eventually my head cleared. I opened my eyes, slowly, and not without effort, adjusting to the light. The sight before me evolved from a formless blur to one of the most beautiful things I have ever seen in my life.

Mistress DeStasio was reclined on an antique fainting couch, her face twisted in pleasure. Her open robe revealed a pair of luscious breasts that rose and fell with each labored breath. The redhead knelt before her, head bobbing up and down with zeal. Her back was crisscrossed with red marks. Mistress DeStasio reached down and raked her fingers through that mane of red hair in silent encouragement, and from the look on her face the redhead got the message. I resisted the urge to touch myself.

It was clear the mistress was nearing climax. Her face took on a tense, determined look, and her hips were moving impatiently. Then Mistress DeStasio grabbed a fistful of hair and ground the redhead's face into her crotch. She cried out, head tossed back, then sank down into the sofa with a sigh.

I was panting for breath as if the orgasm had been mine. Mistress DeStasio toyed absently with the redhead's sweat-dampened hair, swirling it around her fingers while the woman nuzzled against her.

"Some wine, pet," Mistress DeStasio muttered.

"Yes, Mistress."

The redhead dropped a kiss on Mistress DeStasio's belly, then got up. I watched her cross the room, then turned back to find the mistress looking at me. Her face had that wonderful glow women get after sex. Her gaze made me blush, and that seemed to amuse her, for she smiled as if I had just told her the cutest little joke.

Looking at her, I was mesmerized. I would have done anything for her. What I wanted to do was crawl over there and pick up where the redhead had left off. Something told me the mistress wanted the same thing.

Mistress DeStasio tore her gaze from me when the redhead returned with a goblet of wine. She took it with a nod, then cupped the woman's breast, giving it a gentle squeeze that made the redhead purr. Then she flicked her thumbnail over a stiffened nipple, piercing the skin. The redhead cried out, but I think it was more in pleasure than in pain. A single drop of blood formed on her nipple and dripped into the goblet of wine. The mistress sipped from the goblet then smiled, dismissing the redhead with a wave of her hand.

I should have been terrified being alone with this woman, but I wasn't. In fact, I had never been more excited than I was at that moment.

"You are even lovelier than Jillian said you were," Mistress DeStasio told me.

I blushed again. "Thank you."

The mistress took a long sip of wine while she considered me. "Yes. Very nice indeed. She has such a good eye for these things. Come join me."

I did as she commanded. Sitting next to her made my insides tremble. She offered me the goblet of wine. I took it, then, with some reluctance, drank. If any blood remained I could not taste it, but the act itself was my first step down a dark path, and we both understood the significance of the gesture.

"Mmm," I murmured.

"The vintage suits you, then?"

"I think it does, yes."

The mistress smiled. She plucked the goblet from my hand and set it aside. Then she was kissing me. Her mouth, soft and warm like velvet, crushed against mine with such power that I was grunting under the strain. When she began stroking my breast those grunts became moans of sheer pleasure. Her touch was demanding, and she coaxed my nipples to erection in no time.

Feeling bold, I threaded my arms around her neck and pulled her with me as I lay flat on the sofa. There wasn't much room, but Mistress DeStasio made the most of what we had, repositioning herself above me on all fours, then kissing me again. She dragged her lips down to my neck, and I had visions straight out of a "B" horror movie: her biting me, drinking my blood. It didn't happen.

The mistress kissed her way lower, lingering over my breasts, her tongue flicking over stiffened nipples until I was squirming on the sofa with a need I had never known before. I was absolutely desperate to feel her mouth other places. Well, okay. One place. Mistress DeStasio continued lower still, planting warm, wet kisses across my belly.

When I felt her breath on my inner thighs I moaned and spread for her like a cheap whore, opening myself wide, inviting her into me, offering up my cunt as a plaything for her amusement. She took it, took me. The mistress dipped inside me, hungrily lapping at my pussy lips, fucking me with her tongue, leaving me breathless, whimpering just like the redhead before me.

But she denied me orgasm. I was so close to reaching climax I could taste it on the back of my tongue, but Mistress DeStasio lifted her mouth from my cunt before I tumbled over the edge.

Frustration made me tremble. I wanted to scream!

Mistress DeStasio crawled on top of me again. I caught a glimpse of a wicked smile before she pressed her lips against mine once more. When she slipped a hand between my legs I moaned with an even greater need than before, arching off the sofa to push more of my slick flesh into her grasp. Her fingers danced inside me with such skill, I returned to the pinnacle in moments.

"Please!" I begged. "Please finish me off!"

"How badly do you want it, Alyssa? Will you give yourself to me?"

There was more to her question than playful teasing. I knew what she was asking. Somehow I just knew. It's probably not a good idea to make such an important decision when you are on the verge of coming, but I've found there are times when you just have to toss logic and reason out the window and give in to your passion. I realized there would be no turning back once I answered her, but nothing could have stopped me.

"Yes," I gasped. "Anything. Just please . . . Mistress . . . do it."

Mistress DeStasio laughed. She had me now. Her fingers quickly seized the button of flesh at my center and rolled it without mercy, wrenching groans of pleasure from me. As I wriggled on the couch in ecstasy I felt the warmth of her breath against my neck. The pressure continued to build within me. I was so close . . . so close . . . Her mouth at my neck . . . so close . . . Something sharp pricked my skin . . . so close . . . Her fingers deep in me . . . so close . . . so close . . .

I came with a tremendous shudder. Mistress DeStasio sank her fangs into my neck at the moment of climax. It was glorious. The sensation of her sucking my blood was like nothing I had ever experienced, and it set me off again. I trembled underneath her once, twice, thrice, caught in a downward spiral from which I could never escape. Never. Never.

it took another two feedings for Mistress DeStasio to make me a vampire. *Vampire.* Even now I stumble over the word, like someone learning a foreign language. I don't look forward to the inevitable conversation with my mother. It was hard enough bringing home a woman for the first time. Wait'll she sees my fangs. Ah, well.

I realized very early on I was Mistress DeStasio's flavor of the weekend. It was just a romp for her. Did I want more? Maybe. But no one got more from Francesca DeStasio. Making love to Jillian helped me get over it. I won't go into details about *her* prowess in bed, but in a word . . . Wow! Between bouts of vigorous sex I learned that Jillian was not a vampire. She was bound to the mistress for eternity but remained human to deal with the outside world I have now forsaken.

My interview with Francesca DeStasio was the scoop of the century in fashion circles, even without pictures to go with it. She was quoted in my article as saying she never thought of herself as photogenic. The mistress was not without a sense of humor. Nori was so tickled by the article she didn't make a fuss when I told her I would be working out of my apartment from now on and that I wouldn't be available during normal business hours.

I used to joke that I was a creature of the night. Now I really was. I sacrificed my mortal soul and joined the undead. Why? For a good lay. I know, I know. Stupid, right? But ask me. Ask me if it was worth it. Was fucking Francesca DeStasio worth the price?

Yeah. It really was.

should know; she makes her living as a dancer. She lives alone in her apartment full of lace shawls and feathered fans and dried roses and glitter, with only her cat, a Russian Blue named Juniper, for company. She has admirers who bring her chocolates, which she gives to me because she is allergic. Her skin is almost blue-pale, and her body is so painfully thin that her domed breasts seem almost out of place. She thinks nothing of changing clothes in front of me, standing there in nothing but shoes and stockings, her flapper dress half-pulled over her head, pink nipples crowning dainty breasts, shaved, swollen pussy framed by her lace garter belt. She doesn't know how I feel when I see her like that.

Jasmine Lee is twenty-six; I am nineteen. I have never been kissed, Jasmine has been kissed by too much. Too much love has left a dark imprint on her soul, she says. It was my innocence that attracted her to me, she says. I am curved in the places she is flat; my hair is light and curly where hers is dark and straight. I am as needy as she is independent. I long to curl up beside her and suck the brilliance from her being, taste her mouth and throat like a greedy little vampire.

Jasmine Lee is eccentric and self-centered. She does not call when she says she will, but my cell phone will vibrate me out of sleep late at night or trill in the middle of a class. I am studying classics at the university, and I lock myself in the library for long hours, throwing myself into studying to combat the loneliness I feel. I long to be with Jasmine all the time, but the friendship is always strictly on her terms. I have no other friends, I have no lover, no one fascinates me like Jasmine does. I can only think of her. The way her body emanates a scent as delicate as her namesake. I've never seen her in sweat pants or tee shirts like a normal person, I do not think she owns any. I've never seen her lose her cool or exhibit any of the weaker human emotions.

Jasmine Lee

BIANCA JAMES

Jasmine Lee is my best friend. I met her standing outside the cabaret show where she worked as a burlesque dancer. She was smoking a clove cigarette, and after she'd finished, she'd taken a roll of violet mints out of her purse and offered one to me. When the square sugar tablet melted in my mouth with the taste of purple flowers, I knew I'd found my love.

Jasmine Lee powders her face to the color of a bedsheet with Chinese powder, paints her eyelids the color of shimmering lavender dusk. She wears matte dark red lipstick like a 1920s movie star. She applies coat after coat of glitter nail polish to her fingernails until they are encrusted like jewels, like ten sparkling miniature disco balls. Jasmine Lee carries a silver beaded bag containing her cigarettes, her candy, her pharmacy of pills. She wears cat's eye sunglasses, her pin-straight black hair cut in a Louise Brooks bob with bangs. Jasmine Lee is stick thin because she is allergic to so many things: peanuts, walnuts, shellfish, legumes, dairy, wheat, chocolate, and strawberries. If she eats even the smallest amount of any of these things, she will die. I seldom see her eat at all.

Jasmine Lee does not keep boyfriends. She had too many when she was too young, she says, and got burned out on sex. There is not a man alive who can satisfy her, she says, she needs too much, and they only know how to take. She

But things change when she invites me away on a trip for the weekend. We leave late at night, long after the sun has set and the commuter traffic has died away. We travel in her big black car, and I stick my head out the window like an eager dog, sucking up the warm night wind. It is summertime and I am on break from school. Everything is dark except for factories that look like Christmas lights tangled up in machinery. Our soundtrack is Lotte Lenye singing the *Three Penny Opera* in German: "And if we don't find the next whiskey bar, I tell you we must die," she croons in a voice that is almost frightened. I feel sad and romantic staring out into the darkness. We stop at a truck stop in the middle of nowhere so I can use the bathroom, and Jasmine orders food for me while I'm gone— a grilled-cheese sandwich, french fries, and a vanilla Coke. The entire time she sits there and smokes, not removing her sunglasses, not saying anything. I offer her my French fries, but she says no, they might have been fried in the same oil as shrimp. I eat until my belly swells, and fall asleep in the car. The next time I open my eyes, we've arrived at an unfamiliar place. It's so far outside of town that there's no light but the stars. It's so dark that I get frightened. What if we get lost and can't find our way back to the car? Jasmine grips my hand in her surprisingly strong one, and leads me to the cabin that she's borrowed for the weekend. She doesn't say whose cabin it is. She lights candles in the big room, where there's a wide bed and a wood burning stove. Jasmine tucks me into the bed and tells me she'll come back soon, she's going out for a smoke. I fall asleep before she comes back.

When I wake up, it's already the next afternoon. Jasmine is asleep next to me in the bed; she's naked, her sunglasses gone, her face powder smudged. I make no effort to wake her, pausing a minute to watch her beautiful sleeping figure, dusky lashes resting on her pale face. It feels unbearably hot in the cabin. There is only one small window hidden behind some dusty curtains, and it is stuck fast. My entire body feels sticky with sweat. There is nothing resembling a kitchen or bathroom, just the bed and the stove, a fur rug and a low table. There is no water, but a half-empty bottle of whiskey on the table, so I take a pull from that, choking as it burns my throat, then savoring the spreading warmth in my guts.

I go outside to explore. I can't see anything for miles, just trees and a lake. I decide to go swimming, to wash the grime from my body. Feeling self-conscious, I enter the lake wearing my long black dress with my underwear underneath. I am a bit tipsy from the whiskey, but the cool water feels good against my sticky skin, and I swim out to the middle of the lake. It is breathtakingly beautiful here—the water seems endless, and the tall pine trees and the orange and red colors of the sunset are reflected on the lake's surface. But as it gets darker, I realize I've swum out too far, and I panic. I start swimming back, but I've lost my sense of direction and I can't remember which way I came from—the water looks endless on all sides. I feel weak and dizzy from the booze, and remember I haven't eaten since the cheese sandwich at the truck stop the night before.

My arms and legs get tangled in the long dress, and I feel myself sinking, as if something was pulling me deeper down. The feeling is strangely narcotic, and I stop resisting as my oxygen begins to run out, swallowing deep gulps of lake water.

Moments before blacking out, I feel strong arms around me, pulling me up and out of the dark and back to the shining surface. Her mouth, pushing air into my lungs, her arms pulling the soaked garments off my tangled limbs. I cough up water, and see it is Jasmine who has rescued me. She is nude, her hair and skin is wet and glossy from the water and she looks like a seal or a mermaid. The sun has disappeared from the sky, but in the twilight I can see that I am not far from the shore at all. Exhausted, I collapse against Jasmine, comforted by her bare skin against mine, the length of our bodies pressed together. We don't say anything, but her thigh is buried between mine, and we kiss a wet kiss. All of my buried desire comes rising to the surface, and I press my vulva against her leg as hard as I can, but she pulls away from our embrace, leaving me squirming in frustration.

"We've got to get back to land before it's completely dark," she says. She instructs me to wrap my arms around her neck, and she swims a slow crawl, towing me back to shore.

She dries me off with a towel and tells me there's somewhere that she wants to take me. My clothes are at the bottom of the lake. I have nothing to wear. She tells me she'll lend me some clothes, even though she is much smaller than I am. She finds a leather corset and a long black gauze skirt to squeeze me into. The corset zips up the front and laces up the back; she pulls it tight until it bites my flesh and I can barely breathe. Jasmine dresses differently that usual—black leather pants so tight that they outline the seam in her cunt, with boots and a white silk camisole. She drives us down a road that leads us into the forest and out to a roadhouse on the other side of the lake. I'd read about places like these, but I never really believed they existed. The house is decorated like an antique bordello, with dusty tasseled drapes and long velvet couches. There are women in elaborate sexy costumes everywhere. I wonder if it's some sort of brothel at first, but I don't see any men. Maybe it's some sort of weird secret lesbian bar? Jasmine keeps a protective arm around me as she talks to the women. I can't seem to focus on what she says to them. I am distracted by their eyes watching me, cruising my body. As painful as the corset is, I know I look good—my waist is cinched impossibly small while my full breasts spill from the top. I'm not used to this sort of sexual attention from anyone, and it turns me on.

Jasmine keeps handing me red cocktails that taste like pomegranate and cherry, and I keep drinking them. Before long, I'm having difficultly standing, and I stumble off to find a bathroom so I can piss. I open the door, and it's not before I've gotten inside that I realize someone has followed me in— not Jasmine—and has locked the door behind us. She is a tall woman with long, curly blonde hair and green eyes, and is dressed in some sort of low cut velvet gown. She comes up from behind me, and pins me against the sink, so we're both reflected in the mirror. She plays with my hair with one hand, the other hand pressed against my artificially flattened belly. "We look a lot alike, don't you think?" She whispers in my ear, then licks it gently. "We could be sisters . . . "

I close my eyes. I'm so drunk and horny, I still need to piss, and I don't care that this woman isn't Jasmine; she's sexy, and I'm just curious to see what she'll do to me. She half unzips the front of my corset and pulls out my breasts. She cups the breasts in both hands while kissing and sucking my neck, grinding her crotch into my ass, barely covered by the thin gauze of the skirt with no underwear beneath. I moan a little as she pinches and rubs my stiff nipples between her fingertips, the porcelain of the sink pressing against my mound and belly, making me feel full to bursting. She shoves one leg between my legs to spread them, then pulls the skirt up over my ass and tucks the hem into the waistband. She gives my ass an appreciative squeeze before reaching down under to stroke my wet cunt with her fingertip. Then, without warning, she glides a single digit into my slippery pussy. I gasp, because the feeling of her finger inside of me is only making my bladder feel fuller. She swirls her finger inside of me, pressing the pad against the front inside wall, while my clit rubs up against the cold ceramic sink. My hips swivel around that single digit, as if I were her puppet and she were jerking strings attached to my cunt. And before I know it, I'm coming, my breath coming in sweet, raspy gulps, and my cunt is leaking hot piss onto her hand, down my thighs, and onto the floor. I feel her teeth pressing harder against my throat, the pain increasing the intensity of my orgasm. We are interrupted by hard pounding on the door, which forces the women to rip her finger from my cunt, and her teeth from my neck.

It's Jasmine, and she does not look pleased. She says nothing; she just takes my hand and jerks me out of the bathroom. The blonde woman is laughing now, and suddenly I feel very drunk and foolish. Jasmine half-drags me down the hall to a bedroom, where she slams the door behind us, and locks it. She stands to face me, arms crossed.

"What the fuck were you doing back there?" she asks me.

"I had to piss," I reply feebly.

"Yeah, and look at yourself: you peed all over the place." She slaps me. I burst into tears.

"I'm sorry, Jasmine," I sniffle. "I didn't see her come in. I didn't know what she would do to me."

Suddenly, Jasmine looks sorry for mistreating me. She gathers me back into her arms, and says, "Now, now, I forget how innocent you are sometimes." She kisses me again, and her lips are so soft, the kiss cuts right to the source of the tears, soothing the ache in my heart, and I feel my cunt throbbing again. Her mouth tastes like flowers.

"Did she draw blood?" she asks softly. She lifts my hair up off my neck to check. "There's just a little bruise here, thank god she didn't pierce through . . . "

"What would have happened if she did?" I ask, but Jasmine does not reply. She has me sit down on the big bed and strips off the too-tight corset and piss drenched skirt. I feel incredibly relieved to be naked. "Let's get you cleaned up," she says.

Jasmine brings a pitcher of water and a basin from the dressing table and washes my legs, checking the cloth after she wipes my pussy to check for errant blood spots. There are none.

"Maybe I should take you home," Jasmine says, towering over my supine body.

"No, I'm fine," I lie. "I want to stay here, with you," I say, trying to sound sober.

Jasmine kneels down before me, and she says "What did she do to you? Show me where she touched you."

"She stuck her finger inside. Just one finger."

"Like this?" Jasmine asks, and I am pierced on her finger.

"Yes," I moan. I am so horny, my nipples are hard, my cunt is wet, I am praying she will not stop.

"It was your first time," she said. "But you did not bleed."

"No," I reply.

"I am going to make you bleed," she says.

My cunt tightens up around her finger. I can't bring myself to say no. I want it too badly.

Jasmine unzips her leather pants. They're the kind that unzip all the way around, front to back, and I can see her shaved mound protruding. She takes her other hand, and slips it between her legs. I think she's just masturbating at first, but then I see her remove something from her pussy, an impossibly thick, cruel looking black dildo. It slides out of her cunt, slick with juices. There's a D ring where a belt buckle would normally be in her pants, and she fits the dildo through the ring, and adjusts it so it's pulled tight against her belly.

"I don't think that will fit inside me," I mumble, a knot of dread tightening in my stomach.

"Don't worry about that for the moment," she says. "Just remember it's there."

She withdraws her hand from me for a moment, and dips her fingers in a glass of red liquid, her fingers dripping and scarlet. Without further ado, she shoves three fingers in me at once. I scream out loud, as the quick, sharp pain tears through me. She's fucking her hand in and out of me, corkscrewing her fingers, and adds a fourth finger, until the better part of her hand is inside of me. I am stretched, torn and bleeding, and Jasmine starts sucking my clit and labia furiously, sucking up the blood that flows from my torn cunt. I am surprised to discover that the pain only adds to arousal. Every time she stretches me open a little further, there's a heavy rush of pumping blood to my vagina, my clit feels more swollen and tender. I'm at the brink of orgasm, in a transcendental state for what feels like hours, and when my cunt finally contracts into strong contractions of orgasms, I feel the blood pump out of my wounded pussy and into Jasmine's greedy mouth. I lay there, softly weeping as Jasmine continues to feed from me. I am starting to feel light headed and faint. I've never bled this much before, not even on my period.

Finally, Jasmine rises, her face smeared in my blood, and lies on top of me. I feel the head of her cock nudging my sticky pussy. I turn my head away from her, try to close my legs against her, but she sinks her penis into me, and I am awakened to a fresh blaze of pain.

I can sense the excitement in Jasmine as she kneads my breasts in her palms; she's breathing heavily, thrusting into me with her hips. She nuzzles and licks my throat, then whispers in my ear, "You have given me your blood, your innocence, you belong to me now . . . " She's going to bite my throat. I can feel her sharp teeth against my neck.

But there is one thing that Jasmine hadn't counted on—I am bigger than she is, and though I am young and mortal, my hunger is strong. Before she could bite me, I pushed her away and rolled on top of her, her dick still lodged in my cunt to the hilt. I fucked myself deeper and deeper onto the dildo lubricated with my own blood, pinning Jasmine's wrists to the bed with my own hands. She gives a hearty laugh. "So you're the kind who likes to flip the script, eh?" She says, amused. I knew she was just playing along for my sake, but the very fact that she refused to take me seriously allowed me to do what I did. I licked her throat, locating the throbbing vein with my tongue. And I bit back, hard, taking a chunk of flesh with my teeth, the blood gushing forth, soaking everything: my face my hair, jasmine's pristine white shirt. She screamed in agony, but as I drank from her, I found myself growing stronger, holding her struggling wrists, pinning her hips with my tensing thighs. I would not let her escape me, now that I finally had what I wanted. I drank and drank of Jasmine's blood that tasted like meat and flowers, until she laid there, dehydrated, a pale husk of the magnificent being she had once been. I stood above her now, plump and glowing, nude and bathed in blood, and her body began to shrink in upon itself, collapse into dust and ashes, until there was nothing left at all. I had no regret. I had everything I wanted.

You see, I never so much wanted Jasmine as I wanted to be her. I had always suspected this about her, but I'd never had the proof. She had thought I was a lot more innocent than I really was, but I was prepared. I was not sure what she intended to make of me—to make me her slave, her blood donor, her companion, or if she'd just planned to kill me, but I could have never been happy that way. I was hungry for her power, you see, it was what had attracted me most to her.

I unlocked the door to the room, and I found everyone else had gone; I was alone in the house. I took a shower alone, rinsed away the blood in the shower, and stared at my newly created self. My skin was white and paper sheet flawless, my eyes glowed preternaturally. I had everything I wanted. I found the car keys, dressed myself in the clothes I found in a closet, and drove back to the city. I knew the way without consulting a map.

Blood Tells

The Vampyre Relates a Story to Her Half-Mortal Daughter

MARÍA HELENA DOLAN

MUST WE KILL to obtain a complete feeding? No, Mi Queridita. And there are even times when we do not wish to do so for any of several reasons.

What might these be? Very well, I shall present one such instance.

Understand, Mi Vida, boredom is the true curse of my kind. We walk through the centuries night after night, seeking solace, or amusement, or simply relief and distraction from the accumulation of memories. We each must individually find ways to address that immutable fact. You cannot imagine how insufferably tedious this can become at times.

But to illustrate my point regarding a complete feeding, I will tell you a story, which being Lesbian you can perhaps appreciate.

One evening, it would be, oh, perhaps forty years ago now, I found myself suffering from just the sort of difficulty I spoke of earlier. This unsettled frame of mind birthed a mood that caused me to ambulate about rather aimlessly. Lamentably, there simply seem to be times when a certain unassuageable restlessness ensnares me. As it did on this particular hot summer night.

With a sharp clarity now, I can recall passing through a row of houses in the East Lake section of your metropolis, my awareness partially submerged within my desultory ennui. Undoubtedly this preoccupying inattention accounted for the fact that I only gradually became aware of the faint aroma that had been so subtly tracing my olfactory sense. It must be stated that our powers of smell vastly dwarf those of canines, and we often hunt based on what this sense informs.

At any rate, I had been unconsciously following this strengthening scent. So I stood still for a moment, breathing in deeply once to identify the aroma. Ah—it was a woman's bloods I smelled. There is naught like unto the intoxicating blend of smells that bespeak menstrual blood. Indeed, the only question was how I had managed to disregard the heady bouquet up to this point.

No matter, for now I hone in on this exquisiteness, shifting my head to the side so as to better savor and analyze the redolent scent. Yes, most assuredly this is that nectarous blood, profuse, copious, and strong. Indeed, much stronger and pervasive than one usually encounters, given the paddings and pluggings and various concealments women perforce use to inhibit their flows.

No, this flow is decidedly uninhibited, and I must locate its source quickly or else be driven mad. Striding down a dead-end street where the uniform size and structure of dwellings fitted so closely together presents a saw-toothed wave-form against the dark sky, eagerly I locate the house where this inebriating aroma originates. I feel the moon rise behind me, and she now shimmers against the glass as I stand transfixed before a large, wide window. The lunar deity and I both stare at the woman on the other side.

From the scattered works and materials about her place, I deduce that the woman must be an artist, working mostly in paints and clays. Well-built and sturdy she is—not at all possessed of that loathsomely boyish stick figure so prized of late. No, this creature is assuredly a woman, rounded and of substance.

The only clothing she wears is a small T-shirt, so frequently washed that it fair shines and the original coloration can only be guessed at. Her waist, hips, thighs, legs, and feet are quite bare, allowing her blood to travel wholly unimpeded as she moves about her capacious kitchen and ample living room.

I have never beheld such a fantastic apparition before. Her blood, hot and sweet and strong, flowing quite freely down her thighs, adorned with the occasional thicknesses. Her flow travels in streams, strong red currents that glisten wetly as she shifts her weight or moves across the floor.

Upon reaching her knees, the streams begin to distinctly separate, spreading into individuated tributaries and running in numerous starkly scarlet rivulets, all cascading farther down along her tan calves and shins to her feet. As she stands still for a moment, it seems as though red roots have taken hold at her base, reaching motile trunks and branches up to her weep hole.

When she moves again, some clotted masses of uterine matter drop out of her body directly onto the white floor tiles, there forming intriguing if inscrutably irregular patterns. These are joined by the persistently flowing streams, all swirling together in a primordial soup of creation. She is making art, using her body as the medium and the floor as her unyielding canvas!

The sight and smell of that sacred blood being celebrated

in such a primeval fashion engenders a piercing and violent hunger within the core of me. This hunger rises fiercely, until I am sick with desire. My stomach lurches, my mouth hosts a biliousness in its nether portions, my entire being trembles with a monstrously yearning awe. Yet I must somehow find the strength to steel myself and hold fast to the spot outside her window, so that I might not imperil her profound artistry.

She bends forward to examine the pattern work, considering her creations from various angles and levels. Is she perhaps receiving messages from all the woman ancestors of her line? Can she be divining the future with these scrying traces upon the floor? Does she not know that I behold her in her veridical glory and anxiously await her?

I can restrain myself no longer. I *concentrate* upon her. And she turns and faces me. Black-haired and black-suited as the night I am, and greatly intent upon my quest. She regards me with an unafraid apprising stare. Taking her unflinching viewing as assent, I lift the aged window all the way up into its track, feeling the leaden counterbalances as they move audibly but unseen within the frame.

The night silhouettes me as I shift into the house. I stand before her with a slight tremble, hands clasped behind my back so I may more easily restrain the impulse to seize her.

The woman regards me up and down and appears only curious. I hear her strong thoughts: Why am I here, and what do I think of her art?

Giving a slight bow as though this were all a practiced part of a hallowed ritual, I bend down easily and place my forefinger into one of the beckoning red trails. Moving carefully with a slow and steady rhythm, I outline my own design therein, reverently tracing across small puddles and over major splashes alike. When this consecrated task is complete, I raise the wetted finger to my lips and lick the substantive blood very carefully from my own flesh. Eyes closed and senses fully alive, I savor the flavor of her, of Life Eternal.

Opening my eyes again and looking directly up into her face, I see knowingness and acceptance suffusing her smile. Uncoiling from the floor, I stand and face her fully.

We willingly walk toward each other, meeting in the middle of this tiled menstrual hut. When we are within arm's length of one another, she raises her arm with the palm outward so that I will stop. And through some unimaginable effort, I do. She then gracefully directs her hand down to the parting point of her black-furred mound, catching some of the flow. Still smiling, she raises that hand to my lips, offering me the stunning essence of herself.

Taking that bloodied hand between my own, I upturn this cup of flesh to my lips and drink down her exquisite offering with reverential gratitude. Then I press her palm against my mouth, leaving a pattern upon my now-luminous face.

In concert we move to the couch, a rather large and ungainly thing in outline. However, it is covered with a handpainted drop cloth bearing scenes out of legend: satyrs and wood nymphs, fairy queens and elven subjects, twining vines full of grapes that transform into fantastic serpents and labyrinthine patterns.

Ah, such an interesting and talented woman. She must remain among the living, to create more art. I will be well-satisfied with the flow of life from between her legs.

She readily lay down upon the cloth, one leg resting over the back of the couch, the other dangling off the front with her foot touching the floor. And there can be no refusal of such an offering.

Hardly able to restrain my eagerness, I kiss her mouth, smearing her own blood across her face. Our lips and tongues slide with slippery ease across each other repeatedly. Placing my hands upon her hips, I pull her middle down upon the flat of the couch.

I kiss down her neck, feeling the wild enticement of her strong pulse. To avoid this all-compelling allure, I immediately place my face between her legs. And I begin to work my mouth upon her nether-mouth. Nearly collapsing from the intoxicating smell and my own excitement, I endeavor diligently to grant her the pleasure she deserves.

I am like a jubilantly drunken dolphin, leaping and diving for sheerest joy in the warm waters near the island's coast. I drink and drink from her salty shallows as her pleasure causes the flow to increase, pushing past her cervix and into my world.

As her body quickens and heart races, she grinds furiously against my red-soaked face. Blood pours across my neck and down my chest; and like a famished foal at her mother's fount, I drink and drink her down.

Her explosions contract and twist her whole body, over and over as she cries out and clutches me hard. Even after she is obviously spent, I continue to pleasure her and suck the sanguineous sustenance until she is still and dry. Her exhaustion forces sleep upon her.

Despite my engorgement and satiation, I stand and run my hands from eyes to cheeks and mouth, scraping remaining blood off and spatulating it into my greedy mouth. I place my hands up to my long thick hair and through it, ensuring that her essence bathes me completely. I am thoroughly drunk with the blood, the smell, her pleasure. I enfold my arms around myself to hold me still until I regain some composure.

After a while, I gaze down upon her and feel great affection and gratitude. Bending over her prostrate form, I very tenderly place a kiss upon her lips. Wiping a drop of blood from the corner of my eye, I lightly apply it upon her lips. Thus when she wakens, she will have something tangible to prove to herself that it was not a dream.

My eyes linger upon her fine face and frame for one last look, and then I am out of the house the way I entered. I slide the window down behind me and smile to the gibbous moon as I go forth into the notably changed night.

Some years later, I immediately recognized and so purchased some of her work from an Atlanta gallery. In fact, you may recall seeing those canvases upon the wall in my study when you were small: "Red Composition #10" and "Blood Tells." Yes, Mi Perlita, the very ones you were so fascinated by as a child.

And so, as I say, it is not necessary to kill in order to have a most fulfilling feeding.

Transubstantiation

LESLIE ANNE LEASURE

Jacoby wears gingham dresses and daisies. Her skin is Victorian white. I'd say porcelain, but it's been said before. Six hundred and thirty-six times in the last 205 years, to be exact. Well, that's when I started counting, anyway. China is a close second at 532 times, the last time by that sweet baby butch thing who skulked around the bar after Jacoby one too many times. I remember the sound of her body sighing to the ground in the alley. Jacoby is a redhead, Irish, still with that damn soft lilting brogue. It kills me every time. Not me really, but it definitely kills.

The things I know about Jacoby could fill several books and a good number of porno flicks. She grows orchids, multiple variations. In the small hours of morning, before dawn, she steps out of her clothing, picks one orchid, always a color different from the one of the day before, and slowly, damn slowly, traces the petals across her entire body. I don't know why she does this, if it is only for the pleasure of it, the precious touch of something like skin, without the blood to distract her. She is fastidious this way. The first time I saw her do it, I almost remembered how to breathe again.

She keeps hummingbirds in an aviary that she lights at night and darkens during the day. They sip red sugar water. Perhaps she likes the irony: things drawn to red, then gone.

She reads Tolstoy and Turgenev. She giggles her way though Gogol. She always, always, brings you to orgasm before she drinks. It's beautiful, the flow of ecstasy into death.

I could say that I'm the patient hunter, stalking my prey. But the only part of that sentence that is true is the stalking part. It's obsession: pure, banal, divine obsession.

Picture nighttime in a small midwestern city, the Amoco sign rising on the horizon like the moon. Another girl child, maybe eighteen, probably not, she is found sleeping in an unlocked church. Although Jacoby can't enter the church, she waits for evening to fall deeply. She waits for the girl to return. She takes her by the hand to the Amoco station bathroom, where she strips the girl and bathes her in warm sink water and kisses. Jacoby's hands are heartbreakingly gentle. She likes her women to come like thunder and go like lambs. The edgy, brittle, tough girls, fragile under the glass of loss and heartache. She breaks them, and when they cry she sings lullabies, right to the point when they move into joy. When she drinks, their eyes are prisms.

I've become careless over the years. I think this is the first time she sees me as she exits the bathroom. I'm leaning against a red car, smoking. She is done sooner than usual. Hungry tonight.

"You," she says. It is easy to say she is wanton in her satiation, but it's more than that. She cocks her head with a smile. "Bolshevik revolution?"

I had been following her for more than one hundred years before that, but I nod. "Anastasia?"

"Delicious." Jacoby loves lost girls. She indicates the body in the bathroom. "Yours?"

"Not at all."

"No . . . she wouldn't be, would she?" Jacoby is thoughtful

and lifts her hands to adjust the flowers in her hair. "You love hyacinth."

I do. "Yes."

"And . . . " she takes a step closer and very slowly, orchid slowly, traces my jaw line, "women."

"Yes."

She drops her hand. "Isn't it lovely to walk past mirrors without seeing yourself?"

I wonder if she's known all along that I've been there. I wonder who she used to see reflected. "Yes. But then sometimes I forget I exist."

"Ah. If a vampire falls in the forest . . . " she laughs. "But you can hear the sound of one hand clapping now, can't you? It sounds like a quiet ocean."

I don't know what to say to this, but she doesn't seem to expect an answer. She takes my arm and walks me across the parking lot.

"You know I could kill you," she says.

Her hand burns, a crucifix. "I do."

"What's your name?"

"Does it matter?"

"In some Australian tribes, when a person dies, it is forbidden to speak his or her name for fear of haunting. And say it has a common meaning—fire, water, stone—then they would come up with a whole different name for it that everyone had to use." She doesn't break stride but gives me a sideways glance. "'And from there the Lord scattered them abroad over the face of all the earth.'"

"Give me a new name then, and I won't haunt you," I lie.

"If I give you a name, will you wear it like a collar? Will you fall to your knees for me?" She flirts.

We are so dramatic. I grin and continue the game. "If you ask it."

"Ah. That I might," she lilts. "But you know I have no use for vampires."

"So, if I speak your name, you won't haunt me then?" I flick my cigarette into the ditch at the edge of the highway. I speak her name. "Damn, Jacoby."

She releases me, looks away, narrows her eyes against the moon. "The King Kalevide bound the servant of death in unbreakable chains after his beloved died. But when the king died, his spirit was too restless to seek wisdom in heaven, and so was sent back to guard the gates of hell in the place of his enemy."

"Such is love," I say. Morning is not distant, and the late-night semis hurtle past us like trains. "My name is Joan Darcy."

"Joan of the dark castle." She plays with my name. Another truck, a few more steps. "Do you hear the voices of dark angels, then?"

"Not lately," I tell her.

"Two hundred and five years," she says suddenly. "Is this love?"

"You knew?"

"March 21, 1800, the ascension of Pope Pius VII. You were dressed as a cardinal, committing two major transgressions right there, I believe: A woman. A vampire. How did you manage to enter the basilica?"

"Dead women make good bishops," I tell her. "I slipped out for a bite."

"Nun?"

With a wince, I make the sign of the cross.

"Evil." She laughs and checks the sky. "Hmm. Morning. Your coffin or mine?"

I know she's planning to kill me; I'm planning something else. "Yours, of course."

Of course, I had planned on being more careful. Jacoby is older than I am and wily as hell. If it came to a fight, I'd probably end up the worse.

I wanted to taste her. I wanted to crush her body against mine with my hand at the small of her back. I wanted to enter her, with each finger in turn, and then together.

But most—oh, but most—I wanted transubstantiation.

I catch her wrist, the wooden stake about an inch from my chest.

"Do you know I've been following you for five hundred years?" she says, still pushing the stake toward me. She is stronger, and in my surprise, I lose a quarter of an inch.

"No."

"I'm a better stalker," she says. "You lack subtlety."

I step back a pace but no farther. I feel the plaster wall behind me. "That's true. But I have something else."

"A death wish?" She makes one furious push and then suddenly releases me.

I sink against the wall, watch her pace across the room. "Hardly."

She leans against the vanity. She has painted the mirror with orchids. "There's a passage to the sewers through that door. Go. Now."

I turn, knowing she won't stake me from behind, and head for the sewer. Not a bad first date. I hear her covering the aviary, singing the birds to sleep.

I was made at the fall of Athens. The city burned. At that time, I was an initiate in the temple of the oracle, in the city for study. The woman who made me was drunk with blood that night. She didn't bother to hide what she was; her lips were red with life. She swept through the city, sipping terror.

When she took me by my arms, she whispered, "My

darling, blood is only water filled with the breath of the gods."
I remember how she tore into my throat. I remember ecstasy.
She fed me, and as I sank to my knees, she held me steady.
Total surrender. Death. Immortality. The transformation into
the profane was beautiful and holy in its way. And, yes, I was
profane. We both were.

Her name was Horatia, but we, her lovers, never spoke
her name. We slipped through cities seducing wives from
husbands, girls from their chores. Horatia was amused by my
desire for the priestesses and later the nuns. If Jacoby has a
thing for bad girls, I've always had a thing for holy women.
There is just that slight shimmer around the body you can
see when you're undead. Maybe it's because you don't have a
soul anymore that the strength of another's is like a beacon, or
maybe it's just me. But I couldn't help it; I've always wanted
them. I'm no stranger to obsession, although I've often called
it love. Sometimes heady and quick—a startling of her quiet
study, a seduction of a bride of Christ—they always wanted to
save me. I played the part well, dark and seemingly lost. In
the end, their hair fell across my face, and I entered them with
my hands and tongue before I drank my desire. Horatia said I
was looking for what I thought I didn't have. "You always want
purity, but you already have it," she would tell me after I fed.
"Pure evil, my darling."

HORATIA CREATED MORE vampires than any of the
undead I've known.

"It's a rush," she told me once. Whenever she fell into one
of her dark moods, she slipped out and came in with another.
It always seemed to make her happy for a time.

This is ultimately why I left her. I didn't know what I was
looking for, but it wasn't her coven of sycophants. I did want
purity, and pure evil was enough for me then. I never bothered

to restrain my wants; there didn't seem a need. Even when they begged for their lives, they were just sweeter. I lived this way for centuries. I can't apologize for it; this is who I was, what I was made to be. It's funny, in a way, to realize Jacoby was watching me all those years.

I don't know exactly when things changed. It happened over time, perhaps. But slowly, no matter how many I killed, no matter how many loved me first, I began to feel an emptiness, a kind of boredom. And one night, at the turn of the nineteenth century, I saw Jacoby. I didn't realize she was a vampire at first. The sun had just set, and the evening vespers to celebrate Pope Pius VII's ascension had begun. Had I glanced at her a second before or a second later, things might have been different. But she struck me with all the beauty of life and death together. Her shimmer had nothing to do with a soul. I thought it must be a spell of some kind. But I was suddenly as helpless with desire for her as with any of my mortal loves. Maybe it was my own despair, seeking relief, any relief, and she seemed to be some kind of ideal, lovely and shimmery, and yet what I was. I think at that moment I knew she would be my salvation. Then, I didn't know what that would mean, only that I had to follow her.

I see her again a few nights later, after dinner. Jacoby is pleased with herself and wipes a drop of blood from her lips. The dead girl is slumped inside an old-fashioned phone booth.

"Tight squeeze," I say, stepping out of the shadows.

"*Hmm.* Well worth it," Jacoby hums. "I seem to remember more than one tight place you've taken advantage of in your day."

I laugh, and we walk for a minute in silence. She doesn't look at me but slows her pace to my own.

"So, I have to ask you, Why exactly is it that you followed me for so long?"

"Ah, so we come to it, then," Jacoby says. She seems pensive and doesn't answer right away. We are walking away from the center of town into the residential streets. It's a college town, and students hang out on their porches drinking beer and shouting invitations to the street. One group has a blow-up children's pool, and they all slosh around, splashing each other.

"I first saw you when you were mortal, before you went to that temple. You know how you can always tell when a girl isn't quite like the others? The way you led your sisters and brawled with your brothers. And then I saw you with that young girl in the village."

The young girl in the village was the first woman I tasted, in the mortal sense. Alone, the act itself would have changed me, but unfortunately, her father caught us in the act. Which is why my father sent me off to temple. Although senators were screwing boys in the senate, girls were definitely not.

"It was pretty hot," I say.

"Yes, it was." Jacoby shoots me a look. "But then they sent you off, before I could have my way with you. When I saw you again, you were a vampire."

"And?"

She grins and shakes her head. "Well, you were amazing. The number of women you had . . . three in a night. You were like a force of Nature."

"Would you have killed me then, when I was mortal?" I asked, imagining how things might have been different if it had been Jacoby instead of Horatia. I thought of the girl in the phone booth.

"I think," she says and finally looks at me directly. "I think I would have made you."

I don't see Jacoby again for weeks. And I look. More than once I risk dawn at her window, but although the hummingbirds whirr through their caged world, still fed, I don't see her. Finally I give up for a while.

I've lost her before, in the mid-1920s. As it turns out she had headed to the New World, while I was traveling Egypt, which is where I found the Omega Codex.

This is actually when I found out about transubstantiation, at least in the vampire sense. And the vampire sense actually predates the other definition. The problem is, the codex is devilishly hard to translate, an obscure Coptic dialect mixed with letters I've never identified. At first, I thought I was reading more buried "heretical" texts about Christ that the church had edited out early on. But then I realized the codex predated his death by more than a century. The texture of papyrus, the size of the sheets of the page gave me a timeframe. What caught my attention was the constant mention of blood. Well, really what initially caught my attention was the woman I saw reading it the first time. In retrospect, it would have been easier to find out what she knew about the codex before I killed her, but at the time, I was looking for a meal, not information. It was only when I skimmed a few phrases, and decided to take the book back to my home that I realized she might have been more useful to me alive. Or even undead, but then, I've never made another vampire. I didn't want to be like Horatia.

But the codex offered me hope, unconnected to my obsession with Jacoby. In translated bits and pieces, it became clear that it was a text about vampires. At least it seemed so to me, even though it never used it in words I recognized. "That which neither lives nor dies" seemed to be clearly vampiric. But what got me excited, in a way I hadn't been in ages, is the few lines that I could translate:

I was that which neither lives nor dies
I am beyond death, beyond undeath,
transubstantiated
beyond purity, beyond impurity
beyond omega
beyond beginning.

IN THE YEARS following, I pieced together more. It's a cryptic instruction manual of sorts. Or a long spell. Maybe it's just wishful thinking on my part, but the long and short of it seemed to say this: If two vampires who have never made other vampires (this is a critical point in the codex, I'm not sure why) "meet completion together or alone" (this part is still unclear; if you can do it alone, why do you need two?), they will be "beyond omega, beyond beginning." How someone can be beyond an ending and a beginning at the same time was beyond my understanding, but I kept coming back to it every time blood tasted like ash.

WHEN I DO see Jacoby again, it's like this: I wake from sleep, and she is straddling my hips, her right hand wrapped around my throat, her left circling my breasts.

"Is this what you want?" she says as I open my eyes.

I sleep nude. She is out of character, wearing a 1920s black velvet opera cape, clasped with silver. The skirt is velvet too, and I know she just drank because her thighs, naked against my own, are pulsing hot.

I don't move, and it's hard because what I really want to do is push my body into her hands. But not like this. One compromise and the whole thing will be lost. So I stay still and say, "No."

"No?" she pinches my nipple hard and bares her teeth. "You're lying."

I open my hands at my sides and say again, "No."

"I know you want me."

"I do. Just not like this." I want to tell her now, all of it, but I can't. Not yet.

She tightens her grip at my throat. "If you were mortal, I'd snap your neck."

It's a risk, but in one quick motion, I scissor my legs and slap her hand away. We roll, wrestling, until I'm holding her down on the bed by her wrists. It is adrenalin, and it won't last long. "Jacoby, listen."

She spits a Gaelic curse, followed by a few choice phrases in Russian, but she stays still. I release her hands and edge off the bed, facing her. I pull on my old silk smoking jacket, a gift from a mortal boy who had a talent for clothes.

"OK, here's the thing. I have a question for you."

She sits on the bed, drawing her knees up. "A question?"

My bedroom is a concrete block and black iron sconces. I pace to each candle and light it, even though we can both see perfectly well in the dark. I just like the effect, and I needed time.

"Actually, two." I say and light the last candle. I turn, lean against the wall, and face her. "Do you ever get tired of this?"

"Of what?"

"Being a vampire. The whole creature of the night thing."

She laughs, but it isn't an easy laugh. I know she's going to lie. "*Hmm.* Immortality, eternal youth, power. What's not to like?" She says it lightly.

"The fact that nothing ever changes."

She stretches her legs out on the bed and leans back on her hands. Her back is slightly arched, and I want to take the three steps to the bed and arch her yet farther.

"Everything changes, Joan. Clothes, countries, gods, literature. We've seen a hundred lifetimes. More."

"Everything changes but us." I say. "I used to love it—being on the outside of things, standing above it all, watching mortals live and die. But now..."

"A mid-death crisis?" Jacoby is cruel and yet knows exactly what I'm saying. I don't answer, and I watch her settle into seriousness. This is how I know her. This is how I love her. "All right. I get it. But there isn't exactly an alternative."

"There is."

"Sure, sunbathing, wood sticks, fire . . . none pleasant."

"No, I don't mean that."

She looks at me sideways and pulls her cape around herself tighter. In this moment, she is like a little girl playing dress-up. "What's the other question?"

This is one I'm not ready to ask yet. The codex is unclear on this point. I pull the sheaf of copies of the codex from the little chest where I keep them. "Have you heard of the Omega Codex?"

"That's your second question?"

"No," I say. "But have you?"

She gives me a wry grin. "Is that what you were doing all that time in Egypt back in the '20s? You became such an ascetic. *Hmmm*. And you missed all of those sweet flapper girls, my little monk."

"How did you . . . ?" I am still surprised she knows so much of my movements. Here I thought I was so stealthy.

She shrugs. "Ah, Joan. Didn't I tell you I was subtle?"

"But why?"

"Tell me about this old codex." She laughs. "Omega. Such an obvious title. The end of what? Another apocalypse myth?"

I hand it to her. "It's in Coptic, I think."

She stares down at it for a minute, and I know she can read it. Maybe better than I can. "It is actually a mix, there's some . . . Aramaic, I think."

"Oh."

She slowly flips pages, scanning the inscriptions. "What do you think it means?"

I am standing by her, looking over her shoulder at the pages. "I'm not sure, but it seems to say that two vampires can change into something else, something more powerful if . . . Well, I'm not sure. I think it says if they complete each other or something like that."

She smiles and raises her eyebrows at me. "This passage? Right. It means 'if there is love between them.' And then there's a lot of stuff about candles and designs on the floor, typical mystical writing. Oh, and sex. Definitely sex."

"Oh." I step back, blushing, as much as a vampire can blush.

"It's probably trash, Joanie. Wishful thinking. We are already beyond life and death." She snaps the book shut.

I shrug. "Maybe. Have you ever made anyone?"

"No, I haven't," Jacoby says slowly, understanding what I am asking. "You are not serious about trying this. With me? You hardly know me."

This feels like dangerous ground. How much do you know someone when you are standing outside of her life, observing her actions for two hundred years? Is what you know real or a projection of what you want? But I am stubborn after all.

"Look, Jacoby. There's something here, with us. Seven hundred years of combined stalking can't be all wrong." I don't want to sound too serious, but damn, why did she follow me for so long if it wasn't some kind of love?

She looks almost frightened for a moment and gets up, as if impatient. "All right, yes, I can admit it. But it was a crush. That's all."

"Are you sure?" We are standing inches from each other, and I take her hand.

"No." It's an unwilling response, and then she seems to catch herself. "But, Joan, you can't count on me."

"Why not?"

She shrugs. "What the hell. When do you want to do it?"

I want to hug her wildly but hold back. "I think it says something about the full moon."

Jacoby nods. "Yes, that's in two nights."

"Two nights then. Here."

"Yes." She turns and leaves without another word.

I mean, when you think of it, what the hell is love? Revelation? Because when you start telling truths you become closer to someone? Truth? Because truth changes all the time, depending upon angles and images. It's like a place you know, when you leave it and come back, something indefinable has happened. Then it's inexpressibly lonely. Familiar and different.

Is it a kind of prayer? Something that brings us closer to some kind of god, a way to express hope and longing for the divine?

I couldn't get her out of my mind the next day. I couldn't sleep, couldn't feed. I didn't want to look for her. I felt like if I saw her before the ritual, maybe she would change her mind and tell me then. But I couldn't help myself. I would just look, watch her in the way I had for so long. Yes, perhaps this was obsession. Perhaps vampires are incapable of the kind of love that would preclude following someone. But this was just an excuse. I think it was just that something about her, about thinking about her, freed me from the horrible feeling of aloneness and emptiness that had filled me in the past hundred years.

I followed her, just one more time, I told myself, like an addict tying off for another fix. Just one more time.

I don't know, still don't know, if she was aware of me that night. Jacoby left her place just after sunset. She wore a white shift, barely decent and yet oddly innocent. When she passed, she smelled of lilacs. Jacoby headed for one of her regular haunts: a gay bar by the train tracks. I waited outside. The cars passed, and the taillights seemed hypnotic. I knew what was going to happen. An hour later, Jacoby came out of the bar, a little leather dyke in tow. They were kissing, and Jacoby did her usual turn, pressing the girl against the wall and covering her mouth when she started moaning. Then came the bite. And then, yes, and then I watched as Jacoby made a shallow cut at her throat and pressed the girl to her to drink her own blood, making her vampire. I thought briefly of Horatia as I stood there. And I have to say, love or no, I stood there crying.

I knew she didn't love me. Maybe she was fascinated by my love for her. Or maybe she was crueler than I gave her credit for. That what she had said the night before was all some kind of gruesome set-up. Or maybe she was as scared by what I was proposing as I was. And I asked myself, Is this love for me or an obsession with what I can't have? I suppose if love requires a soul, then it is moot. But maybe there is something within us, something inherent and unique to every person, that recognizes something in someone else and says yes. Like a favorite color, there is no reason to choose one over another, but still we do and I don't know why. But I couldn't help it. I loved the way she moved, how she made me feel, yes, even the translucent hardness that shimmers like my mortal angels'. Maybe that's what those girls would transform into if they were made. I wondered, Would the ritual still work? I wondered if I should go through with it anyway, just to see. I wondered if my own want, call it love or not, would be enough. And maybe I thought that she was just scared, that she really might love me after all, in her own way. Behind it all, I believed that somewhere in her was that woman I loved. Maybe that was stupid or wishful thinking or selfish. I don't know. And then I thought, maybe this is what unconditional love should be: that no matter how a person behaves, that recognition remains. And maybe that is something precious, and maybe it counts. Or maybe, finally, it is the ability to love without expectation or possession.

Her kiss is as I've imagined it. We've painted signs on the floor, spoken words I didn't quite understand, invoked the profane, the holy. Her hands are cool as they slide across my body. The candles burn in their sconces. The moon, our sun, shines through my one window, white and yellow light intersecting through the darkness. We are naked quickly. I lay on top of her, slide her legs apart with one knee. Our bodies press together.

This is more than blood lust, more than lust. I think of her when she was mortal, the daughter of a minor lord. Seemingly chaste, riding horses, the wildness constrained by mortal rules. I love that her immortality freed her from that, even at the price. I love her laugh, her grace, her words. I slide down between her legs, palming her thighs apart, and press my lips and tongue to her warmest place. It feels like sweet eternity, and when she cries out I don't stop. I keep wanting this moment to last. This rare vulnerability, her naked wildness, her hair across her face, her fingers in my hair. And I want to give her everything I am, in simple gratitude for this moment.

The world shimmers. I moan against her as the transubstantiation takes me. What does it feel like to be changed? Maybe Horatia was right in this: My blood felt as though some god had exhaled fire into my body. I remember pain, a flash of fear, and then feeling as though I could experience everything, from my own ecstasy to Jacoby's hidden pain, to the love and pain and joy and sorrow of all the mortals around me. With an inhalation, I understood mortality is all of this: beyond beginning, beyond ending.

Breathless, I crawl up her body and we kiss again. "I love you," I say.

She looks up at me, her eyes widening for a second, and what is there is all the beauty I love in her. A flash of wonder, and then it is gone. "You're mortal."

"You're not." I knew she wouldn't be.

"No," she said, and then she smiled. I'd seen this smile before, hundreds of times. She reached her hand up to touch my face. "Warm."

She rolls on top of me. "Warm," she says again and runs her hands up and down my torso. This time I surrender to her touch, pushing my body up to her hands, arching my back when she is inside me. And I can't hold back, and I keep saying "I love you" over and over as she breaks me.

When she leans over me with that smile, the one I know, the one I've watched, I know she doesn't love me. Or she can't. And I can't stop myself from crying. When she tears into my throat, it feels for a moment like a greater pleasure than orgasm. I think, *Just give in.* Oblivion is tempting in the face of this grief. For a moment, I let her drink. I know I love her; this is all I can give her, this is all she can give me—death.

Then I reach under the pillow for the wooden stake, and with my last strength ram it through her heart.

And then I lay there, covered with the dust of her, weeping and waiting for the sun to rise.

A Vampire in Vegas

M. J. WILLIAMZ

THE CROWDS BUSTLED around me as I made my way
through the streets of Las Vegas that warm summer evening.
The city literally pulsated with lifeblood. As overdue as I was,
I could easily have lost myself in the rhythmic flow running
through the masses, but I had a mission.

I had spent the night before at the blackjack tables with a
remarkable woman. Her name was Marisa. Marisa Donatelli.
She didn't know I knew her name, but that was OK. The less she
knew about me the better. I was lucky to have found a woman
like her so quickly in such a city. She was just what I needed. I
came to this, one of my favorite cities, in search of just the right
person. I knew the moment I saw her that she was the one.

As I made my way to the San Marcos, I recalled the previous
night. In a city as teeming with diversity as Las Vegas, it's easy
to get lost, go unnoticed. That's not always easy for beings like
me, but it was easy here.

To make myself even less noticeable I had commandeered
a taxi from a poor unsuspecting driver. Having just dropped
off a call girl and her date, I made my way to the airport in
search of another fare.

I sat there, engine running, searching the hordes to see if
anyone interested me. There were people everywhere, trying
to decide if they wanted to pay for a cab or take the shuttle. I

didn't really care what they chose. None of them appealed to me . . . until I saw *her*.

Dressed in a tight black dress that accentuated her small waist and curvy hips, she strutted through the crowds. She knew that both men and women were watching her, enjoying the view of her full breasts under the plunging neckline, where the diamond pendant hanging from her necklace rested perfectly on her cleavage. She was very comfortable with the attention, as though she was used to it but didn't expect it. I definitely liked her style.

As I opened the door for her, she slid in gracefully with barely more than a glance at me. I was enjoying the view too much to care. Her dress had shifted slightly, revealing tantalizingly shaped thighs. Oh, this could be the one, I thought. I would know shortly.

Tossing her bags in the trunk, I read the luggage tags: Marisa Donatelli. A good Italian name, and I do so love Italians.

"Where to?" I asked, careful not to look in the mirror as I climbed back behind the wheel. One distinct advantage to driving a cab in Vegas: All the fares are too self-absorbed to realize there is no reflection of me in the mirror. But why take chances?

"The San Marcos," she replied. Her voice was low and smooth. She was all class.

I chanced a glance in the mirror and saw that she, too, was too self-absorbed to notice me. Knowing she would definitely notice me later, I took advantage of the time to look into her eyes, deep into her eyes. And there I saw it: the slightest bit of uncertainty. That's all I needed. My first instincts had been right. She was not an ice princess. She was ripe for cultivation.

In between glances at the road, I continued to study her in the mirror. Her arms were tan and toned. Her fingers were long, shapely, and well manicured. And missing something. I saw a white line on her tan finger where obviously a wedding band had been for years. I licked my lips in anticipation. Oh yes. She would definitely be the one.

She turned her head to look out the side window. I allowed my gaze to travel back up, past those beautiful breasts, past the diamond necklace, right up to her neck. Long, gracefully shaped, wrinkle-free—it was the perfect neck. I could make out her pulse beating there. My own pulse raced. She would be mine, but I had to be patient. In the end, she would surrender herself to me. I turned my attention back to the road as I felt the thrill of anticipation sweep over me.

At the hotel, I opened her door for her, grabbed her luggage, and even carried her bags inside for her. She tipped me well, again showing class. I didn't need the money, but I appreciated the gesture.

"Marisa Donatelli," I repeated back to myself as I walked back out into the night. "You have no idea how different this particular Vegas experience will be for you."

There was no reason for me to get back in the cab. It had served its purpose. Instead, I milled around in front of the main entrance of the hotel, blending in with the multitudes for a few minutes before reentering the building and making my way to my room. Not that I slept there, but I kept a room there, just in case.

I took a quick shower and quickly donned a perfectly tailored black silk suit. The white shirt under it, with its wide lapels gave it a less formal look.

Once dressed, I ran scented oil over my short, black hair and knew I was looking good. I didn't need a mirror. I knew from memory that my features were striking: my high, strong cheekbones, deep blue eyes, aristocratic nose, and lips that were made for kissing. In truth, I am a handsome woman. I was never really considered pretty, not even when I was alive.

The time had come to find Ms. Donatelli. First stop: the registration desk. Putting on my cockiest swagger, I approached a young blonde desk clerk. She was cute, with dimpled cheeks and sparkling blue eyes. She was also very well endowed. I allowed my gaze to linger over her tight sweater for an extra moment before raising my eyes to meet hers. I smiled my most charming smile, reached across the counter and fingered her name tag.

"Hello, Angie," I said, my eyes moving quickly from her name tag back to her eyes.

"Hi, there," she blushed.

"I was wondering if you could help me out a bit tonight Angie."

"Really," she squealed. "How?"

"Well, I met this woman," I began. "She told me she was staying here. I'd like to send her flowers or something, but I'm worried that maybe I'm being played. So, just to be safe, I want you to check for me and make sure she's really staying here."

Angie shook her head, sending her blonde curls swirling. "I'm really sorry. I'm not allowed to give out any information about our guests."

"Ah, come on, Angie," I continued, having no doubt she would eventually give me the information. "It's not like I'm asking for her room number or anything. I just want to make sure she's really staying here."

"I wish I could help you," she said. "But rules are rules,"

"Look, Angie," I said, looking deep into her eyes. "Just pull up her name in your system. That's all you have to do. I can't see the computer screen. You don't need to say anything except yes or no. OK?"

"I really shouldn't . . . " She was starting to waver.

I took a hundred-dollar bill out of my money clip. I dragged it slowly across her chest until she took it from me.

"Yes, you really should." I told her.

"OK," she acquiesced. "But all I'll say is yes or no."

"That's all I'm asking."

"What's her name?"

"Donatelli. Marisa Donatelli."

She typed the name as I stared into her eyes, which were focused on the screen. You mortals really have no concept of all the talents we have. Centuries of living only at night have allowed us to hone our vision far beyond that of any living being.

The screen came up, as I knew it would. There, reflected in Angie's eyes, I saw Ms. Donatelli's room number: 29269.

"Yes" was all Angie said.

"Thanks. You're a doll," I replied as I set off in search of room 29269.

Ms. Donatelli's room was easy to find, as were the elevators she would have to use. I slowly walked past her room and, using the keen sense of hearing that I've developed for self-preservation, heard her moving around inside. Pleased that she hadn't left for the evening, I positioned myself by the soda machine off to the side of the bank of elevators and waited for the delectable Ms. Donatelli to surface.

It wasn't long until she appeared. I grabbed a soda and got on the crowded elevator with her. Pressed together, side by side, I caught a faint tease of a familiar scent. You know when you think you smell something, but then it's gone? And there is a memory attached to it, but you can't wrap your brain around it because it's gone too quickly? That's what happened to me. It was something from long, long ago.

I let the scent go and focused on the woman beside me. She didn't seem to notice me, but, as close as we were, I was very aware of her. I could hear the pulse beating in her neck. I trembled with anticipation. It had been too long. I had deprived myself way too long. But what better way to end a dry spell than with this delectable Italian morsel?

Once off the elevator and out into the casino, I was careful to maintain a safe distance. She was easy to keep in my sights, though, as she played her dollar slots and drank her cosmopolitans. I don't know how much later it was that she left the casino and made her way up the strip. Following her was much more of a treat than a challenge. She had an exquisite shape, and I found myself mesmerized more than once by the sway of those heavenly hips.

she entered another casino and this time made her way to the blackjack table. I hung back and waited patiently for a seat to open next to her. I enjoyed watching her play. She was confident and played well. She radiated a "Don't mess with me" aura. I knew that wouldn't apply to me. She would let me much closer than she could possibly anticipate. I bit my lip thinking about it. She was truly a worthy prize I couldn't wait to claim.

She had amassed quite a pile of chips by the time I was able to join her. We made brief eye contact as I sat down. I gave her a perfunctory smile.

"Haven't I seen you before?" she asked, her deep voice soft as velvet.

Oh crap! I thought. Obviously she had been more attentive than I realized. Or maybe I just looked familiar?

"I don't think so," I answered curtly, quickly looking away and pretending to focus on the game.

She had my nerves on high alert. Sitting that close to her already had my senses at a heightened sense of awareness. Her recognizing me sent my sensors into overdrive.

I felt her glance over at me again. I guessed she was still trying to place me, but she soon seemed to lose interest as she got back into the game.

Ms. Donatelli fared much better than I, but that was to be expected. I was far too focused on the tasty treat to my right. I could see her pulse throbbing in her wrists, and that memory came back to me again. I smelled something familiar again, something from long ago. And then I realized that it was her perfume. It was a very expensive brand, made for centuries from the same recipe. It was subtle yet intoxicating. My first girlfriend had worn it. The name of the perfume? "Donatelli's." But of course, I smiled to myself. No wonder she carried herself the way she did. She came from money. Glancing again at the white line on her ring finger, I wondered if Donatelli was her maiden or married name, not that I needed the details. She was there to serve one purpose and one purpose only. Details didn't matter.

As I sat there, I became aware of a loud, steady thumping that seemed to grow louder still. I recognized it as the pulse in her neck beating as her heart raced. I found myself mesmerized by the beat. Feeling that I was about to get carried away, I forced myself to look elsewhere. I looked at everything except that pulsating area that I so desperately longed to taste. My breathing became labored, and my own pulse raced. I couldn't fight it. I glanced over and saw the vein popping on her neck. The mortal eye would never have seen it; my eyes would never have missed it.

As I stared, transfixed at the vein, she ran her long, thin, perfectly manicured fingers through her hair. As her wrist blocked my view, I noticed the time on her watch. It was four-thirty in the morning. Shocked at the time, I immediately gathered my chips and left. I had get to The Crypt before five.

The Crypt is a hotel and casino off the strip. Built to resemble a mausoleum, all its sleeping quarters are underground, and they're all coffins. They lock the door to the downstairs at five o'clock every morning. Amusing as it is to see such a vampire wannabe subculture, it's nice to have a place like The Crypt where I can feel safe from curious mortals.

The next evening, I rose automatically at sundown, fully rested. Moving quickly, I cut through the crowds and arrived at the San Marcos. Heading straight to my room, I took another quick shower and dressed for the evening: a pair of gray slacks and a lightweight plum-colored blazer, with a white crew-neck tee underneath. Again, no mirror was needed to tell me how good I looked. I know I'm irresistible. I just needed to make sure Marisa realized that.

I took up my post at the soda machine again and waited. I just stood there putting coins in the machine. Nobody cared enough to notice that I kept hitting the coin return.

Suddenly there was that scent again. My pulse immediately quickened. I looked up to see Ms. Donatelli walking down the hall. She, too, was oblivious to me standing by the soda machine. I took advantage of this and allowed my eyes once again to admire those shapely legs, all the way up to where they were hidden under her skirt. Again I marveled at the shape of her derrière as it swayed away from me. My gaze moved up higher until it made its way to her shapely neck. She was wearing her hair in a chignon, so more neck was revealed. I found myself salivating, just looking at her.

The elevator arrived, and we boarded together. She looked

at me. "Blackjack last night."

I smiled at her and said, "You're right. Blackjack last night."

"I thought I had recognized you," she said.

"Oh yeah. Maybe you had seen me around the hotel."

I decided that the time had come. I stared into her eyes and felt her eyes boring back into mine. I knew I was right. Let the games begin.

"So, what are the plans for tonight? Are you going to hit the tables again?"

"I don't really know," she responded. "I think I might just wander around for a while."

The doors opened in the lobby. I waited for her to exit to the right, and I intentionally started to the left.

"Well, good luck," I told her, trying to sound more nonchalant than I felt.

Mixing once again with the throngs, I kept her in my sights at all times. Once I believed there was enough distance between us, I began to follow her.

I watched, amused and intrigued as she played slots in one casino, then made her way to another and settled in at the video poker machines. I walked up behind her just as I saw the cocktail waitress making her way through the crowds.

"Fancy meeting you here," I said. She looked up and smiled at me. A warm, welcoming smile. Our eyes met, and I felt encouraged.

As the waitress approached, I joked, "Can I buy you a drink?"

Her smile broadened. I ordered us each a drink and sat down at the next machine.

"Any luck with the slots tonight?" I asked.

"I'm doing all right," she replied, "although I feel as though my luck is changing."

Stunned into silence, I began putting coins into my machine.

The waitress brought our drinks. We sat in comfortable silence, sipping our drinks and playing our games.

She spoke first. "By the way," she said, looking over at me, "I'm Marissa."

I met her gaze. "Ronnie." She put her hand out, and I took it in mine, bending low over it to tenderly kiss her knuckle.

Her skin was warm in my hand. I felt the pulse speed up in her fingertips. I knew she was attracted to me. She was as good as mine already.

"It's very nice to meet you," I said, relinquishing her hand and sitting back down.

"How long have you been in Vegas?" I asked, even though I already knew the answer. I wanted to hear her soft, low voice again.

"I just got here last night. And you?"

"A couple of nights ago."

We played quietly for a few more minutes.

This time, I broke the silence. "Well, I think I'm about ready to hit the tables. Would you care to join me?"

"Actually," she replied. "I'm getting pretty hungry."

I bit back a smile as I said, "I could really go for a bite, too." I added, "May I take you to dinner?"

I swear she blushed. She looked away for just a moment, just long enough for me to kick myself for being too forward, but when she turned back to me, she was filled with that confidence that attracted me so. She looked me right in the eye and said, "Yes. I'd love that. I'd love to have dinner with you."

"Wonderful," I said. "I know a great little steakhouse that's off the beaten path. The clientele is quite a mixed bag, but the food is to die for."

"Sounds intriguing," she said and I could tell she meant it.

I stood and offered my arm. "Shall we?"

I took her to The Crypt. The restaurant was done in a

medieval style, but it was very comfortable. I hadn't lied about the clientele either. There were wannabe vampires mixed in with well-dressed men and women and even the occasional gay or lesbian couple. Everyone was dressed nicely, and the atmosphere was hushed and elegant.

As we sat in the lounge waiting to be seated, I felt her stealing admiring glances when she thought I wouldn't notice. As I gave our name to the maître d', I felt her gaze move over me, head to toe and back to head again. She *almost made me blush.* I really thought I was past that after all these years.

After the waiter had taken our orders—she ordered halibut; I ordered steak, rare—I leaned back in the booth and decided to cut to the chase. After all, this was Vegas. I didn't know if she'd be here tomorrow. She didn't know if I'd be here tomorrow. So why waste time? I looked her right in the eye and asked, "So, do you wanna talk about it?"

She glanced back at me, a brief flicker of confusion in her eyes. She quickly masked it. She tried to look almost offended, I believe. "Talk about what?"

I glanced down at her empty ring finger, back to her, and said, "You must have worn it a long time. It's not there now. I just sense that there's something under that cool exterior . . . maybe some inner turmoil. I just wondered if you'd like to talk about it."

She opened her mouth to speak, seemed to think better of it, and looked away. She looked back then and said, "You got all that out of me from blackjack last night and video poker tonight?"

I smiled somewhat self-consciously and tried to act sheepish and shy. "I love to know what makes people tick. Obviously I'm interested in you, and I just wondered what was going on inside. That's all. There just seemed to be something, but I couldn't quite put my finger on it."

She smiled, reached over with her right hand and rubbed her empty left ring finger. Without even looking up she said, "I didn't love him anymore."

"Well, you know," I replied, "that happens."

"This was a little different."

"Why's that?"

"You sure ask a lot of questions for having just met me."

I quickly backpedaled. "I'm sorry. I didn't mean anything. I didn't mean to offend you. I just wanted to let you know that, if you wanted to talk, I'm a good listener." She smiled warmly at me then and said quietly, "I'm sorry. I didn't mean to bite your head off."

"That's OK," I told her. "I'm sure I came across extremely nosy, and I'm really not like that."

I reached over and took her hands in mine. She looked up, and as our eyes met I said, "I'm serious. I'm sorry. Will you forgive me?"

She nodded, then pulled her hands away and took a sip of wine. It had only lasted a moment, but the feel of her fingertips in my hand sent chills down my spine. I could feel the pulse in each fingertip. I again felt it racing at my touch. I knew I had made the right decision.

Dinner was pleasant. I was glad I ordered my steak so rare. The blood dripping from the steak helped. It wasn't Marisa, but it helped. I knew it would keep me from doing anything too rash.

When the waiter came to clear her plate, she still had half her dinner left. I asked if she wasn't happy with it. She said it was delicious, but that she had had enough.

"So, are you one of those women who thinks they have to act like they eat like a bird?" I asked.

At that Marisa laughed, a deep, healthy, genuine, rich laugh. It was the first laugh I had heard from her, and it was music to my ears.

"No," She denied it. "It was just really rich, and I have had enough. Honest."

I smiled and said, "So I suppose dessert is out of the question?"

She laughed again. "Most definitely."

"Well, then," I pushed, "let's go have a drink."

"I thought you were ready for the tables."

"Let's have a drink first."

We went into the nightclub there at The Crypt, which was decorated in a Gothic style. I looked across the table, into those deep brown eyes and knew that night was the night. I couldn't possibly wait any longer. It had to happen that night.

Marisa seemed very comfortable at The Crypt's nightclub, The Vault. The vampire crowd tended to be androgynous or blatantly homosexual, but she was fine. I was very happy to see that. I felt the surroundings could work to my distinct advantage.

We sat there watching the people dance, and I asked her how she was doing with it all.

"I'm fine," she said, as if it were a ridiculous question. "I'm actually really enjoying seeing this other side of Vegas."

The band finally slowed the tempo, and I asked Marisa if she'd like to dance. She surprised me by accepting.

As we danced, she allowed me to pull her close. She rested her head on my shoulder. I could feel the blood coursing through her. I tried to focus on everything around me, anything to keep my mind off the blood flowing through her. I managed to maintain my equilibrium through the song. We made our way back to the table. This time she reached across and held my hands. Her pulse was really racing. Part of me wanted to pull away, and part of me wanted to take her right there.

I asked her if she wanted to dance again. She said she'd

rather wait for another slow song. True to her word, the next slow song found us making our way to the floor, and it wasn't long before I felt her hand tracing my cheekbone as she gently pulled my lips to hers. It was my turn to have my pulse race. Not only did her lips on mine send shock waves through my body, but I could also feel the blood flowing in her lips, just under the surface. Knowing that I shouldn't, I began to trail kisses down her cheek to her neck. My mouth moved to where her pulse was beating in her neck. I felt my fangs begin to extend. She was so close, I could have had a taste right there. I kissed my way back up. I felt my fangs recede again. That had been a close one.

When the song ended, she looked at me and said, "I can't believe I'm saying this, but let's get out of here."

The cab ride back to the San Marcos was sheer torment. She was snuggled up against me. That she wanted me so desperately was such a turn-on, but having her that close and not tasting her was driving me mad.

Once in her room, she fell into my arms and kissed me with a passion that truly surprised me. She opened her mouth to let my tongue in as she took my hands and placed them on her breasts. I groaned in pleasure and began fumbling to undress her.

As she stood naked in front of me, I quickly undressed myself and gently laid her on the bed, lowering myself on top of her. I loved the feel of her warm skin against my bare skin. She immediately spread her legs, and I lay between them, rubbing my curls against her wetness.

I began kissing my way down from her mouth, down her neck, her chest. Each kiss, every nibble caused my fangs to protrude further from their protective sheaths. I dragged the pointed tip of one fang over her taut nipple before taking it in my mouth and sucking on it. She arched her back and pushed herself against me, writhing underneath me.

She took my head between her hands and guided my head lower. I kissed under her left breast and felt her heart thudding there. So much blood in one area. With a mind of its own, my mouth opened wide, but Marisa gently pushed me away, lower still.

As I kissed her flat, firm belly, I caught the scent of her arousal. No longer needing her to guide me, I slid down and took her clit in my mouth. Sucking on that swollen spot gave me such a surge of power. She was mine already, in one sense. She was moving against me, pressing me harder to her. But there was also the rapid throbbing of her clit as all her blood raced to that one area. What I wouldn't have given to slice it open with a fang and drink. But since I had waited that long, I could wait a little longer.

I slid my fingers inside her, going crazy with the pleasure it was giving her. She met me stroke for stroke as she moved on me and against me. Her breathing got labored. I knew she was close. I sucked harder, drove deeper, pushing her closer and closer until at last she arched up, cried out, and fell back to the bed, obviously satiated.

I, too, needed release. I felt like I'd been pounding against a wall but couldn't break through. My wait was almost over. She was still in a post-orgasmic stupor. I knew that the blood was starting to flow away from that delicious area. I turned my head just to the right and drove my fully extended fangs into the femoral artery carrying blood down her thigh. *Whoosh!* Her blood gushed into my mouth and sent me crashing through that wall. Over and over I climaxed, the taste of fresh blood taking me over the edge again and again.

I realized that she was starting to wonder what I was doing. She was coming back to reality. One more suck off that luscious leg before I slowly kissed my way back up her body, as I pressed my wetness against her fresh wounds. My juices would cause the holes to shrink and be hardly noticeable in the morning.

As her eyes focused on me looking down on her, she asked, "What was that all about?"

I smiled. "Oh, I just gave you an incredible hickey. I hope you don't mind."

She smiled back at me and then rolled over so I could spoon against her. I had enjoyed this one in every way, I thought as I lay there waiting for her to fall asleep.

Once her breathing steadied, I eased myself out from around her and took my exit. I went to my room and gathered my things. Vegas had, as usual, been wonderful, but it was time to go. It had served its purpose well. As I waved down a taxi for a ride to the airport, I wondered where I would end up next. It really didn't matter. I wouldn't feed again for a while. Marisa Donatelli would stay with me for a very long time.

Magdalin

CRYSTAL BARELA

The bridge crossing the Spokane River was nearly empty at this hour. I pulled my scarf tighter around my neck and scanned the sidewalk in the park before returning my attention to the rapids below. The cool spray was jarring. This frigid wetness was reality, not the dream that had brought me here.

I know who killed your sister.

A dream of Magdalin; a figment of my prepubescent imagination. The imaginary friend and lover of a teenage girl. I thought my psych classes were taking me past this.

I shivered, checking my watch. Apparently, not. My dream was late.

"Just on time, by my calculations," chuckled a familiar voice in the dark.

Startled, I cried out, my hand flying to my chest. I didn't dare turn around. The voice was the same. French accent carried deep in her chest, as if she had smoked two packs a day for three hundred years.

She laughed again. "Very nearly, *ma cherie.*"

My heart was racing, and my legs weakened. I placed a hand on the iron railing for support and turned to face the voice.

"I apologize." She was tall and slim, pale as milk under the soft moonlight. Her black hair was parted in the center and fell to her shoulders. "I didn't mean to startle you."

Magdalin.

"*You* know of my sister's murder?" She was no more that twenty-five, only a child at the time of my sister's death. She was also a living dream. I laughed. Those psych classes I'm taking hadn't taught me shit.

Magdalin took hold of my arm. I tried to shake her hand loose, but her grip was firm.

"I know of many things, sweet Jodi." I paled at the use of the endearment. Only my Magdalin called me "sweet."

She stepped closer, nearly flush to my body. "You are in danger, *ma cherie*."

She pulled me against her, squeezing me hard.

"Do you recall Waldorf?" She breathed into my hair.

Waldorf: tall, fair, and angelic. He had been Carmen's boyfriend.

"He died the same night as Carmen."

Magdalin nodded, releasing me. I pulled my jacket closely around my shoulders as she placed her pale hands on the wrought iron railing. She was clothed in black; certainly not dressed for an early spring in Washington. I stood beside her, set my gloved hands next to hers, and watched the swiftly moving water beneath the bridge.

"Please, you are cold." She said, gesturing toward a twenty-four-hour coffee house on the corner. "We will take coffee as we talk?"

Without waiting for my response, she led me down the block, her hand on my elbow. The doors of the Rocket Bakery were soon in front of us. We found seats at a table in the corner, and she ordered coffee for us.

"I knew your sister and Waldorf well."

"How could . . . " Her fingers silenced my lips before I could blink.

"Please listen."

The waitress brought our coffee, and I held my tongue. I wanted answers. I'd wanted them for so long.

"I understand your frustration. Twelve years have passed."

I was eleven when my sister was murdered. Decapitated. They'd never found her head. Or Waldorf's."

"No, Waldorf lives."

I shook my head. That was the second time she seemed to respond to an unspoken thought. I wasn't sure what to make of any of this. Her moss-green eyes were sincere.

"I share with you secrets that no mortal knows."

Mortal?

"You will find them difficult to believe." She took my hand in hers, pressing it between her own.

I will tell you what happened.

Magdalin's eyes wouldn't let mine go. Her lips weren't moving, but I could hear her voice clearly in my mind.

Jodi, your sister . . . Her voice stilled, and her eyes darted away as if trying to look behind her.

The air in the coffee shop grew cold, and I looked around nervously, the hairs rising on the back of my neck.

A man sat at the table behind Magdalin. He was slight and dressed all in black. Sunglasses were perched on his long nose, and his hair was buzzed to a shadow along his scalp. The shop had been empty when we entered, and I hadn't seen anyone pass through the door since we'd been here.

Our eyes met over his dark frames. He pursed his lips in a mockery of a kiss and waggled his fingers at me, then smiled, showing a flash of fang.

I shook my head. I was losing it.

"Is there a man with a buzz cut and sickening smile behind me?"

I nodded.

"I want you to get up from the table and walk to your car."

"What's happening?" My heart began to race.

"Listen!" She leaned over our table and put her hand behind my neck, bringing my face close to hers. "Get to your house and lock all the doors and windows."

I shivered. The temperature had dropped to the point that I could see our breath mingling.

A vampire cannot enter your home unless you invite him in.

I shook my head, clutching my purse to my stomach.

There was a shifting of chairs as I stood. My eyes darted around nervously. A couple all in black, shades on, sat kitty-cornered to us. The man stood, resting his palms on his table, his eyes on me.

I took my keys from my purse and turned toward the entrance. Near the door there was another man dressed in black. He was large, his muscles flexed beneath the black T-shirt, pale, his lips red, his eyes hidden behind sunglasses.

"Magdalin," I whispered, my hand coming to rest on her shoulder for support.

Run! I will protect you!

I walked as calmly as I could toward the door. None of the patrons seemed to be aware of what was happening, and neither did I. Something wasn't right. What if more of these people in black were outside?

As I stepped out into the night air, the glass door swung shut behind me. The tinkle of bells on the handle followed me out.

MY CAR WAS parked two blocks away. Scanning the street for anyone suspicious, I ran as fast as I could. With my arm extended, I pressed the unlock button on my key chain over and over. I was sure that at any moment I would feel the weight of the muscled man in black upon my back. I cried out in triumph and relief, as the familiar tones of my vehicle unlocking beeped ahead of me, headlights flashing.

I yanked open the door, locking it as soon as I was inside. I was safe. I leaned back against the leather seat, closing my eyes, slowly regaining my composure as I caught my breath. This was crazy! I laughed. I let that woman get to me. There are no such things as vampires. I stuck my key in the ignition and turned the steering wheel.

The heat was sucked from the air.

Filled with panic, I hit the gas. Something heavy fell on the roof. I cried out, looking up at the ceiling and back at the road. The metal buckled under the weight of whatever was up there.

I put the pedal to the floor, swerving on the road. A driver in oncoming traffic honked his horn. Whatever hit my roof was still there, and it was moving, its denting sounds echoed in the car's interior. I picked up speed as I rounded the corner onto my street, going sixty on the quiet streets of the residential neighborhood.

I slammed on the brakes in front of my home. The tires squealed, and the seatbelt cut into my shoulder. Something flew from the roof, landing in the street half a block away. A large black shape lay in the road, unmoving.

I unbuckled my belt and left the car cautiously, keys at the ready.

I couldn't take my eyes off the form on the road. It looked like the man from the coffee shop. What if I had killed him? I hurried up the sidewalk and backed up the stairs onto my porch.

He moved.

I started and fell against the screen door.

He got to his knees, shaking his head, long, dark hair

brushing the street.

Oh shit! I opened the screen door and jabbed my key at the lock, my hands trembling.

I looked over my shoulder as the key slipped home.

He was at the foot of the stairs! Blood was oozing from his temple and his T-shirt was torn.

A flash of black flew into his chest.

I turned the key and stepped into the house, locking the door behind me.

I ran to the picture window. It was Magdalin, and she was not nearly as big as my attacker. Somehow she had managed to throw him onto the street. I had never seen anyone move so quickly. Her feet never seemed to touch the ground as she leaped and flew around the man. She moved like Jackie Chan, running up and down his chest, throwing trash cans. She swung the neighbor's House for Sale sign like a bat, hitting the man in the head. He flew through the air, landing across the street in the neighbor's rhododendrons.

What should I do? Call the police? Or maybe a priest?

Keep calm. I ran to the back of the house, double checking that the back door was locked and then made my way through the kitchen and dining room, securing windows. I took the stairs two at a time and hit the second floor, checking windows and making sure the latch on the attic was tight.

I backed against the wall in the hall and stared down the stairs at the front door. The door was shaking on its hinges.

I wasn't going down there. Not for anyone.

Jodi!

Magdalin's voice was squeezing my brain. I closed my eyes tight and brought my hands to my head.

Open the door!

Her voice was a whisper, but it echoed in my skull. I could feel it under my skin.

Don't be afraid!

I crawled down the stairs to the rattling door, unable to stand and look through the peephole. My head beat like a drum.

Turn the knob!

I turned the knob.

"Invite me in!" Magadalin cried. Her back was to the door. Dark hair hung down her back in a sheet. Not a hair out of place. I shivered. Her shirt had been torn, and I could see her bra and muscled stomach, red blood flashing in the moonlight. "Now!"

My head was ringing with her voice and I found myself unable to say no.

"Please, come in."

Magdalin backed into the foyer, slamming the door shut and turned the deadbolt. I collapsed on the bench in front of the upright piano, my breathing scattered but my head blessedly silent.

"Are you okay?"

I nodded, still catching my breath. I stumbled along the hall toward the bathroom, wondering if I was going to throw up. I dropped to the floor in front of the toilet and wrapped my arms around the porcelain. The smooth surface was cool relief against my aching head. Who were these people in black and why did they want to hurt me?

"You secured the windows?" Magdalin stood in the doorway, arms on the jams bringing the gash on her side into view. I nodded and pulled upon the cupboard door under the sink, looking for bandages and first aid cream.

"The nausea will pass in a moment, *ma cherie*. Sorry, I was so insistent."

"Sit," I gestured to the toilet, and she maneuvered around

me in the small space and sat on the seat.

"Will they be back?" I whispered, on my knees in front of her.

"I'm afraid so." She leaned forward and kissed me on the forehead.

I sighed and reached for the first aid cream.

"I told you I'm fine."

"You're bleeding," I corrected. She laughed.

"Sweet Jodi." Magdalin's hand went to my hair, pushing a soft blonde wisp behind my ear. "You are too." She brought a finger to my lips, pulling it away with droplets of blood on its tip. Her eyes met mine.

Magdalin sucked her finger into her mouth, swallowed its entire length. I watched, transfixed as her tongue caressed the red liquid from her finger. I had this absurd urge to join her tongue with my own.

I leaned forward between her legs, my hands undoing the top button of her shirt, then the next. She was real and sitting in my bathroom. My heart was racing. I undid another, then the next, my fingers shaking by the time I reached the last button. I slid the shirt from her shoulders, my pulse racing, my blood moving more swiftly through my veins.

I looked down at the wound, a gash from below her armpit to her waist. It didn't look deep. In fact, the blood I had noticed earlier had all but vanished.

"You should remove my bra, Jodi."

I brought my arms around her torso, my hands taking hold of the elastic behind her. The hooks wouldn't come free and I struggled. I laughed under my breath as they came loose. She really didn't need a bra. Her breasts were small, her nipples nearly black in contrast with her milky skin. The nubbins were tight and puckered.

I coughed nervously and reached for a washcloth. "Who

did this?" I said, dabbing against the wound. The blood had stopped.

"Our friend at the coffee shop," she replied, moving against my hand as if she liked the sting.

"He's not my friend!" My voice caught, and I began to shake. This was all too much. My childhood dream friend was in my bathroom. No one had ever wanted to harm me in my life. And now a gang of Goth-obsessed punks had taken a dislike to me? It was absurd! I wiped my tears away impatiently.

"*Ma cherie.*" She pulled me against her, my face in her breasts. She made soothing noises into my hair, and I found myself rubbing my wet cheeks on her creamy smooth skin, nuzzling her. She smelled of something familiar. Earth?

"You are tired, Jodi." She stood, pulling me to my feet beside her. "Come, I will put you to bed." Magdalin leaned over me, tucking the sheets around my waist before lying down next to me. She settled me into the crook of her arm.

"We will sleep, yes?" I nodded, tired beyond sleep, staring up at the ceiling. "Not talk of any of this until tomorrow?"

She was real. Her arm was under my neck, and her long pale fingers on my breast, playing with my nipple. The skin was becoming flushed as all of the blood in my body seemed to rush to that point. I didn't move. Fear turned to desire in my veins. My hand covered hers, and she looked down at me.

"Are you not tired, sweet Jodi?"

I nodded. Her lips neared mine. Soft as butterfly wings they skimmed, tasting slowly, nipping gently, before seeking entrance into my mouth. We explored, tongues tracing, teeth clashing. The coppery flavor of blood mingled with our saliva.

Magdalin moaned low in her throat.

Her hand skimmed beneath the sheet. Her fingers slid over my stomach and easily through my clean-shaven pussy.

"So wet, for me, sweet Jodi?" She rubbed my mound. One finger slipped into me, then the next. I had never felt so hot.

Everywhere she touched, the blood seemed to follow, as if she were a magnet and I were made of metal beads that followed her hand's movements.

Magdalin began a steady rhythm, her mouth latching onto my breast like a suckling child. I was begging her, my hands tangled in her thick dark hair as she fucked me, her fingers a blur, her thumb circling and circling.

My heart roared in my ears, and there was a sudden sharp pain in my chest. I looked down. Blood was streaming in rivulets from around her lips where she sucked, black against my skin. My blood was pumping into her!

I began to struggle. Her eyes caught mine.

Shhhhhhh.

She continued to work her hand in my hungry cunt, sucking and pushing until my body convulsed around her fingers and my cries echoed off the ceiling.

I woke suddenly and sat up in bed. I was alone. My heart faltered as I took in the bloody mess that was my sheets. Oh Christ! I would never get the stains out. The sheets were caked with dark brown stains. It looked like someone had been murdered. Blood was dried on my breasts and down my stomach, caught in my belly button. I brought my hands up to my left aureole and examined the holes there. There were two deep puncture marks.

I laughed. This could not be happening! I looked around the room, and aside from the bloody puddle I was sleeping in, there was no sign of Magdalin. She was here to help me! I ripped the sheets from the bed and threw them in the laundry basket. I wasn't a fucking buffet!

I stepped into the shower and turned on the spray. The

water ran down the drain, pink with my blood. After the blood was washed off I could see the bruising surrounding the holes. I stepped from the shower frowning. My breast was killing me. What did one do when bit by a vampire? I took the antiseptic cream and rubbed the cool ointment on the angry red holes. Maybe garlic would work better?

I thought I'd turn into a vampire, but I had woken in sunlight and I was still here, not a pile of ashes. Maybe they had to bite your neck and not your breast for that to happen?

Was Magdalin lying in a coffin somewhere? The thought gave me the chills. I pulled on my robe and took the sheets with me downstairs. I stopped in the kitchen and put on a pot of coffee. Maybe that would give me the ability to think. A little caffeine would feed the brain.

I pulled open the basement door and took careful steps down the old wooden stairs. I flipped the switch that lit up the corner by the washer and dryer.

I had too many questions. I set the basket on the dryer, then turned on the knob for the washer, added detergent and shoved the sheets in the well.

What kind of mess was I in? All I had wanted was answers, and what did I get? Attacked and molested!

"Molested, sweet Jodi?"

"*Shit!*" My heart nearly flew from my chest. I turned to face Magdalin. She was lying on the old ratty sofa that had been a part of my college furniture before I had inherited this house from my grandmother two years ago.

Magdalin's hands were behind her head, a smile on her lips. I was relieved to see there were no coffins about. It was then that I realized there were no windows in the basement.

"I thought you had gone," I said, crossing my arms over my chest.

"And leave you with so many unanswered questions?" She

sat up, her hand rubbing the back of her neck. She looked tired.

"Of mind, Jodi. Of mind." She patted the sofa next to her. I hesitated.

I had watched that movie. What was it? I couldn't remember, but I did remember that the guy had to be bitten three times before he became a vampire. Maybe that was how it worked. But then again, in the Brad Pitt movie it didn't work that way. Fuck!

"Why don't you ask?" she said, raising a brow, and I laughed to myself. I forgot! How silly! She can read my mind.

"Am I a vampire?"

"Are you hungry, Jodi?"

I shook my head.

"Not for food, *ma cherie*, but for blood?" Her eyes darkened. "You would know if you were a vampire. You would ache with a thousand hungers, your brain expanding in your head, pressing against your skull, urging you to feed." Her tongue licked her lips.

"If you were a vampire you would still be asleep, hibernating until it was dark. You would wake with only one thought on your mind: feeding." She patted the sofa again, and I reluctantly went over. I saw what she had done to that guy last night. Why did I think I had a chance to do anything other than what she said?

We faced each other on the couch, and she took my fingers in hers, her eyes searching. "With me, there is always choice, *ma cherie*." Her voice was soft, seductive. "I will never touch you against your will."

I found myself hypnotized by her gentle timbre. I was leaning toward her, breathing in earth and trees. I shook my head desperately and let go of her hands.

The string snapped. Yeah right, I thought, cursing. A choice.

She chuckled, leaning back against the arm of the sofa.

"I'm getting my coffee, and then we'll discuss this!"

"As you wish."

I stomped up the stairs, squinting as I went into the bright sunlight of the kitchen.

"CARMEN HAD MET Waldorf at a bar downtown called The Crypt."

I snorted into my coffee.

"Amusing, yes? Well, it is known for its darker pleasures. There are many who frequent this establishment who play at being bloodsuckers."

I leaned back against the opposite arm of the sofa, and she pulled my feet into her lap.

"This century it has become a fad to be one of the undead," she confided.

"My sister wouldn't . . . "

"You are such a child, Jodi!"

Child! I tried to pull my feet from her lap.

"Listen! You were no more than eight when Carmen met Waldorf. What does an eight-year-old girl know of such things? You think your sister would share her love of blood with her little sister!"

I felt tears welling, but I willed them back, trying to calm myself. Her hands were soothing. She rubbed my feet in slow circles, pressing her thumbs into my arches.

"She met Waldorf, and it was love at first sight." Magdalin smiled, her eyes turning up at the corners. "There is such a thing, yes?" Her fingers circled my ankles as she spoke, massaging their way up my calves. "He admitted he was a real creature of the night. That he needed blood to live, and she volunteered to be a donor."

"Donor?"

"One who allows herself to produce blood for her Chosen rather than become a vampire herself," she whispered. She was facing me now. My robe had fallen open, exposing my thighs, and her hands slid over the muscles. Heat climbed higher, my thighs spreading.

"Why would Carmen do that?" I mumbled. My thighs were hot, my blood coursing beneath Magdalin's fingers.

"For love, *ma cherie*," she assured me. Her lips followed where her hands had been. I couldn't focus on the questions swimming in my head. It was all about the blood in my veins.

She nipped her way inside my thighs, tiny love bites leaving a trail of blood for her tongue to lap up. I moaned beneath her, loving the heat of her over me. She kissed and soothed her way to my wet and swollen sex. My clit, throbbing with the weight of my blood, rose toward Magdalin like an erect little cock, heavy with need.

She blew against me, and I cried out, begging her to touch me.

"Are you sure, sweet Jodi?"

Magdalin blew again, and my hands took hold of her hair, pressing her toward my pussy.

"As you wish."

Her tongue licked up my wet heat, lapping at my slit like she was starved for me.

I've waited twelve years.

I moaned, and she wrapped her lips around my clit, her tongue circling the excited bit of flesh.

So rich. So delicious.

A cold finger climbed into my hole, then another, pumping in time with her sucking.

Come, ma cherie! Come!

I grabbed my breasts gasping at the pain, legs tensing as my body lengthened.

I screamed as her teeth sunk into the skin around my clit, my blood rushing from my body and into her mouth. I could feel the heavy wetness flowing from me, my entire being emptying down her throat. Her eyes were wild; like an animal, she gorged herself on my fast-pumping life force. I arched against her and pushed her face into my pussy, unable to stop the need. The blood was seeping past her lips and down my thighs. The hot liquid squirted onto my belly and breasts as it rushed from me.

Magdalin's face and hands were painted red. Her green eyes glowed.

My limbs felt heavy. I was dying. This was the end. I wanted to tell her to stop, but I couldn't summon the strength.

"AS I WAS saying." I blinked, the bright light of the upstairs bathroom.

"What?"

"Your sister and Waldorf were madly in love, and Craven Beauchamp was jealous."

"Craven?"

"Beauchamp. Not just of their relationship, but of Waldorf's power. As leader of our coven he had great strength."

I couldn't focus; my limbs were weighted, and I watched them float on the water, seemingly separate from my body. I was in my claw-foot tub.

"What happened?"

"Well, Craven decided to have your sister for his own."

"Downstairs."

"She nearly died."

"Magdalin!"

"*You* nearly died, Jodi." She knelt next to the claw-foot tub and pulled my wet body against hers, her lips against my forehead. "I am so sorry. I did not mean to lose control like that."

I looked down at my body and saw the ragged puncture marks above my sex. I swallowed hard.

"You make me feel like a fledgling vampire." Magdalin sighed. She dropped down onto the bath mat and rested her chin on the lip of the tub. "So hungry and alive." Her hand lifted toward my face, and I flinched. I couldn't help it.

"We must learn of each other so this does not happen." She met my eyes. "You overwhelm me . . . your beauty, your spirit, your taste . . . It will not happen again."

"Damn straight!" I tried to stand, but I was still weak. The hot water sloshed around me, wetting the floor.

"Jodi, please!" She stilled my movements. "We have no time for this! Beauchamp and his coven will return this night!"

"So! I am not going to invite them in . . . What do I have to fear?"

"You will stay in your house always? Afraid to enter the night? I am only one woman. I may be strong, but they are many." *Please listen,* ma cherie!

"The man at the coffee shop was Craven Beauchamp, and he wants you dead."

"Why?"

"Because you are Carmen's sister, and as such Waldorf cares for you."

"I haven't seen Waldorf in twelve years!"

"But he's seen you, *ma cherie.* He's had someone—me— watching over you all this time." It was true.

"But, why . . . "

"Waldorf was hoping you would grow to be much like your sister."

"That's sick!"

"Yes, it is, but his obsession is as great as Craven's." She stood and offered me her hand. "You may have the look of Carmen—the hair, the figure, the smile—but you are not like her. You could not hear Waldorf's call."

I stepped from the tub, and Magdalin wrapped a towel around me. "What do you mean?"

"There is no connection with him. He would enter your mind and speak with you but you could not hear him." She led me into the bedroom. The bed was made with fresh linens.

"Please sleep. We have a few hours, and I will prepare."

I lay down between the cool sheets, trying to absorb the situation. This was all too much. Feuding vampires fighting over me like I was property.

"Magdalin!" She turned from the doorway, hand on the knob. "I can hear you!"

I know. You always have.

I found Magdalin at the dining table. There were a dozen guns laid out on the wooden surface. I picked one up. It was cold and heavier than I would have thought. "I didn't think you could kill a vampire with bullets?"

She opened the gun, spun the barrel, and took hold of my hand before emptying the bullets into my palm. They were golden in color and light.

"Oak," she said. "If you hit the heart, you'll kill the vampire instantly."

"I doubt I could hit a wall directly in front of me!"

"You hit a vampire anywhere, and it will be like hitting a mortal with a normal bullet." I tucked a gun into the waistband of my jeans.

I picked up a bottle filled with clear liquid and raised a brow.

"Holy water."

"But how can you . . . "

"Touch this? You have seen 'CSI'? Yes?"

It was then that I noticed the latex gloves on her hands. I laughed.

"As long as it does not get on my skin I am fine." There were a good four dozen of the bottles on the table. "Holy bombs. You must throw them hard to break the bottle."

I picked up a large pendant in the shape of a cross. I traced the gold design, heavy with stones.

"Put it on."

I slipped the pendant over my head. It was heavy and felt foreign between my breasts. *Turn it over.*

Mon amour, ma force. My love, my strength.

Our eyes met, and my heart fluttered.

The doorbell sounded. The man I thought was dead was standing on my doorstep, not looking a second older than the last time I had seen him. Waldorf was a tall man, his hair as mine: a white blonde that many thought came from a bottle. I didn't know about him, but mine was actually a product of my mother's genes. He was slender and willowy and could easily have been mistaken for my brother.

"Jodi, may we come in?" There were a dozen others with him looking like they had just left a 'Matrix' convention. All of this leather and vinyl was a bit much. Couldn't they dress like normal people? Wouldn't that make them less conspicuous?

"Of course," Magdalin said, pushing the screen door open. Waldorf stood still, waiting for the invite. If I allowed him in my home I was agreeing to have this war with the man who killed Carmen. I was agreeing that I would put these vampires, Magdalin, and myself in danger. I didn't want this.

It's the only way, ma cherie.

I met Magdalin's eyes and she took my hand in hers. I squeezed her fingers tightly.

"Come in, Waldorf," I said, and he crossed the doorway, immediately pulling me into his arms. His embrace was bruising and I pulled away nervously, stepping closer to Magdalin.

"You look so like your sister." There was wonder in his voice. "Does she not, Magdalin?" Their eyes met, and she nodded.

He gestured for the others to join him.

"This is Larz and Josephine. They will help from the inside. They are my most skilled warriors. Present company excluded, of course." He gave Magdalin a bow. "The others will set up a perimeter around your house."

Perimeter? I felt completely out of my element. I excused myself and went upstairs. I needed a few minutes away from the chaos my life had become. In the bathroom I leaned against the sink. Look at me? My skin was translucent, and the bags under my eyes could hold my entire wardrobe.

I reached into a drawer, took out an elastic band, and pulled my hair into a ponytail. If things got crazy it would be better if I could see my attackers. Sneakers, and I would be ready to kick some vampire ass. I turned from my reflection and gasped.

Josephine was standing in the doorway, arms crossed over her breasts. Vampires didn't have reflections. That was creepy.

"Did I startle you?"

"Yes." I brushed past her and went into the bedroom. I dug in the closet for my sneakers. Finding them, I sat on the bed. "Can I help you with something?" She was taller than I, a sword hanging from a black leather belt around her waist. She looked like a pirate.

"Can you tell me why they are obsessed with you?"

"Craven? Haven't the foggiest."

"No."

"Waldorf?" I tied a lace. "Probably has to do with my sister. Some weird Freudian thing."

"I am speaking of Magdalin," she said, walking into the room. The air grew cold, and my eyes shot to the window.

"Do you feel that?" I ran to the window, peering out into the darkness. Josephine came up behind me. The glass began to crystallize in front of us, working from the frame and spreading over the pane until we could see nothing.

"Feel what?" She breathed against my neck, and I turned. Her fangs had grown becoming visible, and my heart began to race nervously.

"The air is so cold," I said, trying to push past her. But she wouldn't move, and I knew I was in trouble. I took hold of the cross around my neck and pressed it against her chest. Nothing happened. Fuck!

Josephine laughed, her chuckles crawling over my skin.

I began to chant Magdalin's name in my mind, willing her to hear me, willing her to be here. The bedroom door flew shut with a loud crash. Josephine picked up the cross in her gloved hand and pressed the tip against her cheek for a moment. The stench of sizzling flesh filled the room, raising bile in my throat.

"You must touch my skin, dear girl." She ripped the chain from my neck and threw it against the wall.

What was the fucking point of giving me the damn thing and not telling me how to use it?

Something flew against the door, causing it to shake on its hinges.

"Jodi!" It was Waldorf.

I'm coming, *ma cherie*! And Magdalin.

Waldorf hit the wood again, and I was impressed with the old house's tenacity. I rammed my shoulder into Josephine's chest, but she didn't budge.

Her arm whipped around my chest and pulled me back against her body; the other went around my waist, lifting me from the floor. I couldn't move my arms from my sides. I kicked my feet, trying to knock her off balance, but her boots were planted on the hardwood.

The door flew open, smashing against the wall and hanging from the bottom hinge. Madgalin, Waldorf, and Larz were framed in the doorway, the light in the hallway behind them.

"Let her go at once!" Waldorf commanded, but Josephine's hold tightened, making breathing difficult.

Stay calm. I was trying, but this situation didn't lend itself to a calm state of mind. They inched into the room. I was trying to watch Josephine.

I felt her pull the gun from my jeans. She swung her arm in front of me and fired. Larz fell to the floor. She was going to kill all of us.

It's okay, ma cherie. *I will save you.*

"Her blood smells sweet, Magdalin." Josephine sniffed my neck.

"Let her go, Jo."

"I gave you ninety years!"

"Let's talk. Please!"

Josephine's mouth latched onto my neck, and the air was sucked from my body.

NO!!

This was no gentle nip, no delicate puncture, and certainly no seductive kiss.

It felt like a rabid dog had attached itself to my throat and was ripping my head from my body. Pain replaced the blood in my veins as my life force sprayed the walls.

Jodi, hold on!

I fell to the floor, unable to move. Blood continued to pump out of me, discoloring the wooden floorboards and the carpet.

Josephine was thrown into the wall above the bed. The plaster crumbled around her and fell onto the mattress.

Gentle hands held me, pulled me into an embrace. Ma cherie! I tried to focus on Magdalin's face, the green of her eyes, but she was a blurry shadow.

Forgive me, ma cherie.

And then there was her kiss, as soft as moonlight on my neck. Her teeth slid into my skin like butter, my blood rushing from my body and into her heart.

I will take care of you, sweet Jodi.

The Serpent Tattoo

E. C. Myers

one of the drawbacks to becoming immortal at the age of
nineteen is that you end up being carded for eternity.

"I.D.," the bouncer grunts, flinging a muscled arm across
my chest to block my way. I can't give it to him. I left my I.D.
in the future, and even if I had it he'd never believe that I'm
375 years old, well above the legal drinking age in this time.

The bouncer smirks, and I consider grinning back, so he
can see my canines. Then again, he probably couldn't tell the
real thing from the store-bought fangs most of the girls wear
at The Raven Club.

There's a meaty smell to him: a hint of prosciutto. I don't
want to touch him, but a little hypnotic suggestion goes a
long way.

I rest my hand on his arm, my crimson nails gently digging
into his sweaty skin. His eyes start to get that misty look, when
he suddenly shakes it off. I'm impressed—he didn't look like
he had the mental capacity. I'll have to use more force.

"Hold on," he says. "Didn't I let you through earlier?"

Of course. My past self must be here already. "I just stepped
out for a smoke," I say.

"Go on in." He waves me through. "Hey, wasn't your hair
red a little while ago?"

"My hair hasn't been red for a long time."

"Must have been someone else," he says. "I see a lot of girls coming and going." I guess he's not that bright after all.

I enter the club and spot Erin, my past self. She's sitting on the far end of the bar by the jukebox, which used to be my favorite perch. What's unexpected is that Cece, the vampire who sired me, is with her.

This presents several problems. The Raven Club is Cece's territory, and I'm infringing on her hunting grounds. I won't even be able to stay here unless she gives me permission. Perhaps worse than that, Cece also has claims to Erin. At this point in my past, I had no idea that Cece was a vampire. We dated for several months before she turned me, and our relationship didn't last much past that. Few do. The breakup was painful; after nearly four centuries, it still stings, but I know I'm better off without her. Cece is a sexy woman and a good lay, but once she has her hooks in you, she's a total bitch. She can afford to be; she's been around at least twice as long as I have.

If Cece's here, I may not get a chance to talk to Erin alone. If I didn't owe it to Leah, who was waiting back home for my decision, I would turn right back around.

It's too late anyway; Cece has spotted me. A vampire always knows when another of her kind is around. I catch her eye, then bow my head in the traditional request for entry. She hesitates for a tense moment before returning the gesture, an understandable delay since I'm a complete stranger to her.

I know if I'm careful, Erin probably won't recognize me as a future version of herself, but Cece might. It looks like it might be too late for that, too. Cece's eyes sweep from me to Erin then back to me. She frowns. I decide I'd better get downstairs and out of sight.

Feeling dozens of eyes on me, the hottie in the tight black tank and matching velvet miniskirt, I cross the room to the spiral staircase that leads to the basement lounge. Erin and Cece watch me as I pass them. I strain to parse their conversation from the cacophony of music, talking, and clinking of glasses in the club.

Cece whispers, "Check that one out."

Erin gives me the once-over and says, "Yeah, she's hot."

"Would you fuck her?"

"What kind of a question is that?"

"I would," Cece says. "In fact, I think I already have." Erin stares sullenly into her margarita.

Downstairs, I sink deep into a misshapen couch just behind the stage. It's still early so it's empty of the usual tangled mass of arms and straps and leather that will become a fixture later, when the lights go out along with people's inhibitions. I try to ignore the strong odor of body fluids that have seeped into the cushions.

Seeing Erin and Cece together brings back a lot of memories, but not the ones I was after when I came here. It also reminds me of my own argument with Leah, the one we play out with disturbing frequency and little variation.

Leah has been pestering me to turn her into a vampire by her twentieth birthday. If I love her, she says, then I would want to spend an eternity with her. Eternity is a long time, I tell her. You don't know what might happen. I remind her about my breakup with Cece, and she accuses me of never getting over her, which is ridiculous. She warns me that I'm wasting time, that she's not getting any younger, and that I'd better make up my mind soon. There's an implied threat there, and I know it wouldn't take her long to hook up with another vamp. I ask her why she wants to be a vampire, and she says it should be obvious. Then she storms out.

I'm worn out just thinking about it. I promised her I would come to terms with whatever issues were preventing me from committing, then make a decision. Which is why I'm here: to see how a person is changed after being turned, other than the obvious. With that as my goal, I figured I might as well go back to the beginning.

several guys solicit sex from me for the cost of a cheap drink. Even if I were available, none of the yuppies, frat boys, or pseudopunks here are my type. Even the Goth girls I once lusted after at Erin's age no longer hold my interest; my tastes have matured over the years, and they are children compared to me.

Finally the waiting is over. Erin stumbles down the stairs but steadies herself with a hand on the banister. She's had quite a few drinks already.

She pauses to shakily light a cigarette. The tiny flame of the lighter briefly illuminates her face, reflecting off her oversized tortoiseshell glasses—I can't believe I ever liked those—and giving a healthy glow to her pallid skin. I marvel at her exquisite paleness. I had always thought of it as a nice side effect of my vampirism, but apparently I had possessed it all along. That's probably what drew Cece to me in the first place, knowing her tastes, along with my naiveté.

Erin pulls deeply on the cigarette, and I can almost taste it. I quit long ago, but I still miss the pleasant burn of smoke in my throat. It's nothing compared to drinking fresh blood, of course, but it's as close as humans can get.

I'm about to stand, planning the best way to approach her, when Erin makes it easy for me. She wobbles toward the couch—toward me. Her red hair falls over her face, and she pushes it away, tucking it behind an ear into the frame of her glasses.

I haven't seen myself in a mirror in several lifetimes, and I had forgotten my appearance. Erin's auburn hair falls to her waist in soft waves, and I remember something else: how proud I had been of that hair. I stopped dyeing it in the mid-twenty-first century, leaving it a natural brownish blonde, and I wear it much shorter now, a length more practical for hunting.

She comes closer, and, along with the secondhand smoke, my nostrils also catch her fragrance: cinnamon and butterscotch. Each human has a unique scent, whereas vampires all smell the same, like iron and earth. Maybe that's what makes them so attractive to us, besides our dietary needs.

Erin plops onto the couch, and the strange contours of the old worn cushions off-balance her, so she shoves up against me. I grab her, hold her up. I don't want to remove my hands from her shoulders—her body warmth is addictive, like nicotine. I settle one arm comfortably behind her, around her waist, and she doesn't seem to mind.

"Sorry about that," she giggles. Her voice sounds odd, like hearing myself on my voicemail message or in an old home video.

"That's okay," I say. "Are you all right?"

"No." She looks at me curiously, cigarette dangling from her lips as she pulls her hair back. It cascades behind her, tickling my bare arm. "You seem familiar. Have we met?"

"You might have seen me around," I say. In your mirror. "I'm Morganne."

Her eyes widen. "Really? That's so cool! I always wanted to change my name to Morganne. Ever since I was a little girl."

A wide goofy smile stretches across her face. For a moment she looks simple, innocent. She's still a child. That's the way I remember myself.

"What are the chances of that?" I say.

"I guess this is fate, then." Erin blows out smoke, eyeing me nervously through the wispy gray whorls.

"So, you want to tell me your troubles?"

"My girl—my *ex*-girlfriend and I were just admiring you upstairs."

"Ex?"

"For now." She sighs. "We had a fight. We do that a lot lately. She actually suggested I ask you to join us tonight. I suggested we didn't."

"You're not into threesomes?" I ask coyly.

"I don't want to share her." She glances away. "Or you."

"Oh."

"She's sulking upstairs, but she'll get over it." She sounds more hopeful than certain. I know that she's wrong.

"I really like your outfit," Erin says.

"Thanks." I had picked up the clothes on the way to the club when I stopped for a bite to eat. Someone had probably found the dead girl by now. "Yours is nice, too."

Her black-and-red corset, long black dress, striped stockings, and the little silver bat choker are the uniform of the Goth vampire wanna-bes. They're a little embarrassing, but even though no real vampire would be caught dead in them, they do a good job of showing off her curves. They certainly got my attention.

Erin takes another drag of her cigarette, then offers the last of it to me. "I'm Erin, by the way," she says.

I shake my head to the cigarette and she leans over to stub it out on the floor.

"Hey, I could use a drink," she says. "How about you? I'm buying."

"Thanks. I'll have a Bloody Mary."

"Be right back." She struggles to get up from the couch, so I give her a little boost from behind. As I brush my hand against her ass, I realize that she, too, has eschewed underwear tonight. Maybe some of our habits never change.

I watch as she lurches to the small bar at the side of the basement. She grabs hold of the counter as though clinging to a piece of wood floating on the ocean.

It's strange seeing myself the way I was back then. I remember myself as timid, shy. Erin doesn't match that image at all. Is it just the alcohol? Or have the years changed my impressions that drastically?

Erin seems like another person entirely. She's both a stranger and someone I knew better than anyone else, once. It's hard to believe that any part of her is still inside me. That's why I'm here: I need to remember what it's like to be her. I need to know how much will remain of Leah if I change her.

I spot Cece descending the stairs, her eyes on Erin. I get behind Erin, asserting my own claim to her. Wrapping my arms around her, I whisper in her ear, "Let's dance."

She puts down our drinks with a twenty-dollar bill and lets me whisk her onto the dance floor. A hyper beat blasts from the speakers. "I love this song," Erin squeals. She seems ready to lose her balance at any moment as she dances to the frenetic music.

"Who's the band?" I ask.

Cece stands at the bar, arms across her chest, glaring at us.

"Zombina and the Skeletones. They're cool," Erin says.

Cece threads her way toward us, the strobe light showing her progress in flash frames of bright relief.

I move quickly, the way I do when I'm striking to kill, which I suppose I am in a fashion, but this time my target is Erin's mouth.

I press my lips against hers. She jerks for a second, surprised, then relaxes and kisses back. I taste tobacco, vodka, and something else, something sweet. Erin. Her lips are warm, and through them I can feel her heart throbbing. She is so alive.

"Oh," she says when we finally break off. Her face flushes from embarrassment. I had thought it would be weird, like kissing a sister, but it felt . . . right. It seemed to be the same for her. I want more. I want more of *her*.

"That was great," she whispers.

A hand pulls my shoulder roughly from behind. I turn, and Cece slaps me hard. "You don't belong here," she says. "She's mine."

"Cece!" Erin says.

"That's interesting," I say. "Because if anyone has an interest in what happens to her, I think it would be me."

"Do you know who this is?" Cece says to Erin.

"Cece, I'm sorry—"

"I think we should discuss this in private," I say to Cece. She stares at me for a moment, then turns and stalks away.

"I'll be right back, Erin," I say. "I think I'll want that drink when I get back." She nods, her lips pressed tightly together.

Cece waits for me in the hallway outside the restrooms. We size each other up.

She looks like the Cece I know. I've known her for 375 years, but for all intents and purposes, she has just met me, which gives me an advantage.

"What do you want with her?" she asks.

"I just wanted to talk."

"That looked like more than talking. I've put a lot of time into this relationship, and you're not going to step in when I'm about to turn her."

"Is that what I always was to you? A project? A challenge?"

"You were never a *challenge*," she sneers.

"Well, I'm not trying to steal her away from you, if that's what you're worried about. I just want to talk to her. Let me have her for tonight."

She considers. "No."

"You've always been a bitch, Cece. I don't know what I ever saw in you."

"Still upset about my dumping you?" she asks. "I did dump you, didn't I?" She takes a step closer to me, puts her hand on my arm, runs her nails lightly along the top of it. "You're not here for her, are you? This is about getting back at me, isn't it?" She leans in. "You want to spare yourself the pain." Her cool lips brush against my neck. "Or maybe . . . you want me back?"

I can't believe she's actually trying this on me. It's an amateurish move; in fact, she taught it to me.

I groan softly at her touch, rotating my head back and exposing the neck to her lips and tongue. I know her timing; she won't make her move right away. I bend my head and nuzzle her cheek with my nose. I play my lips behind her ear, down her neck and below her jaw. Her breathing grows heavier.

I never had patience for this tactic. I sink my teeth into her neck and tear out her jugular along with a sizable chunk of flesh.

Astonished, Cece stumbles backward, her hand clamped over the open wound. Without a heart to pump the blood, there is no arterial spray, but the life will drain from her quickly enough. Vampires are resilient, but not even we can survive this much damage.

Cece collapses at my feet, the only sound the gurgling of blood in her throat. I look down at her and realize what I've done. "Damn," I say. I think I'm finally over her.

I find Erin sitting on the couch, nursing her drink. I take my Bloody Mary and wash down Cece's blood.

"Where's Cece?" she asks.

"She's cooling off."

"She seemed really upset."

"Don't worry about it."

"Hey, did you put on lipstick?" she asks.

I rub the back of my hand across my mouth. I had cleaned most of the blood off in the bathroom, but my lips are always red after I feed.

"It's getting late," I say.

She nods. "Why don't we go?"

"Thanks for walking me home," Erin says. She yawns, briefly displaying two rows of perfectly normal human teeth. I keep one hand on her arm to guide her so she won't weave all over the sidewalk. We had already stopped once to let her vomit in the gutter, which reminded me uncomfortably of the first time I killed someone. That had been messier, blood and bile disgorged all over her drained and lifeless body. Blood is definitely an acquired taste, whether you're undead or not. It comes in a range of flavors, as different as merlots and cabernets, according to individual victims.

"I'm happy to," I say. "I couldn't leave you alone."

"It's just . . . I'm drunk." She laughs. "And, and, and . . . did you hear about the attack in the park?"

So they found the body. "No. What attack?" I shift her arm over my shoulder and pull her closer to me as we walk. It helps a lot that we're the same height.

"This after— This evening, a girl was killed in the park." She touches the choker around her throat. "Her throat was cut or something, and she was only wearing her underwear." Erin shudders. "They still hadn't identified her by the time I left my dorm, but I bet she goes to NYU, too."

"That's scary," I say. "There are all sorts of maniacs out on the streets."

"I know, right?" She squeezes me tight. "Where do you go to school?"

"NYU." I never graduated, of course. "Film major."

"Film? Really? Me, too! Maybe that's where I've seen you. What classes do you take?"

I look up and see that we've made it to University Hall. "Oh, we're here," I say.

She looks up and stops short. "How do you know where I live?" she asks.

"You told me before we left," I lie.

Erin leans against the wall and takes a deep breath. "Oh." We look at each other. "Would . . . would you like to come upstairs?"

I smile. "Yes."

We step into the lobby, and I wince in the bright fluorescent light. The security guard—his name, Jonah, springs to mind— eyes us strangely.

"Are you two twins?" he asks. "Or am I just seeing double?"

Erin laughs. She looks even paler in the harsh light. In her outfit, I'm sure she looks more the part of a vampire than I do.

"No, we aren't twins," I say.

"But you're related, right?" he says as he takes her card and swipes it. "You have to be sisters."

Jonah returns Erin's card. "Actually, we just met," she says then grins at me. I reach over the counter and grab Jonah's forearm, pressing my nails into him.

"I forgot my I.D.," I say. His eyes lose focus as I plant the suggestion, "You remember me, don't you?"

He scratches the stubble on his chin, making a sound like sandpaper. "Sure," he says. "But you'd better get a new one first thing on Monday."

"Okay. Thanks."

"You two have a good night," he says as the elevator doors close behind us.

As soon as we're clear, Erin bursts into laughter. "Can you

believe it? He thought we were sisters!"

I force a laugh. It is pretty funny but a little too close to home for my taste. "I guess there is a little resemblance."

"That's why you look familiar! Say, maybe we are *sisters*, huh?"

I press the button for the tenth floor again, but it doesn't make the elevator rise any faster.

"You're drunk," I say.

"Or maybe . . . maybe you're my doppelganger! Yeah. Or a clone."

"Or maybe I'm from your future." She frowns, and I think I've gone too far.

"Oh come on, be serious. We're like the same age."

"Sorry, just trying to—" She places a short, black enameled fingernail over my lips.

A moment later she kisses me. Her tongue probes my mouth, then she pulls away abruptly. "Ow," she mumbles.

I taste bitter iron.

She sticks a finger in her mouth, runs it along her tongue, and winces. She examines the smear of red she finds on her fingertip, shiny with saliva. "What was that?" she says.

I stretch my mouth wide and she stares at my fangs. "Wow. That's nice dental work. My parents would kill me if I filed my teeth like that."

The elevator door dings open, and we step out. All I've had is a taste, but the hunger burns through my body. I press my mouth against hers and slip my tongue over and around hers. There isn't much blood, but it arouses an appetite for more.

As if I have any doubts of where things are leading, her hand slips under my skirt. I catch an evil grin on her face when she touches me. I wonder which of us is the seducer as she rubs her fingers against me.

we're so caught up in the drunken choreography of touching and kissing while trying to get to her room, that before I know it we are sprawled on her bed. My miniskirt is the first sacrifice to the altar of the one-night stand.

She has a hand up my tank top and fondles my right breast while I unlace her corset.

"You're so cold," she says. She caresses the underside of my breast. My spine tingles.

"You're very warm." I undo the final lace and when I unclasp the top and bottom fasteners, the corset slips apart. She sighs with the release, and I run my fingers over her warm pale breasts. I've touched myself before, of course, but this is a new experience. I know how it feels to her, and that turns me on even more.

The corset has left red creases in her smooth skin, and I slide my tongue along them. She shudders, and I reach up, press my palms against her hard nipples, rubbing them, then cup her breasts. I feel her heart beating inches from my hands; I want to reach in and wrap my hand around the warm bloody muscle, dig my fingers into it to touch the core of her.

I claw my right hand and scrape my nails along her breast, five lines radiating inward to her hard nipples. She gasps. Blood wells from the scratches, trickling down the side of her breast like drizzles of strawberry sauce on a sundae. I lick the soft flesh greedily. She moans, a guttural animal sound.

She pulls off my shirt, then lifts her head to take one of my nipples into her mouth. Her lips and mouth are hot. I shudder from the warm wet movement of her tongue against my breast. She reaches a hand down between my legs and begins massaging my clitoris with two fingers.

I reach down to rub teasingly and stretch my other hand across her breast, tracing lazy circles around her nipple with my finger, alternating between fingertip and nail. When she seems ready, I slip two fingers inside her easily. She is hot and moist.

I push deep, then pull out almost all the way, teasing. Pushing back in, I match the rhythm of her massage.

Her face is a mirror of ecstasy as we race to orgasm.

Erin sleeps, and I watch her like an old lover, the oldest I have ever known. She lies in repose, a pale corpse resting on her deathbed, but her heart still beats, her naked chest still rising rhythmically with each breath.

I place my right hand between her breasts, trying to absorb the warmth from her body. She is an inferno, and her heartbeats drive me mad, like The Telltale Heart hidden under the floor. I place my left hand on my chest, between identical breasts, and count. I imagine my own heart pumping blood through my body, my own blood instead of the blood of countless victims.

Erin says something. I tilt an ear to her lips. "Cece," she murmurs.

I slip out of bed and pace the small room, looking at everything but the naked woman. All around me are the pieces of a life, precious and irreplaceable, yet they are the things I left behind most readily when I became a vampire. How can they be both so important and so worthless?

"I didn't say it before, but I like your tattoo," Erin says sleepily. She rubs a hand against her right breast as she sits up, wincing from the pain. The cuts have become inflamed, bright red welts standing out starkly against white skin.

"Thanks," I say. The tattoo on my lower back is of two serpents—one light, one dark—each consuming the other's tail and twisting over each other in a lemniscate, a figure eight.

"Isn't that the symbol for infinity?" She crawls to the end of the bed to examine it more closely, her hair and breasts hanging low. "It's made of snakes," she says in surprise.

"It's a double ouroboros."

"What does it mean?"

"*Ouroboros* means 'tail swallower.' The image means a lot of things: It's about opposites, the cycle of life and death, resurrection."

"Cool." She sits up and pulls her hair behind her head, the motion lifting her breasts and causing some of the wounds to reopen. The scent of blood mingles with the smell of sex in the air. My mouth waters, and my head begins to throb.

"I wish I had a tattoo like that," she says. "So far I've only played with henna. A tattoo seems so permanent. It's like forever."

I turn to stare out the window at Union Square just across the street. The sun will be rising in an hour. Almost time for me to go.

"What really happened to Cece?" she asks.

"What do you mean?"

"I didn't see her leave the club."

"You were drunk. You're still drunk."

"What was she talking about? Who are you?"

I spin around and find her sitting on the edge of the bed with one leg drawn up. I sit down beside her. I try to put a hand on her knee, but she shifts away from me.

"I'm your future," I say.

"What does that—" Her eyes widen.

"You understand?"

"Holy shit." She purses her lips and lowers her head. Tangled red hair slips forward and chastely covers her breasts.

"I should have known," she says finally. "You knew my body too well. You knew exactly where to touch, exactly what I like. Not even Cece knows me that well. And you do look just like me." She shakes her head. "I'm such an idiot!"

"You're not," I say.

"Wait."

"Yes?"

"You can't be from too far in my future. You look my age. But you're different somehow. And your teeth . . . " She brushes her hair aside and lifts her damaged breast, as though discovering it for the first time.

"I come from a long way into the future. I'm very old."

Erin tries to dart away from me, but I grab her arm and hold it in an iron grip. She whimpers and pulls on her arm. Soon she stops struggling and sits there, looking at me defiantly.

"You killed her, didn't you?"

I see something in her eyes, something deep that I know I will never get back, no matter how much I might remember about her, about myself. I wonder what she sees in me. She shudders and breaks eye contact.

"She was just like me," I say. "If I weren't here, she would be. And she wouldn't be so gentle."

"Why are you doing this?" she asks.

"I have to."

"No you don't."

"I do," I whisper.

Part of what I love so much about Leah is her fragility, her humanity, her innocence. I don't know how much of her will be lost when I give her that wish, when I make her into the demon Cece had turned me into. I hadn't been given a choice then, but Leah has one. I have one.

"I won't hurt you," I promise her. "You'll live forever."

I had wanted Leah so badly I had offered to change her. She had resisted, but over time, as we grew closer as partners and lovers, she changed her mind. Had I done the right thing, planting that seed in her mind? Was I taking away more than I was giving her?

"Why?" she asks.

"You'll be happier."

"I won't be human."

"You'll be better."

"I'll be different."

"No. You won't."

I push her down on the bed, raise myself over her with my hands pressing her wrists into the bed. For the last time I look into those bottomless green eyes, as they stare at me in terror. I keep my eyes on her as I lower myself and press my lips to her breast. I flick my tongue out, and her nipple responds instantly. She's becoming aroused, the blood rushing, even while she continues to struggle under me.

Her chest rises and falls more rapidly, and her breathing becomes shallow. Without warning, because there never is one, I sink my teeth into the soft flesh. She cries out and flails her arms, but I hold her tightly. We've moved beyond pleasure now into pain, unstoppable, unbearable, unavoidable pain. There's nothing to do but stay the course.

I suckle at her breast like a newborn, drawing life from her drop by drop, in blood not milk. She moves more slowly, but I keep my grip on her arms. I hesitate briefly before sinking my teeth into her neck, finding the artery and bursting it in my mouth. The hot spray of blood hits the back of my throat, and I swallow, drinking deeply almost to the point of no return.

When I have had enough I push myself up to look at her face. Her eyelids are closed, fluttering, her face contorted in ecstasy and agony. She is close to death now. Now it's time to bring her back.

I bring my mouth to hers, my lips slick with her rapidly cooling blood. At my prompting, she opens her mouth, and my tongue pushes into it. She sucks on it, pulls it. Then without warning she bites into it. I hear her teeth sinking in.

She drinks the blood welling from my tongue. The bitter taste of it fills my mouth, dribbles onto her chin, and still she sucks, drawing the life I have taken back into her. I pull away, my ruined tongue burning. She stretches her head blindly, her teeth gnashing in search of more blood. I give it to her. I slash my thumbnail across my throat and her mouth finds the flow of blood. She drinks and drinks and drinks.

I roll away from her finally and get to my feet. I wipe myself with a damp cloth in the bathroom, and as I dress I look at the gruesome sight on the bed. She lies twisted, hair swept out, blood trickling from the corner of her mouth like sleep drool. Her breast is torn and bloody, and her chest no longer rises. She is a beautiful corpse on her deathbed. The stink of life is everywhere.

I lay my hand to her forehead, nails pressing into the skin. In another twelve hours she'll wake in a panic. She won't know what has happened to her, only that she has been changed somehow, violated.

But she'll be all right. She'll heal. She'll figure things out, and she'll find her way just as I did.

I draw the blinds to keep out the morning sun then let myself out of the room. It's time for me to go home, back to my love.

We are two snakes, light and dark, forever entwined. This is the moment that binds us.

Rune

CHRISTA NORDLUM

Rune waited in the shadow of the alley across the street and stared thoughtfully at the woman coming out of the club. Rune had been watching her all night, a woman dancing alone, intrigued by her independent spirit. She was of average height and build but had a peculiar style. She was clothed partly in military garb, wearing camouflaged cargo pants and visibly scuffed army boots. Her shirt was cotton, pristine white, with a rainbow splashed across the chest. The lamplight revealed to Rune that the woman's hair had once been a dark color but was currently dyed a bright red. Her face was quite fair though, thought Rune, and her eyes soft and revealing.

The wind whipped Rune's dark hair around her long pale face, but she paid no notice. In these moments it was if she was a part of the Earth, unaffected by weather, all of her energies focused. She supposed that despite all appearances she and this woman would have a great many things in common. Before her was a perfect example of one who, like Rune, defied social norms. Rune knew that the world had seen changes, but there were things left untouched by the passage of time. There were always those who were frightened by difference and those who embraced it. There was always dusk followed by dawn. There was always life followed by death, and for Rune there was always a girl. Tonight, it would be this girl.

She was swift and silent as she approached the woman on the street. With guile Rune embraced a submissive demeanor, letting her take the lead as initial pleasantries were exchanged. Her name was Cassie, but it mattered little. Though her hunger was great, Rune found herself enjoying the moment, this slow and secret seduction of her newest adventure, her prey. It came so easily, too, with a perfectly timed compliment, and a slight touching of the hand. Even the elements were playing their part with the cool breeze and the scent of a coming storm on the hot summer air. It wasn't long before Rune was accepting an invitation to accompany the woman back to her home.

Cassie's naked body glistened in the glow of the candlelight, which reflected in Rune's heavy-lidded blue eyes. Rune watched her as she fell sleep, still wrapped in their embrace. Her skin was soft and smooth, her breasts supple, her neck inviting. Rune was addicted to this; she longed for these women in ways they themselves couldn't imagine. She desired all they had to offer her from the fervid moments they shared in bed to the moments after, to the hunger and the feast. Their blood was everything. Blood was the source of life; it was the source of power, the source of passion. This was the reason she existed, the reason they existed.

Rune took a last look and slowly morphed into the demon. Her unusually blue eyes turned a fiery red as saliva-slicked fangs protruded from her mouth. Her human needs were forgotten now as she focused on the prey before her. With her tongue she tasted the salt on the skin of Cassie's neck and then plunged in deeply with her teeth. The body stirred but did not wake as Rune devoured it whole, drinking in her blood, her life force. When Rune was finished, she turned back to her human form and lay next to the body. She silently caressed the skin, still warm to Rune's touch, and thanked Cassie for her gifts before she left.

Rune woke just before dusk. A storm had come and gone while she slept, but the scent of the rain still lingered in the air. Being careful not to fully expose herself to even the muted rays of sunlight, Rune pulled back the dark shades in her room and peered down to the street. People moved about hastily, carrying umbrellas and briefcases. She almost felt sorry for them as they rushed through their small, pathetic lives. Rune reveled in life just as she reveled in death. She closed her eyes and could still feel the woman's smooth skin under her fingertips. She could still taste her blood, warm and sweet, pulsing with life. Rune closed the shade. Today was a new day, a new adventure.

When night came, she drifted down the streets toward the club again, already searching, hunting for the girl. Her eyes scanned the streets and stopped when they caught a flash of light. Rune slipped into the shadows as the woman with the silver necklace threw her head back with an enchanted laugh, exposing the vulnerable spot on her neck just above the clavicle. She had light auburn hair that was pulled back from her face, and her eyes were green, deep and familiar. Rune entered through the club's side door and waited in a corner, the air in the bar already thick with smoke. She watched as the woman came into the room and made her way to the middle of the floor. She started to dance, slowly at first, and then her long, firm body forged with beat of the pounding music. It was all Rune could hear; the woman was all Rune could see.

Rune stepped into the hazy glow of the dance floor and walked toward her. There was an instant connection between them when Rune approached, and when her eyes met the deep green of hers they sent a shiver down Rune's spine. They moved together, becoming one body on the dance floor. Their longing, their heat, their desire became locked in harmony, timed to the rhythm of the music and the sensation of skin against skin.

They moved that way for hours, never leaving the warmth of the one body, always pacing with the music. Their first kiss was there on the dance floor and was initiated by the woman. "My name is Vic," she whispered in her ear. Rune felt a curious sensation in her chest, a tightness that betrayed her usual icy calm. Her senses heightened, and she found herself very aware of this woman next to her, her hands, her mouth, and those deep green eyes.

They moved away into the thickening darkness, still wrapped around each other, still mesmerized by the music and the magnetism between them. When they reached Vic's apartment they wasted little time with clothes, pulling them off on the way to the bedroom. They kissed more passionately on the bed, and Rune slowly pushed Vic to her back and used her mouth and tongue to tease her flesh. With her hands, she caressed her face and neck and massaged the roundness of her breasts. Rune's fingers traced around the now erect nipples and down to the flatness of Vic's stomach and finally stopped to feel the wetness between her legs.

Rune continued to kiss Vic's body, taking in every inch with her mouth, while her fingers steadily stroked inside her. Vic began moaning softly when at long last Rune's mouth reached her center. With each stroke of Rune's hand and each movement of her tongue Vic's moans became louder and closer together until there was a slow and powerful release. Vic tightened her grip on Rune's shoulder and whispered, "I want you," as she pushed Rune to her back. She was both strong and gentle, vigorous and slow. Rune felt her body go from tense to relaxed as Vic expertly ravished her body. Vic pulled her up and kissed her full on the mouth. She was sitting so that her legs straddled Rune's torso, and her body, pressed against Rune's, was hot and damp with sweat. Rune had not felt so warm, so wanted for over two centuries. This woman was powerful and passionate, and Rune's attraction to her was intense. The connection between them was like wild fire: It burned and consumed, it was fast and strange.

There was also something haunting about this woman. The way she moved fascinated Rune, and she knew she would enjoy this final dance with Vic. She would watch as she drifted off and then take pleasure in the feast. Rune would make it slow; she would savor this woman for as long as she could.

They remained one body, there on the bed, holding each other, kissing, not moving. Rune stroked that auburn hair and the smooth skin of Vic's face slowly, softly, until at last she closed those green eyes to the world. Rune took in her naked form and admired her. In these last hours Vic had made her feel as if she were alive again.

The demon took her, and fiery red eyes burned into the sleeping body. They found the spot where Vic's neck met her shoulder. Rune shifted her body on top of Vic, and her tongue licked her full lips. Rune's mouth opened wide as she leaned down to abate her insatiable hunger. As her mouth closed down over Vic's neck, excruciating pain seized her body. Her jaw locked up, and she silenced a scream as she was thrown from the bed. She got up quickly and braced herself over Vic, plunging in to try again, and again she had the same result.

Rune sat in the darkness in the middle of the room. Every muscle in her body ached, and she cowered like a cornered animal. She resumed her human appearance and heard Vic stir.

"Are you leaving?" she whispered.

Rune didn't answer right away, but looked around frantically, searching out all escape routes. Vic sat up on the bed.

"Rune? Are you okay? You're shaking. Come here. Stay with me."

Rune nodded, in shock, and then was vaguely aware of Vic's

presence at her side. She allowed herself to be led back to the bed and under the sheet. There Vic held her from behind and softly kissed her cheek, her neck, her shoulder. Vic whispered in her ear, "Thank you for tonight. I don't normally take home strange women from bars, but you . . . you were amazing."

They had talked very little since they met on the dance floor and Rune noticed for the first time the sweetness of Vic's voice. It soothed her as it resonated within her ear. She felt torn in two, being both attracted and repelled by her. The demon inside growled and fought and pleaded with her not to let this prey live to see the morning, but Rune, still in agony, just let herself be held. Just before Rune drifted to sleep she whispered back to a deeply breathing Vic, "Only one other woman made me feel like you did this night, even in all my years."

The morning light was harsh, even though the sole window faced the west. Thankfully the bed was still mostly covered in shadows. Vic rose first, and Rune could hear her start the shower. For as long as Rune could remember, she had left the women before sunrise; this was new territory. Rune lay there for a moment in a complete daze. She couldn't remember what happened after they made love, why she had not yet killed Vic, or why she was still here. She slipped out from under the sheets and went into the open bathroom door.

The room was already steamy from the hot water, and Rune pushed back the shower curtain, revealing Vic's back streaming with rivulets of water from the showerhead. Rune stepped in and pulled Vic close to her. She kissed Vic down her body, avoiding her neck and starting in the middle of her back. Vic turned to face her and moaned slightly as Rune kissed up her leg and stopped between her thighs. Rune found she enjoyed giving this woman pleasure even more than she enjoyed receiving it.

When the shower was over and they were dressed again,

Vic went to see about breakfast, and Rune wandered into the living room. She was still perplexed about why she was here during the day but also felt unable to leave, as if she were drawn to that spot. She looked absently around the room and her eyes froze on the picture on the mantle. She had not seen that face in 180 years.

Rune flashed back to the spring of 1824. Her mind took her through the many hot and sultry nights, bringing back to her the smell of Victoria's hair, the sweetness of her voice, the way she touched her, and those beautiful deep green eyes. Rune could hear her soft moans, feel her warm skin, see the shocked and disgusted faces of Victoria's parents the night they caught them making love.

Rune remembered how she felt as if she were dying, like her heart was being ripped from her chest when they sent Victoria away and forced her to wed some rich plantation owner. She remembered the night she met Victoria in secret and how angry and jealous she was when Victoria wouldn't come away with her. She remembered where they made love for the last time, in the orchard on the far side of the property, and how Victoria had left her before dawn. In the spring of the following year she had planned to whisk Victoria away for another affair. The very night she had been able to slip from under her father's watchful eye, she had been turned into the demon. Rune began her new life by hunting down her old lover with an insistent rage sweeping through her. She kissed the sleeping Victoria and then drank deeply of her sweet blood.

Rune slowly came out of her reverie and found that she was again engulfed in pain. Her head cleared, and she remembered at once the events from the night before. Vic entered the room, and Rune stood up fast and began to shout, "Who are you? Why do you have her picture?" Rune was shaking again and pointed toward the mantle.

"That's a photograph of Victoria King. I was named for her. She was my great-great-great-great grandmother," Vic said quietly as she moved closer to Rune. Vic's face registered with confusion, then slowly recognition, and finally horror. "That means you must be . . . Oh my God."

Rune began to inch away from Vic, and the two started to circle around each other. "You were the beast that murdered her!"

"How could you know that?" Rune said in barely a whisper, clutching her stomach.

Vic's voice was strong when she answered. "Victoria had a baby girl shortly before you took her life. When her husband found her body, he vowed to rid the world of the beast that could do such a thing. He heard of a coven that communed nearby and took the baby to them. They blessed her with a spell, a protection spell. Now with every generation the story and the spell have been passed on." Vic paused, and her face became pale when she spoke again, "Along with the ability to—"

"Kill me."

Vic nodded her head in response, and Rune, still shaking, backed up toward the door.

"Where are you going to go, Rune? It's still daylight for eleven hours."

Rune grabbed a large blanket from the back of a chair and twisted the handle of the door. "I will see you again?" she asked flatly.

"Yeah." Rune nodded and softly shut the door behind her. She ran quickly through the hallway and down the stairs to the first floor. Her skin started to tingle and burn as soon as she hit the street, and she wrapped the blanket over her head and across her shoulders. The blanket smelled of Vic, and Rune felt a mix of emotions as she ducked into a parking garage to get out of the sun. The demon reminded her of her primal needs, of her hunger, but there was more. One part of her wanted to throw the blanket down and allow the sun to burn her body to ashes. The other part of her wanted to find as many innocents as she could and drain them of their lives.

She found her way to her apartment and shuddered and crouched in a darkened corner of her bedroom, still holding Vic's blanket. Her memory was flooded by the past, and she was forced to relive over and over all of her years with Victoria. The last image she had just after the sun went down was of her night with Vic and she began to feel her pull. She was being drawn to her,. Vic was calling her.

Rune stood and shook off the images and their lingering effect. She morphed instantly into the demon, her red eyes glowing in the dark of the room. She was ready for battle. She burst through the door and left the building on the prowl for the woman. Tonight she would taste blood or be released from her pain. She let out a low guttural growl and turned her nose into the wind. Vic's scent came to her almost immediately. She was close, in the alley near the club.

Rune rounded the corner fast and blocked two kicks and a punch from Vic. She landed a couple of quick punches and pushed Vic to the ground. Vic bounced up easily and advanced again, kicking hard and connecting with Rune's middle.

"You can't win, Rune. You feel it, don't you? You've felt it all day. The spell."

Rune threw more punches, rights and lefts in succession. Vic blocked them all with ease, and her counterpunches landed squarely on Rune's jaw.

"I feel everything, her and you," Rune muttered while clutching at her stomach. "Was it all just the spell?"

Vic hesitated before answering. She stopped hitting Rune, and her eyes were drawn down to her feet. "No. Last night was real; the feelings are what triggered the spell, your feelings and mine. Now I feel Victoria, too, what she had with you, her memories."

Rune was breathing heavily now and propped herself against the brick wall, using it for support. She could sense this was near the end and changed back to her human face, her blue eyes shining with tears that wouldn't fall. "When I was alive I loved her with all of me and I knew I didn't tell her enough. There was nothing in life nor anything in death that I wanted more. Until you."

"There was a time when I didn't believe the story, and I never in a million years thought I would find you." Vic reached up and touched Rune's face. "She loved you, too, Rune. Her heart was broken when she was forced to go away, and then again for almost a year when she didn't see you. She tried to tell you why she couldn't go with you, why she had to stay. It was for the baby. It was so the child would be taken care of. But you wouldn't listen, and when she found out you had died she shut herself away and cried for days. Her very dreams were haunted by you, by your death."

"And then I killed her." Rune looked directly into those deep green eyes, Victoria's eyes. She was ready.

Vic pulled the wooden stake from her pocket and without hesitation drove it solidly into Rune's chest. The pain was immense when it pierced her heart. She could feel her body start to crumble away. Once again she was brought back to that last night with Victoria in the orchard. The scent of the blossoms overhead reached her nose; she could feel the coolness of the grass that held their naked forms; and she saw Victoria one last time in the face of her descendent before Rune closed her eyes forever.

When the dust settled to the ground Vic knelt on the street. Crouched there, she wept until dawn.

Girl Eats Girl

KIM-LIN HOOPER

I glide over her sleeping body without a sound. She lies on one side, her body a pale, moonlit landscape, lily white. It's as if she has been here for centuries, her smooth curves and valleys emerging from hard rock, softened and weathered by time, wind, and water. The white satin sheet flows over her thighs like a river. If I bite, there on her side, how will the blood come? Will it form a stream, running down quick, making a small tarn in her belly button before it trickles off again? Or will it ooze, viscous and slow, a lava flow edging down her back, pooling dark on the sheets?

I settle at her side and lay my hand on her hip gently, not wanting to wake her, and turn her into her back. She stays limp as I move her. I jump as her black eyes open. I grab her wrists and push them down onto the pillow on either side of her head. She struggles, so I sit astride her, pinning her down. It's easy; she is smaller than me and weak.

I lean into her, smell the place where her neck meets her ear, close my mouth around her earlobe. My breasts touch her body.

I'm going to do it now.

I move my mouth down to her neck. No, I can't bear to bite her neck, so I move down farther, to her shoulder. I find a place in the top of her shoulder that my teeth can pinch and hold on to. I hear her suck her breath in. I close my eyes and bite, hard. It takes a long time for my teeth to pierce the skin. I almost think I've botched it. Then she whimpers with pain, pants for me to stop, breathes hard, trying to bear it. I haven't drawn a lot of blood. Red rubies form on her white skin. I taste it with my tongue. It's hot and salty.

HOW did this happen? How long did I sleep?

I awoke, weak in both body and mind. Then I could not lift the lid of my coffin. Lying on my back, I put my feet to the stone covering and sought to raise it with my legs. My strength failed.

"Z'bud!" I exclaimed, though my voice emerged as a cracked whisper, so sore and dry was my throat. I heaved onto my front and raised the lid with my back, on all fours like a cart horse. The stone lid fell to the floor with a heavy thud. It took all my strength and afterwards I lay in the darkness, spent. When I finally rose, my gown and cape had gone. So it was naked that I climbed the steps of the crypt into the church, and in my strange state thought that the walls surrounding me had changed and grown! What sorcery was this! The narrow walls I knew were gone, and I stood in the near darkness, in a larger hall with arched ceilings and rows of wooden pews. Was I hallucinating from lack of blood?

I walked among the pews and out of the church. I found myself under the old yew tree, but what now? So much thicker in the trunk, a mature tree! Its branches arched down to the ground, blocking out the moonlight and the view. My advantage was that the branches covered my naked body from the sight of any passer-by.

It was with glee that I spied a sleeping man, unshaven, with long matted hair, lying on a wooden bench. A drunkard. Easy blood! I resolved to steal his clothes while he slept. He wore leather garments: tight britches and a jacket. I crept over to him. His breath smelled of liquor. I tugged at the fastenings on his britches, unable to work them, so weak and feeble was I.

He awoke then, to both my surprise and his.

"Wvugggh . . . blimey. A naked woman . . . and taking off my troussshers . . . Mmm, I in heaven, poshibly?"

He reached down to his crotch and with grubby fingers assisted me with his fastenings. One button and a mechanism unlike any that I'd seen before, which parted the opening to his britches in an easy swipe. Fascinating. He pulled down his britches and then his undergarments, which were gray and foul, revealing a shrivelled, flopping mouse in the nest of a hairful crotch. Then he took me by the waist to pull me atop him. Despite my revulsion I did not resist and allowed myself to be pulled onto his belly. What's more, the unwitting sot had placed me in close proximity to his foul-smelling neck, loose skinned like a turkey's.

"Thatsch nice, very nice," he said, his hairy arms around my waist. "Are you a prossie, love? Listen, I've no money for yer, but if you fancy giving a poor man a ride, thatsch very kind . . . would be mutsch . . . appreescheeayted."

I did not hesitate to sink my fangs in. He gave a deep bellow and tried to push me away. I clung fast with my teeth, while he rolled me from one side to the other, trying to shake me off. I nearly drained the miserable vagrant, so thirsty was I. He lolled unconscious on the bench as I stood up, strengthened though stumbling, drunk from all the liquor in his veins no doubt. I removed his britches and jacket. The britches fit me well at the hips, he being a thin man, though they were long in the leg. The jacket was large on me.

And so, disguised as a man, I headed for the gate of the churchyard. As I emerged from the cover of the yew I staggered backward, unable to believe my eyes. I was in a broad street lined with tall houses, and though it was night they were covered in bright lights of every color. Tall poles topped with yellow light lined the street. Gone were the fields that used to surround my resting place! What was once a secluded English country churchyard in fields was now surrounded by a town unlike any I'd ever seen before, and lights, people! By Satan's dagger, how long had I been asleep?

I ran into the street, where I saw young women dressed in small clothes that scarcely covered them, their bodies half revealed like brothel girls, their hair all unfastened. They shouted and laughed in the street on the arms of men, kissing them on the mouth. I saw other women wearing britches like mine but with womanly garments from the waist up. My britches were no manly disguise amongst these women! I saw a clock on the side of a large church, and the hour was late, past midnight, and all around us this unnatural light, glowing and illuminating us. The fronts of the buildings were very large windows of clear glass, showing garments, shoes, and many other things in so many colors, with large worded signs above the windows. By day these would be selling their wares, I realized.

Of course I knew by now that I had slept for a very long time, into some later age. Bewildered, I felt the pain on my skin that light causes, brought on by the unnatural lights, which were much stronger than the candles and lamps of my time. I headed into a side street, where there was some darkness to comfort my giddy self. I headed on and rounded other corners. I crouched in a corner by some steps and glanced about me. I was tiring still further and would need more blood soon.

Then across the street I made out a staircase leading down to a cellar, upon which were three women standing in line on the steps. They wore britches like mine, only of blue, and their hair was cropped short like a man's. The black door opened, and they passed in. I crossed the road and headed for the steps, hoping to gain passage. In the cellar there would most likely be further darkness, and what's more, here were women, and I fancied that I could pursue one, follow her when she was alone, and take her blood.

I came down the steps and encountered a black door. I pushed, and it opened onto a small black-painted space with another door opposite. Entering, I saw a stout, curly-haired woman seated in an enclosed booth: a gate woman. Behind her was a clock face, not attached to any pendulum, below which hung many outer garments, most probably capes and jackets like mine. I nodded at her, hoping to gain passage.

"It's three pounds after eleven," said the woman.

I put out my hand and took hers. She looked surprised for a moment but did not draw away. Amusement passed across her ruddy features.

"Woman, I have no money, but if you will offer me passage I will work for you for the night."

She broke into a laugh. "Well, I don't get offers like *that* every day. Look, love, I tell you what, I'll let you in this time, seeing as it's only ten past and you asked so nicely. But don't tell anyone or they'll all want to get in free. You won't get a drink with no money though; you'll have to chat someone up, see if they'll buy you drinks!" She laughed, raucously. "Don't think I've seen you before. Have you never been here?"

"My thanks to you, kind woman. No, I have not been to this place before. Tell me, what kind of place is this?"

She gave me a bemused look. "Go on in love and see for yourself before I change my mind."

I pushed the other door and entered what appeared to be a kind of tavern. It was dimly lit, and I saw women, many of them dressed in britches, others in more womanly attire, seated at low tables with candles, on chairs that were red with thin legs. There was a bar backed by a mirror, so I drew away quickly to one side. Rows of bottles were hanging upside down along the top of the mirror and gentle blue light emanated from the top. Etched onto the mirror were the words THE DUNGEON. Hanging from the ceiling were many chains, fulfilling no function but decoration, as far as I could see.

There was loud music playing of a kind that I found disagreeable at first. I looked around for a man who might be willing to purchase a drink for me. I was thirsty for wine or beer. But there were only women in this place. A tavern with only women! I was used to mostly men in the taverns; the women were either tarting their wares or accompanying their husbands or brothers. A woman approached me. She had short hair in a very bright shade of blonde, standing up in long spikes above her head and was wearing black leather britches like mine and a tight black vest. I noticed that her arms were very muscular. She smiled and leaned on the bar. The barmaid came over, and the blonde woman spoke to her.

"Pint of Four-X please." Then she turned to me. "You not drinking anything?"

"I long to drink a flagon of beer, good Mistress, but alas I have no money."

She laughed. "Well, I don't think they've got flagons, but I'll get you a pint if you like. What do you want?"

"This beer is not familiar to me."

"Well, they've got Budvar, Four-X, Grolsch . . . There's this new organic one as well that's s'posed to be good. I haven't tried it yet. The hippy earth-goddess types seem to like it though."

"Would you choose for me, good woman?"

Again she laughed quite heartily, as if I'd made a good joke. "Right-o. Another Four-X please."

I sat on a tall stool with a red cushioned leather seat and let my eyes feast on the score of women in the place. A fine choice. Many were talking in groups. Five women rose and danced together in a group. One of them was a particularly fine beauty with light brown hair in abundance, a fine shape and clear complexion, a fulsome bosom, and lively large wanton eyes. Most charming was her long, elegant neck, which made my mouth water. She was dressed rather rudely in a black corset. The thought of drinking blood from the neck of a beauty like that did often bring me to a passion that bordered on lustfulness! The corseted woman and another drew away from the group and began to dance together, the one putting her arms about the other's neck, both moving lewdly against the other. They kissed, very long and deeply. One even kissed the other on the neck. I felt my own pulse quicken. Women loving women! Why, in all the centuries of my life had I not seen this before? Were they all like this in here? If so, then for a vampire like me who thirsted after the sweet blood of womankind, this presented me with so novel an opportunity. I had only to seduce one, and then . . . . I was jolted out of my reverie as a flagon of beer, made of glass, was placed in front of me.

"There you go," said my drink-buying woman, as she swung her leg over the stool next to me. "You were miles away. Caught you staring! Who are *you* eyeing up then?" I looked at her smiling face.

"Don't be all offended; I'm just kidding about with you. What's your name?"

"My name is Balasa Anuta Moroaïcă."

"Whoa . . . That's a name and a half. Sounds Eastern European. So does your accent. D'you mind me asking where you're from?"

Now there's a question. I chose honesty. "I am not of this

time and place. Though in a crypt near here some time ago I laid down my head to rest, and then I awoke to find myself unclothed in this unfamiliar and bewildering world where women are bold and lustful and lights are bright even at night, seemingly by some magic, rather than the use of fire."

"Fuck," she said. She was looking at me like I was a mad woman. "I didn't understand a word of that, but never mind . . . I'm Liv. My parents are Norwegian. So's my name. But I was born here, in England."

"Ah, a tall, strong Scandinavian. Of Viking blood perchance? I see it in your coloring." She had a handsome face, with strong cheekbones and piercing eyes, blue as ice.

"Yeah, probably. But my real hair color's plain old mousey brown. This blonde's out of a bottle, of course. Crikey, you're drinking that fast."

"As would you had you not had a draft of beer for a hundred years or more. What year are we, in fact?"

"What *year* are we? Are you having me on?" She regarded me with a confused seriousness. "I'm used to people asking me the time, the date, but the year . . . Well, it's the sixth of May, 2005."

"Zounds!" I nearly fell off my stool. The last time I was awake, the last time I was awake . . . My memory fogs . . . and yet I believe it was sometime in the year of 1667."

"Oh! I really love this track. I'm gonna go and have a boogie. You coming?"

"I'm sorry, I don't understand you."

"Ah . . . too much slang maybe, if this isn't your first language. Do you want to dance?"

Dance? I do not dance. When I have, it has been out of necessity, to gain passage into some great house. I take part in dances to mask my identity from those fathers whose daughters and wives I seek to drink from . . . and those dances are formally arranged, with steps and partners and patterns.

"I am not familiar with this music. I fear I am a little weak for dancing."

"Christ, you're serious-faced, aren't you? C'mon. It won't do you any harm."

She took my arm and led me over to the area where the other women were dancing, writhing and jerking, one in front of the other, while others danced together. My Viking lady bobbed about in front of me holding a cigarette, which she held out to a woman nearby who leaned over and lit it for her. The music was a series of very fast beats, with a female voice wailing out over the top of it at various intervals. I mimicked the Viking and bent and straightened my knees to the rhythm, stiff as a wooden horse. It was not a difficult dance to learn; there seemed to be few rules and conventions, and besides, the drink was quickly making me giddy, so little true nourishment had I taken.

SO I'M IN The Dungeon, feeling a bit bored of the same old, same old, when this really gorgeous woman that I've not seen before walks in, with long, black wild hair and a really nice body, all dressed in black leather, trousers tight around her cute arse, but wearing this jacket that's a bit big and which she doesn't even unzip or take off. Looks like she might have borrowed it off her brother or some mate. She's strange looking, with pale skin and a really serious, unsmiling expression on her face. Maybe she's a Goth. I'm on my third pint already, and I'm sitting with Jules and Sam, and they're chatting away about the cricket, which really isn't my thing, so I get up and go over to the bar, thinking I might start a conversation. The beer'd already made me gutsy, and I was up for meeting someone new.

Anyway, I bought her a drink and we talked. She had this

really old-fashioned way of speaking, with a bit of an accent, Eastern European sounding, so I put the strange turns of phrase down to English not being her first language. Well, they get taught to speak proper English don't they, they learn to speak in a formal way that's about fifty years behind. But she's calling me "good Mistress" and "good woman," and she says, "I'm not of this time and place," and gives me this long speech about crypts and bold women, and I can't remember what else. So I start to wonder if she's an art student on a weird performance art project. Or maybe it's some strange and eccentric way of chatting people up, a false persona or something.

And then, and this really got me, she goes and asks me what year it is. I'm starting to feel like I might be on *Candid Camera* any minute now; it's got to be a wind up. Then they put on Baby D, "Let Me Be Your Fantasy," and it's just such a classic and they haven't played it for ages, so I've got to dance, and I've Dutch courage enough to drag her up with me. And she's looking all wooden and uncomfortable on the dance floor. Then Lou comes round with the vodka jellies, and she looks like she wants one, so I buy it for her. She doesn't seem to have any money on her at all, and I get her another beer. What the hell, it's Saturday night, and it feels good to have someone to treat. I'm dishing out the drinks to this hot woman like some sugar daddy.

After downing those she seems to get a bit more into the music, and she's looking around at all the women, and I think, she's a bit happier to be here, when she starts to look pissed. I thought these Eastern European girls were supposed to be able to take their vodka. Then she starts dancing more energetically and swaying her hips.

I give her a smile, and she stops looking around and looks right back at me, very deep into my eyes, in quite a cunning way, like she's got plans for me. It takes me by surprise, as I wasn't expecting her to be that forward. Then she does a strange thing. She moves closer and puts her hands on my neck, one either side. With her fingertips she strokes my neck from top to bottom, then back up again, slowly with a light gentle touch. I put my hands on her waist and we dance like that: her holding my neck, me holding her waist. Jules catches my eye and winks, makes a very unsubtle thumbs-up to me under the table. I pull her a little closer, and she puts her head on my shoulder, facing into my neck. I realize that she's sniffing my neck. She is breathing in deeply, taking in the scent of me. It's a weird thing to do but kind of sexy, so I put my arms right around her.

She whispers in my ear, "Tell me, where do you live? Can we go there now?"

Whoa. I raise an eyebrow. She doesn't waste time. I turn my head down to hers and she looks up at me, dreamy eyed and almost swooning, practically hanging in my arms. She seems excited, breathless. Nice to know I can still have this effect on women. I'm pretty affected right now myself.

"I've got a flat. It's a taxi ride from here."

"Then take me there."

Don't mind if I do.

So we made our way to the door, and I called a cab. I stepped up to the street, but she hung back behind the staircase. The cab pulled up, and she looked frightened. I took her arm and led her up the stairs, opened the door of the cab for her, and actually had to help her get in. It was very strange. As the cab pulled away I realized she really was scared. It raised some questions in my head. I tend to have a busy imagination. I started to think that maybe she was from a really remote village, where there weren't even cars, and had come over here to escape something, or to get a better life. You hear all these stories about traffickers bringing women over as prostitutes. Maybe she'd escaped some pimp only today and still didn't know where she was. Well, I told myself to stop being so far-fetched, but all the same I was wondering what I was getting myself into. She was clinging to my arm with a grip so tight it hurt. She was staring out of the window like a cat startled by headlights, her head darting from left to right, alert, full of adrenaline. She babbled something about undreamt of speed. I put my arm around her and pulled her in toward me. She leaned her head on my shoulder. The taxi driver smirked at us in the rearview mirror.

As we entered her residence, a long bright lamp on the ceiling burst into hideous, dazzling light. I cried out, "No light!"

"Look, are you OK?" she said as she extinguished it by means of a device on the wall. She looked nervous and worried. "Look, if you're not feeling well or something . . . . I can call you another taxi, so you can go home?"

We stood in a corridor by a staircase. Now in the faint light coming in from the street I realized that to a woman of this time, my behavior seemed odd and that I must reassure her. I did not want to leave. Not now that we were alone, her warm blood pulsing close by me, with only her pale Scandinavian skin separating it from me. I smiled and moved toward her. Her breathing quickened as I pressed myself against her until her back was to the wall, then I put my arms around her and kissed her. She kissed back, and her tongue entered my mouth, but I kept my lips from parting fully so that she would not feel my fangs. I marvelled that I had not tried to seduce a woman before. I had not imagined they could possibly want me as much as I them. Normally, when I find my way, as a bat, into their bedchambers they scream as I transform myself, and I must hold them down, bite immediately. There is no time for seduction. Mine has been a long, lonely life.

"Let's go upstairs to my flat," she breathed in my ear.

We went up the stairs, through another door, which she shakily unlocked, so passionate was she for me. Once inside, I kissed her again immediately to avoid her illuminating other bright lights. She had on a jacket, which she removed. I lifted the bottom of her vest, and she raised her arms to let me remove it. I marvelled at the way her gestures, which I had thought so mannish in the tavern, turned to such feminine, swooning responses the more I kissed and undressed her.

I could have had her straight away, drunk of her blood there and then, but she had unbuttoned my jacket and said in a low voice, "You've got nothing on underneath."

Then she was touching my breasts, and I felt a desire rising in me that was stronger than any I'd felt before. Curious, I decided that I would leave the drinking of her until I'd seen where she might lead me.

She dropped my jacket on the floor and led me by the hand to her small bedchamber. She knelt at my feet and removed my britches. The featherbed, with white silken sheets and a soft covering, was marvellously soft as she pushed me back onto it. With her muscular frame, she was far stronger than me, although at my full strength, once I had a draft of her blood inside me, I knew that I would be able to overpower her.

As she kissed my neck, then my breasts and my belly, I felt almost mortal. She laughed at my surprise as she licked at my cunt, not realizing that I hadn't expected it. I laughed, too, for it was she eating me, like she was the vampire drinking my life from me. And when my body quivered and then shook in a violent climax I fancied that she might have shaken the darkness out of me, as for a moment I had stopped thinking of her blood.

But must is must, prey is prey, and blood lust is what makes me, and so I turned her onto her back and moved atop her. I was weak again now, from the energy that my pleasure took from me, and I shook a little. Should I give pleasure first or take her blood now? I kissed her again, and her lip grazed one of my teeth.

"Christ, you're teeth are sharp," she gasped.

I looked into her eyes and moved my hand between her legs. I licked her neck as my fingers penetrated her. I heard her gasps, felt her innocent, unsuspecting pleasure. Could I drain her life, in the midst of such trust and mutual absorption? Her passion moved me. I moved my hand faster and faster as I opened my mouth over her neck. I could not do it. I could not bite. She cried out, and I felt her body move under me, begin to rock. Then before I had time to pull back, her neck lifted off the pillow with the straining of her body. It hit my fang, which pierced her skin.

"Oh, owww!" She pushed me off her and I fell back, nearly tumbling from the bed. "That was fantastic hon, it really was . . . but you bit me so *hard*." She had sat up and put her hand to her neck. The blood was on her fingers. So hard. Little did she know how much harder that bite could have been.

I came toward her again and tenderly, with all the restraint in the world, licked the blood from her neck. Oh, sweet taste of earth, salt, and bitter wine. She shrunk from me and made a face.

"Jeez, that's strange. That's kind of kinky. Do you really get off on that? Wait a minute, I've got some bandages in the kitchen."

She went into another chamber, and when she returned, she said, "Grrr . . . .I like a bit of bite in a girl. Come into my arms."

I lay back in the bed with her. She put her arms around

me from behind and pulled the sheets over us. Never had I been in such close proximity to a woman without draining the lifeblood out of her. Her skin was smooth and soft, like silk. If there was a way I could drink of this one only partially, without harming her, without taking the life from her completely . . . I found myself drifting toward sleep.

And so here we are, lying in bed together, sleeping in the aftermath of fucking fantastic sex. Except that I woke up a few hours after we fell asleep, and now I'm horny as hell again. There was something almost primordial about the way she made love to me. A kind of pure, unbridled lust in her eyes, like she could have devoured me, eaten me alive or something. It really got me going. And then she bit me. She drew blood, for fucks sake. And now I'm lying awake, looking at her, wondering about her. Balasa. What a strange name.

I get out of bed and go to the toilet. She doesn't wake up. When I get back into the bedroom, I have a strong urge to wake her up to make love again. Well, why not? I stand at the end of the bed, looking at her body. I think of her biting my neck. I think of vampires. I know I have an overactive imagination. Imagine if I were a vampire, looking down at her body, hovering over her as a bat. What if I bite her like she bit me? Could I do it, could I enjoy the taste of her blood like she seemed to enjoy mine?

I glide over her sleeping body without a sound. She lies on one side, her body a pale, moonlit landscape, lily white. It's as if she has been here for centuries, her smooth curves and valleys emerging from hard rock, softened and weathered by time, wind, and water. The white satin sheet flows over her thighs like a river. If I bite, there on her side, how will the blood come? Will it form a stream, running down quick, making a small tarn in her belly button before it trickles off again? Or will it ooze, viscous and slow, a lava flow edging down her back, pooling dark on the sheets?

I settle at her side and lay my hand on her hip gently, not wanting to wake her, and turn her onto her back. She stays limp as I move her. I jump as her black eyes open. I grab her wrists and push them down into the pillow on either side of her head. She struggles, so I sit astride her, pinning her down. It's easy; she's smaller than me and weak.

I lean into her, smell the place where her neck meets her ear, close my mouth around her earlobe. My breasts touch her body.

I am going to do it now.

I move my mouth down to her neck. No, I can't bear to bite her neck, so I move down farther, to her shoulder. I find a place in the top of her shoulder that my teeth can pinch and hold on to. I hear her suck her breath in. I close my eyes and bite, hard. It takes a long time for my teeth to pierce the skin. I almost think I've botched it. Then she whimpers with pain, pants for me to stop, breathes hard, trying to bear it. I haven't drawn a lot of blood. Red rubies form on her white skin. I taste it with my tongue. It's hot and salty.

It's disgusting. It makes me want to gag. "Ugggh!"

Then the next thing I know, she's got her teeth into me, really hard this time, so hard it's really, really painful, like daggers in my neck. I'm lying on top of her, but I can't pull away, she's so firmly hooked into me.

I finally manage to tear myself away, then I push her, quite violently, and she falls onto the floor. But she's really opened up my neck. It's gushing. I feel sick and dizzy. There is blood on the pillow, on the sheets. I look at her mouth, and there is blood all over it. I think I am going to faint. I grab the phone and dial 911. I can hardly talk. I ask for an ambulance. I tell them I've stabbed myself in the neck, I'm bleeding, I'm bleeding severely. I give my address. I lie back on the bed. If she really is a vampire she could get me now. She could finish me off, now that I'm so weak. I'm an atheist; I don't keep crucifixes. All the garlic's in the fridge. But she doesn't. She just looks at me. She looks odd. She looks sad. I open the window next to the bed. When the ambulance arrives, I'll throw my keys down out of the window. I should stay on the bed, not go down; I might collapse.

I hear the siren, see the blue light flashing. I shout out to them, drop the keys.

"We'll be up right away. Try and stay calm."

I look back at her, but she's not there. She's gone. Then there's a fluttering at my left ear. A bat flies out of the window into the street.

Feast

JEN CROSS

I WAS SO hungry that night I couldn't eat. You ever get hungry like that, hungry for something they don't make anymore, some old recipe that got passed right down into the dirt, buried, lost to you and yours, although your mothers, those forebears, would speak of it to each other once in a while over your head while you played under the kitchen table, listening to them talk—pass not so much particular words but a tone of voice, a sigh, something that dripped and was sweet and thick with contagion and cornmeal, and your mouth began to water, and then you made a noise that interrupted them, brought them back to this reality, and then the moment passed and you couldn't quite figure out what had happened? You know what I'm talking about?

That *something* that I'd heard in their voices was what I'd been hungering after for weeks, and it wasn't to be found in my kitchen. Finally, one frustrating Friday night, I gave up ignoring the hunger, and decided it was time to trawl. I tossed my half-emptied dinner bowl and fork into the sink, threw on a quick change of clothes—my sweetest red gingham dress with the plunging neckline, a sweater the color of clotted cream, weathered brown motorcycle boots—and went for a drink, or three, in the hope I might forget to be hungry for a while.

A butch sat at the bar with her back to the world, like

Quasimodo finally run out of town. Her denim jacket vest stretched across broad shoulders like newly poured cement. The boulders of her thighs jutted away from her body, and her boots rested easily on the filthy red linoleum floor. Her greasy blonde hair hung in dregs against her shoulder blades, slicked away from her forehead with something that may have started out as style but now just looked like sweat and a lack of attention after a few days spent under a car. She was gorgeous and filthy.

She held the same position for two hours, while I went through drink after drink, obtusely attempting to banter with a bartender so sullen that she wouldn't even turn on the TV for those of us trying to run away from the voices in our heads. The butch didn't get up, didn't even raise her eyes when asking for another beer. She'd gone through half a dozen pints and a pack of cigarettes in the time that I'd been watching her from the other end of the bar. After I ran out of singles for the jukebox, it was her stillness that finally mesmerized and fascinated me.

Then I noticed the tattoos that ran along her forearms. I squinted to try and make them out, but the bar was too dark, and I was far enough on my way to drunk that, rather than helping me to see clearly, the room just went blurry and seemed to be giggling. I joined in, with a sharp laugh at myself, which got both the bartender's and Quasimodo's attention.

"What?" They said in unison.

To the bartender, I raised my glass in a half-hearted toast and shrugged. She turned back to her magazine while I downed my drink.

To Quasimodo, I then turned my sexiest, which is ultimately my drunkenest, smile, and said, "I was trying to read you."

The woman slid like night across the empty stools between us and presented me with a close-up look at her arms. The jacket was rolled up at the cuffs, exposing the ham of her thick forearms. Down the right, in a thinnish blue-black script, ran a list: *hambre, hunger, faim, fame,* and so on. Skimming the left forearm ran a similar list for the word *thirst.*

I wondered what ran down her back. Don't think I didn't know whom I was dealing with.

"Oh," I breathed. "Thank you." I cocked my head slightly, looked at her through the curl of my bangs, and offered my hand. "I'm Desrée."

"Esse," she said, taking my hand gently in the meat of hers and pressing it carefully and completely to her lips.

"Ah," I sighed as she released my fingers. "So good to meet you." She said nothing, focusing on her cigarette for a moment. I bent my head down over my glass, running my hands through my curly short hair, and considered my next move. My fingers felt hot, and my body swollen . . . well, swelling.

When I looked up again, the big woman was staring at me.

"You're empty." The voice that seeped from Esse clogged every pore I never knew I had. Her voice was filled with crags: a rough-hewn, too-many-cigarettes-and-bourbon, dragged-through-glass-strewn-back-lots kind of voice.

"Yes," I answered, although I didn't know exactly what I was confirming for her.

"You ready—"

"I will be soon enough if you keep talking to me."

" . . . for another?" she finished, as though I hadn't spoken, indicating my glass.

"Oh. Yes." Again I wondered what I was telling her. She raised a couple of fingers at the bartender, who brought her another pint and me another Jack and Coke. She lit a cigarette off the one she was finishing, then inhaled deep and long on the butt, sucking the rest of the life out of it. I felt the suction between my legs, and was suddenly not at all sure that the aroma of my arousal was not mingling with the smell of beer, cigarette smoke, and sweat around us.

"You've been watching me," she said through a cloud of exhaled smoke. I breathed a sigh of relief, as I'd become concerned that she only spoke in one- and two-word sentences.

I nodded. "Yes—uh, that's right."

"Why?"

"Well." I considered this, sipping my drink. There were any number of reasons—her size, her prowess of consumption, her apparent patience, her tattoos—those lips, her goddamn enormous hands. I decided not to give too much away. "You're the only other person up here."

"*Mmm-hmm*," she said, cloudy with doubt.

I took a long drink then, and felt a calmness settle over me. The words *I can wait all night* hovered around my shoulders. I glanced at her, but she'd assumed her position again: folded down over her drink, massive forearms lain on the bar in front of her, right hand raising periodically to offer that fleshy mouth a long suckle on a cigarette. No wonder she went through so many; a single inhalation took the thing down halfway. I felt some weight, like a certainty, press on my shoulders. We sat in silence while our pulses spoke. My heart pounded toward her, telling a story of starvation and longing. Telling a story many years in the making.

Ready, I thought. *Yes.*

So I tipped my head back, exposing the smooth length of my neck, and emptied my glass down my throat. I felt the immediate heat of her attention on me, like some otherworldly thing rising from her shoulders; I imagined her dark eyes blazing. She hadn't moved, but I knew then she'd been watching me just as I'd been watching her—but with a different sort of sight. I felt her throb to life next to me, and felt myself thicken and open in response. The bar was dark and humid. The bartender stayed out of our way. She knows when a jig is up. She did not warn either of us away from the other, although I imagine she thought she ought to have.

Esse stood just as I rose. For all of her imbibing, there was nothing unsteady about her. She offered her massive body as a foil for my consumptive one, which was wobbling on those stupid boots. I opened my purse to settle up, but Esse eased me gently and assuredly away from our stools, shoving open the heavy oak door like a curtain for me to pass through. Outside, the air was warm and damp, late summer making its last stand, and dull brown and yellow leaves shushed under our feet as we walked. She didn't touch me—a fact I found almost unforgivably considerate—but I felt her surround me still. We walked into the night.

In my boots, I stood a bit taller than Esse. Now, I am not a slight girl, some wisp of a thing. I stand an actual five feet ten and weigh substantially more than any runway model who'd boast such a height: Several Naomi Campbells could probably fit inside my skin. I tell you this so you can properly picture my reaction as we reached the curb, which was flooded by some backed-up storm drain. The rain that had fallen earlier in the day had brought down leaves and twigs, and the curbside was filthy and slick with motor oil, runoff from neighborhood gardens, twenty-five-cent-chip bags, and other assorted trash all gathered in the dark waters. I hesitated, preparing to make the leap halfway into the street in order to avoid soiling my boots but suddenly became weightless. I had been lifted as she pounded through the waters. Her hands around my waist and hips were possessive, the way one is possessive with a friend's television when carrying it down to the moving van—there was no grabbing or grasping, no feeling up or taking advantage of her position—and as soon as we reached drier asphalt, she set me down and kept on walking, assuming I would continue to match her stride.

Through my shock, I exhaled and released my belly from its years-long confinement held up against my spine. An open belly is a dangerous thing, and mine had some words for me about a lack of fulfillment.

"Tell me," she said then, and for a second, still caught in my reverie of being carried for the first time since I was seven years old, I thought she wanted to hear about that. But then I felt for her energy and realized she was talking about something else.

"About what?" I asked.

Esse slashed her dark eyes in my direction, trying to read me reading her. Her broad cheeks pushed back, and she offered me the promise of a smile, deep dimple parting the left cheek from itself. "About the hunger. I like to hear."

I unfurled myself into the thicket of the night's dense heat, her attention and desire. I spoke of men afraid of my need, shamed into flinging *slut* as an epithet, when I wanted more than a woman was supposed to, and of women lovers similarly shamed. I spoke of being filled yet left empty, said how I didn't know what was wrong with me and wondered why couldn't I be like normal people, normal women, those women who could come thirty times an hour or come just from the pressure of tight jeans in their crotch. I spoke of the images I didn't want to feed on anymore, a rapist face I'd open my eyes to keep from imagining and how my wide open kisses or fucking was so frightening to some people, alarming, like I was somehow too present for their taste.

I felt my eyes well but cut them to the side and frowned, shutting off the tears. I didn't want to cry with her. I wanted to be the hard woman she'd met in the bar, diamond to her flint, strong enough to strike sparks. We continued to walk, and I felt her attention dance and flicker around me, present but unconfining. I paused to collect my sadness and push it back where it belonged, while we walked along a long row of ornate Victorians, each one tucked in and quiet, eyes shut to the night, even as its surface burst forth with color and frills. We passed a moon garden, walked through the scent of night jasmine and datura.

"I don't need to ask you about yours, do I . . . your hunger?" I said, placing my hand on her bare forearm where it said *hambre* and held her like that for a second, feeling something that could have been a shiver or just the night moving, buckling. She stopped, caught my hip with her right hand, and turned me, using my own momentum, into her body, into those hungry and thirsty arms. In spite of the couple inches I had on her, I felt myself reaching up to kiss her. Our lips met, firm and questioning at first, then my mouth slipped open to take her in. Esse gasped in response, pulling at my very breath.

We fed. Her mouth against mine was alive, full and ripe. The kiss was like a reintroduction, an ancient bone memory rekindled. I relaxed my body against hers, and she held me up. I moved my hands up from her chest to her face, then slid around to scrape the back of her neck with my nails, to finger and pull at that hair. She unleashed a tight, cramped desperate moan, the smallest sort of admission, like she'd slid open a lock within herself. I flooded in response, hardly restraining myself from climbing right into her clothes and riding her wherever she wanted to take me.

Don't think I didn't feel it when she was kissing me. Don't think I didn't know what she thought I was getting into. But she had never met someone as hungry as me, with so much to feed someone.

Her hands popped open like a vise clamp sprung, and

I pulled my hands from her like you'd pull off a lead scarf, trailing my weight across where I wanted her to remember.

"No, you don't have to tell me," I mumbled, sucking at the blood welling from my bottom lip, as we began to walk once again, the both of us rather wobbly this time.

As she turned from me, Esse said to the sidewalk, "They never touch me." I had no response. I knew it was true.

We arrived at my little rental bungalow, stuck like a sore between two ancient Victorians, and snuck in the back door like teenagers past curfew. Without turning on any lights, I led her into the darkness of my kitchen. I was so hungry. I felt like I hadn't eaten in years.

The glow from the streetlights offered enough illumination that the kitchen seemed to throb. Esse placed her hands beneath my arms and lifted me up onto the green Formica countertop. She shoved my dress up my thighs, took the knife I abandoned after chopping onions and garlic for dinner, and tore through my panties.

And, yes, then she fed. The room was filled with the hot metallic pungence of me. I covered her face with my blood and juices. And as she gorged, she plunged into me. I clutched her to my flesh, my hands grasping like an infant's: ungraceful, brutish, and demanding. I took all she had to give. We filled together.

The streetlight outside blinked out, as it does every night. In the darkness, she shoved farther into me, her free arm wrapped completely around my thigh to anchor me. I felt myself burning through and taking pleasure in the damage of her touch. I rode her mouth, my labia plumped and aching for more. I fed.

We were drenched and messy. She kept her clothes on, like they always do. My hands stayed plain and white and shaking. I took her arm, unwrapped it, and bit down hard over where it said *Faim*. I left a bruise that would thicken to purple, then sicken to a yellow-brown. It would warn others away. She was mine to feed from. We were each other's troughs.

other women had seen this hunger in me, but it was as though they didn't know what to do with it, met it with confusion and worry, took the hunger in their hands instead of my body, and then laid it back down when they couldn't get it to close its mouth, stop crying, go to sleep. I blamed myself, blamed the rapist, the one who'd forced the orgasm from my early body and left it always tinged with blood and sharp edges every time it started to creep up on me, slicing through to leave me wounded once again. I wanted to know release, satiation. I wanted to sleep as my lovers had slept after sex, that exhausted knowing of pleasure wound through my body, muscles devastated and joyous.

When the streetlight flicked back to life, I caught a glimpse of the needles in her mouth, the contortions of cheekbone and upper jaw required to allow for the extended incisors. I knew she was allowing me to see. Her face was smeared, and she stood unsteadily. My throat was raw from yelling and I felt like a wet mop or something even less sturdy, a wet rag—ready at any second to dissolve into bonelessness—but still I tingled with vibrations of lust.

She stared at me, reaching for my hand while I panted. "More?" she said, in a voice that laced hope with preparation for denial.

"Oh please, yes." I ached. She lifted me and twisted us so she could drop me onto my kitchen table. She shoved several fingers into my mouth while with the other hand she opened her fly and released her cock. I inhaled those thick meaty fingers. She smelled like cassia bark, like leaf mould in the redwood groves in spring, like cigarettes, like my own cunt. I

FEAST   [255]

wanted it all in me, all her scent and self. I fed.

She leaned over me a moment, free hand pressed against the wood and cheek against my chest, groaning at the attention I gave to her fingers. I could feel the coolness of her cock against my right inner thigh. She twisted my torso to remove my sweater, then slid the dress' straps down over my shoulders to reveal my bare breasts, nipples round and hard. She took nearly the whole of my left breast into her mouth, swabbing with her broad, hot tongue. My head swam, and I bit down on the flesh of her fingers, crying out around them. Her tongue spiraled around and in, closing down on my nipple, which she suckled and stroked. I couldn't stay still, rotating and undulating my hips beneath her. Every stroke of her tongue across my nipple brought another stabbing throb inside my cunt, and I ached into the emptiness there.

She remained surprisingly immobile above me, the steady shore I slammed myself against. After an eternity of attention to one breast, now swollen and raw, she slowly swung her head to the other side, giving my right breast the same treatment. By the time she finished, I was thrashing beneath her, my arms slick against her hair, my legs locked around her solid hips, boot leather scraping against the denim covering her ass.

She released the fat bubble of my nipple with a pop and lifted her broad face. She said, "More?"

I didn't think I could speak, my mouth was so dry from moaning and gasping around her fingers. I spit them out, pulled her head up to mine with both my hands, and kissed her.

"Oh yes, please," I croaked against her lips.

While shifting her hips slightly to get me to unlock my legs, she palmed the length of her cock and led it to the mouth of my cunt, slicking me open with two fingers. The moan slid out of her like a demon released.

"Aw, you're empty—"

Her cock pushed me open, shoved against and into the tight muscle of my cunt, and I cried out in response. She throbbed into me, slid the length out with a yank of her hips, then slowly pushed back in again. There was a gentleness like uncertainty, and I suddenly felt ravenous.

"No, no, Esse, *fuck* me." My voice sounded desperate, and I flushed with embarrassment, suddenly remembering to prepare for her not to be up to the task. But then she rocked her hips in hard, pinning me against the table, and my heart and body fell open.

We might have been there for days, her body hard over mine, slamming into the wet length of me. The sun might have risen and set, the eye of the moon opened to bless us. Both our mouths were bloodied and bruised, and sore streaks of red ran down her back where my nails had dug in under her jacket and tank top. My neck was bruised and pocked on both sides, and I woke every neighbor with my screams.

Then she said, so small against my ear, "Please, I need you." An urgency filled her thrusts. I took my right hand from the back of her neck and slid it down between us, fingering my clit as softly and steadily as I could manage, given my desperation.

"Tell me how you do it. I like to hear," she breathed into my mouth, palming one of my tits as she continued rocking into me. I closed my eyes and felt the gathering in my cunt, the ache, the build trembling in the thigh muscles tensed around her, while the soles of my boots pressed flat against the table.

"Slow down," I panted, "and give it all to me." Immediately, she slid the full length of her cock out of me, paused for breath until I cried out, then pressed back in.

"That's it. Do it like that . . . like that—" She fucked me that way, listening to my repetition like an incantation, like speaking could make it so, till I came, round and high and trembling. My added slickness smoothed the way for her, and she came against me when I wrapped my legs up around her wide hips again. And then I passed out on my kitchen table, dripping onto the phone bill, the gas bill, a letter inviting me to my high school reunion, and an invitation to take a Discover card.

When I woke, we were on my bed, and I was covered with my mother's old handmade quilt. Esse's body was hot and hard next to mine. She'd removed her boots as well as mine and had pulled my dress back up over my shoulders. She snored softly, turned away, but as soon as I began to stretch and move into the morning light, she turned back toward me, somehow surrounding me with her gaze and uncertain smile. Her eyes searched mine, something, something . . .

"More?" I said, shifting my thighs against each other, and brushing a stray hair from her cheek.

"Yes, more, please," was her response. And then she kissed me, both of us grinning, our teeth sharp and clicking against the others'. She rolled on top of me and nudged me back open. The room filled with the scent of us. I opened my mouth and fed.

Master of the Hunt

RAKELLE VALENCIA

IT WAS A dark evening, which I just adored. I loved to wrap myself in darkness. Curled up on an overstuffed, hunter green couch with a deep-violet, velvet throw ensconcing my lower half. I held a cup of black coffee to my nose, breathing in the warm aroma that was once my drug and my master. I can't drink coffee now; it doesn't sit well with me anymore. And I much prefer a different beverage, a drink so much more powerful and compelling that it owns me.

Dog jumped onto the couch, dumping his large body into the cushions behind my bent legs. He put his heavy muzzle across my thigh, sighed, and waited. I stroked his square, meaty head, smoothing the thick fur between his upright ears. His pert ears were always up, flattening only in anger. Running the fuzzy lobe triangles, one at a time, through pointer finger and thumb, I caressed them to their tip. His eyes strained to stay awake, but finally the big wolf succumbed to sleep.

We've been together a while, Dog and I. There was that incident upon meeting when one of us might not have survived. There've been times recently when he has tested the boundaries, this lupine friend of mine, wanting more than his share of a kill. He is a large, black Siberian wolf with silver highlights running along his underbelly. Lanky in body, he is all muscle, weighing close to ninety pounds, a huge specimen for the breed. It hadn't always been so.

I had found the scrawny, young pup on my first blood lust. This was the time that it had come down to him or me. I had been lost in the forest as a youthful upstart, thrown from my horse during a hunt . . . Well, allow me to regress further than that.

It would have been embarrassing to my family of importance if I had not arrived back at the hosting Schloss riding in the pack just behind the hunt master. Hounds baying, formal coattails flying, lathered horses galloping, and I was late. In fact, I wasn't even there.

The morning hunt rode off in pursuit of the fox, following well-guided, highly bred hounds kept on the scent by whippers-ins. I had not even aroused out of bed. The horn blow startled me deathly awake. Pulling on breeches and glossy-shined, leather boots in haste, I grabbed for my formal coat and hunt cap, and raced to the gilded stables.

Mmm . . . I must say how my head pounded in dull rhythm to the slapping of my feet on the cobblestones, jarring my aching neck and shoulders. Too much champagne I imagined . . . or too much evening activity with the hosting princess.

My flight was also hard-pressed in trying to escape the sinking low of humility I would suffer if my family were to hear of who still lay in my bed. On the hunt field I was determined to redeem myself, so much so that no one would dare whisper of last night's events, and the princess who had leapt upon me with wild abandon, like a rabid animal before the silk bed linen had even been exposed.

She had teased me to the room with wine and champagne, whispering absurdities in my ear. And in the darkened hallways her kisses had become so adamant that she had pierced my tongue with her careless teeth, blood smearing both our lips to glistening red. Like others before her, I had only thought of her curiosity to be with another woman. I thought her clumsy with inexperience. But how wrong I was.

When the door of my assigned guest rooms closed with a definitive thud, she tore at my silk shirt to suckle at my breast. Her ministrations of my nipples were harsh enough to make me come immediately in spasms while leaning back against the door. Still, she didn't stop, and I wondered if she were apt to tear the tight nubs off between shearing teeth.

Delighted, I hoisted the folds of her many flouncing skirts to find a rare lack of undergarments. My fingers probed her slippery crease, plunging one into her snug hole so fast that she released my nipples at the shock of it. Her eyes flashed a demonic golden color as she squirmed away from my finger and dragged me to bed, sharp fingernails clawing through silk to mark the pasty flesh of my arms with stripes of angry red.

Rolling around on the covers, we tore at each other until we both lay naked, bodies so similar. Mine had the hunger of a man; to lust, to conquer, to sink what I could into her creamy depths until she screamed her pleasure behind the hand that would cover her mouth. Her hunger seemed heightened, somehow inexplicable, but her hunger was great nonetheless. I knew she wanted me, had to have me, and I would give myself to her in any way as long as I could just be in her.

She lapped at the skin of my neck as I prodded her hungry twat with three fingers, then four. By the fifth finger, she was grasping my skin between her teeth and trying not to scream her pleasure as the little princess pumped and humped my entire hand into her lustful center.

That's when I felt it. She bit me. In answer to the pricks of her teeth and the trickle of warm blood, I curled my hand into a balled fist and rammed her in rhythm to her suckling sounds.

I must have passed out in euphoria when her sphincter clasped around my wrist and waves of her orgasm rolled over my clenched hand. I felt my head swimming like the very life was being yanked out of me. Did I call out to her? My ears rang with her steady sucking of my neck, louder and louder, until my own body was awash with tremors.

I believed that I had fallen into a deep sleep that hadn't roused until the damned horn blast. And I was late for the hunt.

With my imported Oldenburg charger, I decided to dash through the dense forest, a shortcut to catch the fleeing pack and race for the position directly behind the hunt master. I felt would not have had to vie for the coveted position long; lords and ladies would yield. With my last disgrace still on noble minds, riders would hold back in hopes of yet another folly that I had become infamous for, like the one when I passed the hunt master. One should never pass the hunt master; it just wasn't proper. Even if that master was a slow clod riding a farmer's plug, that wasn't fit for a common field-plow draft.

But I digress. Back to the race through the forest that explains that fateful event, between Dog and I. The Oldenburg, my fine, fleet Warmblood, had stumped a root, wrenching a shoe to a clattering racket. He stumbled to his knees but recovered, unfortunately not before throwing me clear of stirrups, saddle, reins and all. The frightened beast ran as if Satan himself were at his heels.

My cussing should have been heard for miles. Not very ladylike. Then again, I was dressed in a man's breeches and known for my rebellious ways. For all of my carrying on there would be no rescue. This I had ultimately known.

I was hungry and my head thumped loud enough for me to hear the rush of blood through my veins, my arteries. The forest was dark, almost black, and I should have been frightened; instead, I found solace in its shroud.

Peculiarly I could smell the musk of scents left by predators to mark their territory, and I could smell a recent carnage cleaned from the moist, mossy ground. My senses had grown extremely heightened, acute as a predator's. Perhaps it was the forest's influence.

My stomach growled, driving me to distraction. Rounding my tongue over my dried lips, I was surprised to cut it on a sharp tooth. I hadn't recalled hitting the ground so hard in my fall that I had chipped a tooth.

No time to think on it, I recognized that I was sucking my own tongue of blood while also craving to lick smooth flesh in such a sickly manner that I shoved a coat sleeve up to pacify my need with the slathering of my forearm's delicate side. There was a pounding, this time from the small purple veins coursing through the thin, exposed wrist.

A new scent on the dense forested air caught me with force, in time to rescue me from the pain of gnawing at my own skin. Prey, the freshly spilled blood of prey, reeked havoc through my nostrils and tortured my mind. I followed new inner callings to come upon a rangy wolf pup, no more than two years old, struggling with the last fight of life from a glen fawn.

My approach was without caution; I was driven from deep within. The black, matted wolf pup flattened to the ground over its prey and growled, showing blood-tainted teeth that I would have groveled to lick clean on any woman. Undaunted I continued forward.

He meant to keep his kill. I meant to have a taste of it. The white underbelly and spotted, soft hide beckoned me to drink from it. Blood gushed from the baby deer's gashed throat and I rushed, thinking even a drop soaked up by moss and mud would be a waste.

Dog, a mere pup at the time, lunged. We both went down in a tangled tussle to roll on the forest floor, not fighting for our lives per se, but fighting for the right to drink of the tender fawn's blood. I grabbed him by the scruff on both sides of his filthy neck then sunk my teeth into him, receiving a mouthful of fur, skin, and sinewy muscle. I sucked of him heartily, having pricked through his jugular vein. But his taste on my tongue was not what I had wanted when the succulent fawn's odor still tantalized my nostrils. I tossed the mongrel from me. With a yelp, he had yielded readily to share in his meal, waiting on the periphery, sulking, until I had had my fill.

That was the first time I had had dire need of the salty, metallic juices. Since then, Dog prefers to keep to the forests and glens, while I do the deed in castle courtyards and town market alleys.

That brings us from the day I was bitten by the rabid, infectious princess to today, thirty-five years later. Dog and I don't look much older than those youthful times. We've aged only to a prime.

I am hosting master of the hunt now. My Schloss has gained in wealth and superiority, by the surrounding royal families withering away to sniveling, sparring offspring in control of each estate. The young, virile heirs had fallen. I'm sure that the stories of their untimely deaths must give the correlating clue as to their demise, brushed away each time by fantasies, ghost stories, thugs and thieves; others' supposed realities.

The little princess remains, the rabid princess that I thought I had bedded, when in fact she had consumed me. We had not spoken until more recently, when my prowling of the defenseless aristocrats, feeding the curse that had befallen my soul, brought our paths to crossing once again. On that one pagan celebratory evening, the infectious, petite girl strolled

over to take my arm and murmured, "I see you are doing well."
And when she smiled, as the moon was high, those sharp
fangs I had years ago viewed as particularly quaint, pierced
her probing tongue, allowing a drop of red to smear her pearly
whites.

A tease. I held back. It was bizarre enough to be at the formal
ball in a man's tailored coat and the starched white breeches
that I had become fond of donning, but to suck from another
woman's mouth in the midst of a posh ballroom . . . no, no, no.
I *tsked* at her behavior, more to gain control of my own cravings.
It wasn't purely the blood lust calling to me because I had fed
earlier. I wanted her. I wanted to run my salivating tongue
over her alabaster skin, suckling in the most tender of spots
until red pockmarks dotted her pale body crying for release.
I wanted my own canine fangs to scratch a bloody path. And
I wanted to bury myself in her musky, mossy personal scent,
tantalizing my nostrils, arousing me in the ways of the dark,
dense, wild forest.

Not here. Not now. Not ever again. I shook her hand from
my arm and left the room. Frustration coursed through my
blood as I mounted a new favorite hunt stallion, riding astride,
charging into the crisp, moist night air and galloping the
shortcut through the solace of my forest.

Keen in the all-too-familiar surroundings, my senses alerted
to the sounds of lighter hoof beats behind me; the fronts shod,
the backs unshod, traveling swiftly, almost blindly haphazard.
I was being hunted. The princess no doubt.

Reining the hefty steed to a skidding halt, I doubled back
off the path through a packed thicket where I knew the heavy
wood to thin then open into a small, hidden clearing. The area
became alive with the soft noises of the night, heard only by a
natural hunter; a predator.

An owl hooted, obtrusively demanding the identity of its

intruder. Deer scurried almost silently, disturbing my ears like raking fingernails on a schoolmaster's blackboard, and the trickling stream screamed over slippery, rounded rocks standing in its path. I waited.

She had made prey of me once before, but the tables were turned. The prim princess ripped by, riding sidesaddle on a silvery-gray mare, golden tresses escaping braided bondage, silk petticoats and skirt flying freely from the bottom of her tight bodice. She spun her head in what appeared to be confusion, that, or she was listening for me. The princess could perhaps even detect my breathing. I knew this because she was what I had become, what she had made of me.

My mount lunged from the thorny thicket. I scented trickles of warm blood oozing ever-so-slightly from scratches marking his square, bold shoulders. We were upon the princess when her nose also caught the alluring odor wafting on the breezes.

She wheeled the feminine, elegant mare near to slamming my stallion. I leapt, engulfing the royal pastry in my hungry arms to fall tumbling upon the mossy earth. Her glint of bared teeth in the shadowy moonlight attested to a snarl and a readiness to bite.

White, glowing mounds of flesh humped tantalizingly just above the princess' strung corset. I was the one to make the bite, marking a fine, porcelain orb with the half-moon shape of my upper front teeth, dotted on both ends by accentuated holes. I wanted to linger and suck what little I could, but her nails slashed across my cheek. I had to roll away. The rabid princess set upon me.

Down I went, flopped over onto my back in the dew-slickened moss and fern, pounced on by my own quarry. Her needy, little cunt already ground over my pelvis as I lay prone on the chilled ground. She sat upright, riding me as if she were on her fancy silver mare, breaking into a trot over my hips, her head thrown back, mouth agape as if she would howl.

She would not conquer me tonight, as my own private needs had not been satiated in some thirty years by another living being. I could not in all of this time love without killing. I could not bite in over three-tens of years without feeding. My strength was never matched, my stamina never met. And Dog had always cleaned up the carnage of whatever I had left decimated from my lovemaking.

With one stealthy twist of my body and a whack of my leg I threw the petite wench from me to land on her belly in the moss and mud. Grabbing at her bare ankles, pulling her to me, my hands walked up her petticoats to find no pantaloons safeguarding her creamy crease. I sunk my hand sideways along her wet crevice, my thumb teasing circles around her puckered nether hole.

Images in my mind blazed of flesh that could survive my sexual onslaught, images that were so wholly encompassing, so passionately inflaming that I slashed at the intricate lacings of her corset, releasing the flesh I had to have and had to devour.

The vampire princess moaned at my invasions, in my mind, urging me to sample of her velvety cunt. I stabbed a pointer finger into her wet lusciousness, wishing I could thrust my entire head into her heaving pussy hole. I wanted to crawl into her, to be a part of her, so desperate was my hunger.

I punctured the meat of her soft sides with jagged, sharpened canines and with an unearthly hand, tugged the locks of her golden hair at the nape of that fine, porcelain neck. Let her howl now, I thought to myself with glee.

I drank of her then, mind, body, and soul, pounding my fingers deep within her orifices, to draw them out and pound again, lapping at the skin along her spine, nipping at her sides, grasping at her long tendrils until I felt my own release building.

She did howl, as her tiny holes wrapped about my fingers, clamping and unclamping until my own body convulsed in time to the waves of spasms coursing through her inhuman flesh. She howled, and my voice rose to meet hers in a death-defying scream that rent the night air.

Screams traveled on the early morning mist, and were what ghost stories and forest legends were made of, scaring small children who would not willingly go to bed when told, and calling four-legged beasts to the woods to feast. Inhuman screams and howls from mouths of sharpened, glinting teeth warning prey to travel far enough at bay and wrapping those that could emit such sounds in a shroud of solitary blackness; a darkened solace.

About the Contributors

CRYSTAL BARELA'S short stories are published in the anthologies *Rode Hard, Put Away Wet: Lesbian Cowboy Erotica*, *Call of the Dark: Erotic Lesbian Tales of the Supernatural*, and *Ultimate Lesbian Erotica 2006*. She will also be featured in the upcoming anthology, *Lipstick on Her Collar*. When not writing Crystal enjoys the outdoors, photography, and spending time with the love of her life. Visit http://erotikryter.blogspot. com/ to find out more about Crystal's writing or e-mail her at erotikryter@bluebottle.com.

BETTY BLUE regrets not killing more people. When not prowling the dark alleys of San Francisco in search of depravity, she can be found sipping tea and cheating at kitten poker. Betty's fiction has appeared in *Best Bisexual Erotica*, *Best Lesbian Erotica*, *Best Women's Erotica*, *Best Lesbian Love Stories*, *Hot Lesbian Erotica*, and *Best of Best Lesbian Erotica*.

TULSA BROWN is an award-winning novelist in another life and genre. She began writing erotica in 2003 and her short fiction has appeared in over a dozen anthologies. She was a runner-up for the 2005 Rauxa Prize for erotic fiction, and in 2006, her gay romance novel *Achilles' Other Heel* was published by Torquere Press. Her mother does not know what she is up to.

Jen Cross is a writer, writing group facilitator, and member of the dyke erotica collective *Dirty Ink*. Her stories appear (some as Jen Collins) in such anthologies as *Set in Stone*, *Back to Basics*, *Best Fetish Erotica*, and the forthcoming *Glamour Girls* and *Naughty Spanking Stories A–Z 2*.

Longtime activist María Helena Dolan makes her home in the Atlanta area. Her stories, essays, and columns have appeared in numerous publications and anthologies, including *Southern Voice* and *Best Lesbian Erotica*. She loves good wine, home-grown organics, dark chocolate, the resident feline supremacists, and her sometimes astonished but always intrigued Old Lady.

Jewelle Gomez, writer and activist, is the author of seven books, including her novel, *The Gilda Stories*, which was the winner of two Lambda Literary Awards (fiction and science fiction) and over the past 13 years has become a cult favorite. She was on the founding board of GLAAD and the Astraea Lesbian Foundation. Visit her at www.jewellegomez.com.

Kim-Lin Hooper lives near Oxford, England, with her girlfriend, her gay ginger cat, and his long-haired boyfriend. She writes short stories, works in arts development, and is planning to study for an MA in creative writing. "Girl Eats Girl" is her first published story.

Bianca James is an ex-Goth, nomadic genderqueer activist, writer, and translator of Japanese. Her writings have appeared in *Best American Erotica 2006*, *Ultimate Lesbian Erotica 2005*, and many other anthologies, magazines and websites. She recently appeared on *The Tyra Banks show*. Visit her myspace page at http://www.myspace.com/scandalpants.

J. T. Langdon is the Taoist, vegetarian, lover of chocolate responsible for the Lady Davenport's Slave trilogy, *Sisters of Omega Pi*, *Hard Time*, and *Kiss Me Quick! 69 Short Stories of Lesbian Lust*. Despite numerous requests to leave, some made with the business end of a pitchfork, JT continues to live in the Midwest. Visit the author online at www.jtlangdon.com

Leslie Anne Leasure received an MFA from Indiana University. Her fiction has appeared in *Blithe House Quarterly* and *Best Lesbian Love Stories 2005*. She was a fellow at the Ledig House International Writers' Residency. She received an honorable mention from the Astraea Foundation in the Emerging Lesbian Writers Award competition.

E. C. Myers struggles to stay awake in the city that never sleeps. The products of his nocturnal writing have appeared recently in several online fiction magazines. He is also a graduate of the Clarion West Writers Workshop, where he learned the real meaning of "sleepless in Seattle."

Christa Nordlum lives in St. Paul, Minnesota, with her partner. When she is not writing, she enjoys reading, hiking and other outdoor activities. She works now as a pharmacy technician and aspires to obtain a pharmacy degree from the University of Minnesota.

Amanda Tremblay holds a degree in English Literature and enjoys writing short stories and screenplays. Amanda is currently directing a feature length independent film titled *The Book Club* (www.smartistic.com). Amanda lives with her partner and two dogs in northern Nevada.

Once upon a time Rakelle Valencia had published short stories and/or co-edited anthologies for Alyson, Pretty Things Press, Suspect Thoughts, Cleis, HAF Enterprises, Alice Street Editions (Haworth Press), and Winsor Publishing. She is a noted national private clinician of Natural Horsemanship and Equine Behavior and Language and speaker for Purina Mills' annual Horse Owners' Workshops.

M. J. Williamz, who describes herself as a true creature of the night, lives in Portland, Oregon. The fresh northwest air and the women who enjoy it provide plenty of fodder for her imagination. M. J. has had several short stories published and is working on her first novel.

Kristina Wright's fiction has appeared in over thirty anthologies, including *Ultimate Lesbian Erotica* (2005 and 2006); four editions of *Best Lesbian Erotica; The Mammoth Book of Best New Erotica, Volume 5*; and *Call of the Dark: Erotic Lesbian Tales of the Supernatural*. Kristina lives in Virginia and is pursuing a graduate degree in Humanities. For more information about her life and writing, visit her web site, www.kristinawright.com.